MURDER AT THE ROMAN BATHS

An absolutely gripping cozy murder mystery full of twists

JEAN G. GOODHIND

A Honey Driver Murder Mystery Book 7

Originally published as
Wicked Words

JOFFE BOOKS

Revised edition 2022
Joffe Books, London
www.joffebooks.com

First published by Accent Press Ltd.
in Great Britain and the USA as *Wicked Words* in 2014

This paperback edition was first published
in Great Britain in 2022

Cover art by Dee Dee Book Covers

ISBN: 978-1-80405-481-9

CHAPTER ONE

The bucket of the digger had wicked-looking teeth along one edge that made a grating sound as it tore into the concrete slab protecting the top of the cesspit. At first there was only a crazy paving effect, a profusion of cracks and crumbling like crushed bits of bone. The concrete was roughly three inches thick, the metal mesh that kept it together becoming gradually exposed.

The cesspit was no longer used; the washrooms in St Luke's Church next door in the parish of Much Maryleigh were now connected to the main sewer and water supply. The cesspit was on the field side of the churchyard wall, away from the graves of villagers more recently buried and those from centuries ago. The field itself was no longer a field but an environmentally- friendly burial site though unlike the churchyard next door, there were no gravestones, only saplings sprouting from the graves of the newly dead. In time the field would become woodland, a place of dappled sunlight and eternal peace.

There were two men overseeing the job; one was driving the digger, the other was looking on. This latter man, the older one, a local by the name of Ned Shaw, looked up on seeing a man he recognised as Peter Pierce. His bottom lip curled in contempt. Pierce was one of the new arrivals in the village. He was running across the field, waving his arms.

His face taking on a deep scowl, the older man signalled the younger man to switch off the digger while he turned to face their neighbour, clenched fists on hips, a ready scowl creasing his face.

'You can't do that,' Pierce shouted as he came to a stop, his chest rising and falling rapidly, his face flushed as he fought to catch his breath. 'That's my piece of land. It's on my deeds,' he shouted breathlessly. 'You've had a letter about it from my solicitor.'

Ned Shaw made no effort to look anything except hostile. Pierce was bluffing. When his sort disagreed with something, they resorted to a lawyer's letter, an injunction, in fact anything that would prevent an enterprise going forward.

'This was my field, Pierce. Long before you arrived, it was my field.'

'It was common land,' Pierce retorted. 'Everyone used it.'

'Including you,' Ned said with a scowl. 'I had no problem with people using it when we weren't using it. Now it's sold.'

'But it has historical significance,' Pierce blurted.

Ned's look hardened. 'Bullshit!'

His family had lived in the village for generations and he made no secret of his dislike for new arrivals like Peter Pierce. He blamed them for his change in drinking habits. In the past he'd taken his custom to the Poacher but it was a smarty-tarty place now, all posh nosh and muted lighting. He now drank at the Rose and Crown, a more traditional place where they still played darts and the height of cuisine was steak and chips.

Leaning on his shovel, he addressed Peter in a no-nonsense manner. 'Unless you want to end up buried before your time, get the hell out of here. The land's sold, you can no longer use it, and no matter how hard you try this field was always on my deeds. It's not common land. It was my land and I could do as I please with it.'

Peter Pierce was unfortunate enough to have a pink, Cupid's bow-shaped mouth. He pouted.

'The people at the university said there could be important artefacts buried here . . .'

Ned Shaw sneered. 'They did a dig years ago. Nothing was ever found.'

'There could still be . . .'

'Bullshit! There's only bodies here now, the first few but there'll be more. Loads more!'

Peter Pierce looked as though he were about to explode.

'You had no right to sell it to these people, these hippies!' he shouted. He glared at the driver of the digger, eyes blazing, his cheeks puffing in and out like a pair of pink bellows.

The driver shrugged.

Ned Shaw stood his ground, shirtsleeves rolled up ready for action, exposing his dark, hairy arms.

The hippy comment was obviously intended for the digger driver, one of the people who had bought the land from Ned.

The Shaw family had owned the land for generations using it as grazing, ploughing it up when they felt moved to, and letting it go to seed for the rest of the time. As he'd explained to Pierce, Ned had no problem with people using it when he wasn't using it; the kids had played here, the courting couples had lain there in August when the grass was tall and golden and the ground warm.

Ned had not been entirely convinced that their venture into an environmentally friendly burial park would work, but they'd showed him the colour of their money and he'd sold the field. Following their purchase they put work his way. The cesspit was on the land he'd sold them and he had rights to do as he liked with it, but Peter Pierce was adamant, insisting the land was his, purely because of the shape of it and a wall. On Peter's side of the wall beyond the church boundary was a stone lean-to that he'd converted into a pump room for his swimming pool. According to him it meant the wall was his.

'Look, I've already told you,' Ned began, his patience grating along with his voice. 'The wall and this land . . .'

Peter Pierce shook his head so hard it looked in danger of falling off. 'Well, I don't know about that!' he snapped. 'I'm going to see my lawyer. I'll have this sorted. You just see if I don't. Until then, stop or I'll get an injunction. You can stop taking this cesspit apart right now!'

He'd come out with exactly what Ned had been expecting. His patience snapped. His fist shot forward, grabbing a handful of Peter Pierce's cashmere sweater. They were nose to nose, eyeball to eyeball.

Anger simmered in Ned's voice.

'If you don't get out of my bloody sight, you're going to be in that cesspit wallowing around in the shit that you say is yours. Right?'

The suddenness with which Ned had grabbed and then released him go took Peter by surprise that sent him sprawling in a pile of leaves and rubbish mixed with a pungent slurry of chicken and goat manure, the basis for this year's compost heap.

'Your missus won't like the smell of you when you get 'ome,' Ned shouted and laughed.

Scrambling to his feet, Peter pointed at him with a shaking finger. 'I'll have you, Ned Shaw. I'll have you yet.'

Ned made a sudden dash forward — only a few steps but enough to send Peter Pierce running awkwardly but swiftly backwards.

'You'll be hearing from my lawyer,' he shouted once he was safely out of the reach of Ned's fearsome hands. 'And I'll report you to the police. Assault and battery. Let's see what you've got to say then.'

The younger man, Gary, jumped down from the cab of the digger, tossed his dreadlocks out of his eyes, and gave Ned a friendly slap on the shoulder.

'Take no notice of that wanker,' he said.

Ned's eyes were narrowed, his countenance concerned. He shook the hand from his shoulder and remarked glumly, 'It ain't you with the police record.'

CHAPTER TWO

Gloria Cross was looking a dream in a black suit with a crisp white blouse, black and white kitten-heeled shoes, and matching handbag.

Her daughter, Hannah Driver, Honey to her friends, was standing opposite her in a white cotton apron splattered with ketchup and brown sauce.

'You're looking good, Mother. Black suits you.'

She was telling the truth. When it came to choosing clothes and looking good, Honey's mother was top of the tree. Honey, on the other hand, could never find the time to look that good. Or smell that good, certainly not during daylight hours. Her mother smelled of a very expensive French perfume.

'Lovely perfume, too,' she said.

'Can't say the same about yours,' responded her mother, wrinkling her nose. 'You smell of grilled bacon and sausages.'

Honey took a sniff of her sleeve. Her mother was right.

Smoothing her skirt elegantly over her slim thighs, Gloria Cross settled herself more comfortably in the best chair her daughter's office could offer. In fact it was the only chair at present. Honey was perched on the corner of the desk.

Her mother's countenance was somewhat downbeat; what with that and the black outfit, Honey guessed that bereavement was on the agenda.

Out it came.

'Sean O'Brian is dead.'

'Oh dear.'

'But at least he died with a smile on his face.'

'Is that so?'

'He was in bed with his wife on honeymoon. You do know he remarried, don't you? I did tell you so.'

'Yes. Of course you did,' said Honey sounding suitably morose, folding her arms and nodding as though she was feeling his loss greatly — which quite frankly she was not. In her opinion Sean O'Brian had been an ageing lecher; she had the bruises on her bum to prove it. Old he might have been, but he had the wandering grip of a manic tarantula.

'He'll be greatly missed,' sighed her mother.

Discreetly, Honey rolled her eyes. It crossed her mind that her mother had never said whether Sean had tried out his lethal pinch on *her* rear. She wouldn't dare ask, and besides, the man was deceased. He would be pinching no more and it was bad luck to speak ill of the dead.

She made an effort to sympathise. 'I'm sure he will be, Mother. His wife will be missing him for a start. What a rotten thing to happen on honeymoon.'

A knock at the door preceded the arrival of Steve Doherty looking a little paler than normal. He also looked terribly neat and clean-shaven. Despite the absence of his usual two-day stubble and the fact that her mother was likely to cramp their style, Honey noticed a promise of things to come in his eyes.

She smiled at him.

He smiled back, though he looked nervous.

'Hope I'm not late.'

He seemed to overcome his nerves a little, his smile braver than it had been.

She liked that and threw in a wink to help him along. 'I appreciate you doing this.'

He shrugged. 'No problem.'

'Have you had coffee?' Honey asked him.

He shook his head. 'No. I'll pass on that. Saw Smudger on his way out. He said to tell you he's off to take a look at a salamander. I didn't know he was into reptiles.'

Honey grinned.

She'd enlighten him later that their steak grill — termed a 'salamander' in the trade — was on its last legs.

Her mother interrupted. 'We were talking about Sean until we were interrupted.'

Gloria Cross did not like being ignored. Her botoxed lips were clamped into a ruby red line and she gave Steve only the briefest acknowledgement — a slight jerk of the chin — before continuing on as though he wasn't there.

'Oh yes. Sean was a very dear man. Such a romantic and an out-and-out gentleman.'

'Still waters run deep,' Honey responded.

The air between Doherty and her mother was as potent as static in nylon underwear, though when it came to lightning hits, her mother was the one throwing it. Since the demise of Carl, Honey's husband, Gloria Cross had made it something of a crusade to find a suitable replacement — suitable in her eyes, that was. Sean O'Brian, old but wealthy, had been one of the suitors she'd suggested for her daughter. And even though the man was dead, she was still waxing on about Sean O'Brian and his considerable assets.

'Of course, it could have been your honeymoon last week if you'd played your cards right. If you recall, he did offer to escort you on that Arctic cruise we all went on — us from the over-sixties club. You should have come. Sean was very well heeled you know.'

Honey rolled her eyes again, this time in Steve's direction. She knew reference to Sean O'Brian's interest in her was intended for his ears. In Gloria's opinion, Steve didn't come up to the standard of husband required for her daughter. He didn't wear a Rolex, drove a Japanese car, and had an inbuilt aversion to shaving.

But Doherty knew how to take a punch. He also knew how to fling a few, only at present it wasn't a punch, it was a finger. Stern of expression, he was wagging it directly beneath Honey's nose.

'Honey, you should have listened to your mother. That man had everything you could possibly want — including his own teeth. And he could fasten his own truss.' Today he wasn't taking it lying down. He was giving a bit back.

Honey stifled a giggle.

Her mother's face was like thunder. 'Well, that's typical of Mr Plod the Policeman. Making jokes at a dead man's expense! Sarcasm is the lowest form of wit, so I hear.'

Doherty held up his hands in surrender but failed to look contrite. He looked more as though he wanted to laugh out loud.

Her mother arose from her chair and stood formidably at five-feet-three inches — five-feet-five if you counted the kitten-heeled shoes.

This was one of those regular moments when Honey wanted to stuff her fingers in her ears. She'd heard all this advice and criticism before and recognised the coming storm and the sharp opinions that went with it.

In her mother's opinion a beefy bank account made up for a man's age, looks, or general behaviour, though she might draw a line if the guy was a slob. The jury was out on her views regarding any other odd predilections.

Honey was under no illusions; Sean O'Brian had been a man with an eye for the ladies and a habit of chancing his luck. Hope springs eternal, so they say, and whatever was springing about Sean O'Brian's person should have stopped doing it long ago.

Honey remembered him with a shiver of embarrassment. He was the sort of guy who still thought himself a wizard on the dance floor though he was older than John Travolta and too old for discos even when *Saturday Night Fever* was in vogue.

He still tried to hold everything together, wearing tight jeans when they were in fashion and two-tone shoes. White locks hung like strands of unbraided rope to his shoulder blades, usually tied back into a ponytail. He'd also been partial to open-necked shirts and had sported a gold medallion amongst his pure white chest hair.

Having been roughly five-feet-four in a pair of elevated heels, Sean O'Brian had also sported a bald patch in the middle of his head, the straggly hairs brushed over to hide it.

A girl's vision of heaven he hadn't been. Still, she mustn't appear heartless. The man was dead for goodness' sake. She composed her expression behind the coffee cup before she made another comment.

'So,' she said brightly, though in all honesty she was aching to get Doherty alone, to give him a pep talk and anything else that might make the task she'd given him easier to confront. But first things first. Keep her mother sweet. 'How old was dear old Sean?'

Her mother sighed. 'Not so old.'

Honey fixed Steve Doherty with a warning look but she could see his earlier exuberance had modified because he had other things on his mind, namely that very special task she'd asked of him, a very special task that only a very brave policeman could do. In fact, a task he had never done before and he was doing it just for her.

But the question she'd asked had hit the right note with her mother whose face lit up at the prospect of handing out information that only she could give. It was something to do with priding herself that she still had a memory. 'As sharp as when I was twenty,' she'd proclaim to anyone who dared think otherwise.

'He was born in thirty-five,' she reliably informed them whether they wanted to know or not.

Honey nodded. 'Uh-huh. That's what I thought.' So too damned old for me, she thought. 'How's his widow?'

Her mother nodded thoughtfully.

'So-so. They had a good marriage though not a long one. Arlene is younger than him of course, but very active. Really sexy for her age.'

Honey was pretty sure that Sean's second wife — now his widow — was old enough to have a bus pass, sixty at least. Their honeymoon had been an all-inclusive deal to some island in the Mediterranean when old Sean had popped his clogs.

Honey hadn't gone to the wedding. Her mother had.

'He's still good in the sack,' she'd informed her at the time. 'Arlene will be good for him. She does like a man who's active in that department.'

It was on the tip of her tongue for Honey to remark that being sexy had been the death of him. She could see by Doherty's face that great minds — namely theirs — were thinking alike.

'So when's the funeral?' asked Honey, refusing to meet Doherty's gaze. She knew if she did then all respect for the dead would fly out of the window as they burst out laughing.

Thankfully, her mother didn't seem to have noticed.

She was already rummaging in her handbag for the taxi fare to her next destination — lunch with friends. She lunched a lot with friends. That's when she wasn't helping out at Secondhand Sheila, the used designer clothes shop that she ran with a bunch of other elderly ladies.

'The funeral's on Thursday. That's why I came to see you. I need a lift so I need you to come. You'll be well catered for. They're doing a great buffet afterwards at the Poacher, that pub slap bang in the centre of the village. It's a bit like the George at Norton St Philip, though not so old.'

Inwardly Honey groaned. It grated to be amenable and funerals were not on her list of favourite events.

'I'm not too sure, Mother . . .'

She'd been to the Poacher and liked it. However, unlike her mother, she couldn't get her head around the social aspects of a funeral. A funeral should be sad and a time for reflection. From experience it was otherwise with her mother and her friends. Funerals had become part of their social whirl. Like a wedding, it necessitated working out what you were going to wear, how special your flowers and cards of condolence would be, and how much you were willing to spend on them. Expense fell in line with social status. It was also a great chance to swap old stories of lovers tried, lost, and sometimes lamented over, besides possible conquests for the future. Her mother and friends were getting older, but the old adage about there still being a fire in the grate when there was snow on the roof held true.

'The girls will be there,' said her mother as though sitting with a bunch of old ladies through lunch was recompense enough. Honey prayed the dishwasher would throw a tantrum so she couldn't go. Washing dishes by hand had its advantages.

The "girls" her mother was referring to were all drawing their pensions. They were great company for each other but not for her.

'And I would very much like to be there, but unfortunately I do have other things . . .'

'We intend giving old Sean a good send-off with a glass or two of sherry and a few bottles of Chardonnay,' Gloria continued as if Honey hadn't spoken, 'which is why I'm asking you for a lift. Mary Jane has offered to take me, but I think arriving in a pink car isn't right. Unless she could borrow your car of course? That wouldn't be so bad.'

'No! You're right,' Honey said hurriedly. 'A pink car shouldn't be going to a funeral. A wedding, yes, but not a funeral. I'll take you.'

The very thought of Mary Jane behind the wheel of a right-hand drive — the right-hand drive of *her* car — was a big no-no. Mary Jane had shipped her pink, left-hand drive Caddy Coupé over from the States and did use it at least once a week. She kept it in a garage she rented from the man who delivered fish to the hotel.

'Sometimes it smells like a fish market but I prefer that to my car being taken by joyriders and turned into scrap,' Mary Jane had proclaimed.

Her mother stood in front of the half-open office door. At a certain angle it gave a pretty good reflection. Her mother was admiring herself, fluffing up her hair and trimming a tinge of lipstick away from the corner of her mouth with a fingernail.

'Good. You'll enjoy it,' she said as she jerked her lips from one side of her face to the other. 'St Luke's for the service then the burial in Memory Meadow.'

The name of the burial site struck a chord. 'Am I right in thinking that's the new place next to the church? The eco-friendly place where you get buried in a biodegradable coffin.'

'It is. But I'm sure Sean's coffin will be both tasteful and exquisitely original. He did like a little luxury in his life. I think this tuning in with nature was Arlene's choice,' her mother said in a hushed voice. 'I don't approve myself though of course we all have to be more eco-friendly nowadays. All the same, there's nothing like a nice piece of mahogany if you ask me.'

'I hope you don't let Lindsey hear you say that. She'll give you a lecture on the devastation of the rainforests. A few million more people buried in hardwood caskets and there won't be any forests left. I didn't know Sean was so modern-minded.'

Her mother threw her a glower. 'Well, that's no big surprise. You never bothered to find out.'

Doherty started to say, 'Well, if that was what Sean wanted, then that was what he should have.' But her mother didn't give him chance to finish the sentence.

'I blame Arlene. She's the one who wants it and swears that Sean was into this environmental stuff. Still, it does mean that she'll have more of his money to spend.' She shrugged at the same time as straightening her scarf. 'Still, she's the widow. It makes no difference what I say. It's her money now — when it could have been yours.'

Honey ignored the sidelong look of accusation.

'The burial ground used to be just a field, and a pretty rough one at that,' Doherty said, thinking of Memory

Meadow. 'I used to have a friend out there. We used to go treasure hunting in that field.'

'Did you ever find anything?' Honey asked him.

'A Roman coin.' He took the coin out of his pocket and showed her. 'For luck. From the reign of the Emperor Claudius.'

'Nice,' said Honey.

'Grubby,' said her mother and shuddered.

'Good pub if my memory serves me correct.'

Memory Meadow was situated in the village of Much Maryleigh. Honey had read all about it in the *Bath Chronicle*. Once a barren field where little grew except for sheets of discarded corrugated tin and old mattresses, the area had been cleared of rubbish and weeds and seeded with grass, and a landscape gardener had been contracted to make it pretty. The result was an eco-friendly place that didn't feel like a graveyard, more of a copse where rabbits burrowed and pigeons cooed from the branches of silvery leaved trees.

'Rich nutrients in the soil,' murmured Doherty.

Honey shot him a warning look. She'd been thinking the same thing, but it didn't do for her mother to know that. People were sensitive. Her mother was also a traditionalist.

Luckily she hadn't heard.

'The girls will gather at my place,' she voiced in a manner that made Honey think she'd *ordered* them to her place.

'Right,' said Honey with a curt nod. 'You've got them organised then.'

'Of course.'

'What time do you want me to pick you up?'

'Right. I need two hours to get ready once I've had my bath . . .'

Arrangements were made, or rather orders were given.

'I take it you've got something that doesn't have ketchup stains to wear to the funeral,' her mother added, her eyes targeting each and every blemish on Honey's apron.

'I have the customary little black dress.'

'That should be fine,' her mother said. 'We don't want Arlene thinking Sean passed you over because you were a slob.'

Honey's jaw dropped. She was speechless.

Her mother gave Steve another jerk of her chin on her way out and he closed the door behind her, leaned his head back, and expelled a sigh of relief.

'She doesn't like me. She'll never like me.'

Leaving her perch on the desk, Honey tugged at his tie, his prime concession to smartness for the ordeal ahead. She couldn't recall the last time she'd seen him wearing one.

Placing her hand at the nape of his neck, she planted a quick kiss on his lips. 'I don't care. Thanks for being so non-confrontational.'

He opened one eye. 'That's a big word for this early in the morning. Besides, I wouldn't dare. Your mother is full-on. Strange how funerals bring out the battlefield general in people.' He paused. 'Do I know this guy who had his eye on you before I did?'

'He was ancient,' she snapped.

He grinned. 'I know how some girls have a thing about sugar daddies.'

'Well not this girl,' she told him. 'And let's get this straight. The minute I heard he had his eye on me I put on my running shoes and kept well out of his reach. Sean O'Brian could teach the Italians a thing or two about pinching a woman's *derrière*.'

He smiled. 'Sounds like fun — though only when it's consensual, of course. Still, at least there's a party after the funeral. That might not be so bad. Wakes have a habit of turning into parties.'

'Possibly, though not if you're designated driver. My mother and her friends do like to indulge in a sherry or two at funerals.'

'I've heard Memory Meadow bury people in cardboard boxes. They advertise them as environmentally compatible, but they're still only cardboard boxes when all's said and done.'

He was rambling now, saying anything for the sake of putting off the dreaded moment.

'Stop,' she ordered, placing a fingertip on his lips. 'Procrastinating has to stop. You have to go in there.'

He groaned and eyed the ceiling.

She tapped his chin.

'It's no good looking up there. You can't get out of it now.' she said to him. 'The Fans of Agatha Christie Association awaits your pearls of wisdom.'

The conference taking place at the Green River was a first and Honey, always open to the main chance, had thought it a good idea to suggest she knew a policeman who could give a talk.

Doherty had jumped at the chance — after some persuading, like an hour or two when he was at his lowest resistance, in bed, his place, and three o'clock in the morning.

'Do you want me to come in and hold your hand?' she asked him.

His cheeks ballooned before he let out a big out rush of breath. 'No need. We'll get round to that later.' He managed a weak smile. 'Now lead me into the lion's den.'

'You'll enjoy it.'

He grinned and tried to look as though he was only joking, that he wasn't really fazed at all. 'The things I do for love.'

Honey wasn't fooled either by that or the look of casual indifference. Steve Doherty was nervous and it was all thanks to her.

He was about to talk about his job in front of an audience. And not just any audience. The fifty or so people waiting for him in the conference room were fully paid-up members of the Fans of Agatha Christie Association (North Somerset and West Wiltshire Branch).

The face of the tough cop was as pale as plaster of Paris.

Honey gave his hand a reassuring squeeze. Her other hand was poised on the door handle.

'Breathe deeply.'

'I am.'

'Ready?'

'Hold on. I need to do something memorable.'

'Like what?'

'An act that will stay in my mind, top up my testosterone, and diminish my nerves. I got the idea from some old book I've been reading.'

She postponed opening the door and looked at him. 'OK. Do whatever you have to do.'

One deep breath was followed by another. Then he took his hand from hers, ran it down her back, and squeezed her right buttock.

'Right. I'm ready now.'

Feeling warmer than she had been, Honey eyed him quizzically. 'What book did you get that from?'

'Not sure. It could have been the *Kama Sutra*.'

Honey grinned and opened the door. 'I should have guessed.'

Honey's daughter, Lindsey, twirled round on her revolving chair behind the reception desk.

Folding her arms, she looked Doherty up and down.

'Poor old Stephen. You look like a Christian about to be thrown to the lions.'

'I feel like one,' he mumbled.

'Do you know that Steve has a Roman coin, Lindsey?'

Lindsey looked amused. 'Does he now?'

'Show her the coin,' Honey encouraged.

'It's just a coin,' he sighed, but did as he was ordered.

'Claudius,' said Lindsey. 'It was while he reigned as Emperor of Rome that Britain was conquered.'

'Is it valuable?' asked Honey.

Lindsey shook her head. 'Not on its own. A whole hoard and you might be talking of serious money. Gold would be best, though the Crown is likely to shout "Treasure Trove" and take their cut before you get anything out of it.'

Mother and daughter only needed to glance at each other and know they were thinking alike. The tough cop had a marshmallow centre — at least when it came to giving talks to an audience. Talking about coins and treasure troves had calmed his nerves, though only temporarily. The moment passed, he was now staring at the doors leading into the conference room.

Like her mother, Lindsey kept her eyes on Doherty as she spoke. 'What did my grandmother want?'

Honey kept her voice down. 'Your grandmother wants a taxi service for her and her friends to a funeral. It's out of town, Memory Meadow. So I'm it.'

'You'd better go.'

'I am . . .' Honey answered before realising that Lindsey was referring to the man standing frozen and still staring towards the conference room.

Honey took Doherty's hand and squeezed. 'OK?'

He looked gratefully down at her and nodded.

'Then I'll lead you in.'

A low buzz of conversation ran among the Fans of Agatha Christie Association. Most of them were over fifty. Their organiser — a man named Charles Sheet — was less than that. The earnest look of a shepherd guarding his flock glowed behind his designer spectacles. His hair was dark blond and shoulder-length. A few hairs sprouted on his chin—not enough to be termed designer stubble. Lindsey had confessed to her mother that she couldn't take her eyes off those hairs.

'I want to pluck them,' she'd said. If Lindsey hadn't said that maybe — just maybe — Honey wouldn't have noticed them, but she couldn't help it. The hairs were wiry and sparse — like copper springs bristling from his chin. She tugged her gaze away and concentrated on introducing Doherty.

'Oh, Detective Inspector,' Mr Sheet beamed. 'My group are so very excited about meeting you.'

Honey took a couple of gradual steps back as the enthusiastic Mr Sheet took over, arms spread wide as he guided Doherty to the platform and called his diverse audience to silence.

She watched briefly as Doherty was introduced and the audience clapped. He stood up. She saw his right hand grip the table more fiercely than it had gripped her right buttock. She smiled. He was going to be all right.

CHAPTER THREE

C.A. Wright had a smug smile on his face. He was lying flat out on a comfortable bed in a nice little hotel in Laura Place. Although small the hotel was beautifully furnished, its ambience as close to five-star rating as a little place could be.

C.A. Wright stretched his short, skinny legs and reached for the glass tumbler sitting on the bedside cabinet. It was three o'clock in the afternoon; he'd left London just after lunch, the journey taking an hour and a half tops. Lunch had been taken at an Italian restaurant just round the corner from the station. He hadn't eaten much but he had knocked back three whiskies and a bottle of red wine followed by a Drambuie.

The bottle of Glenmorangie he'd brought with him was already showing the strain, there being about two-thirds left.

Never mind, he thought as he smiled blearily at the amber liquid. There were still the bottles in the hotel fridge. They had an honesty policy here: you owned up to what you'd drunk. He grinned at that. Who the hell was stupid enough to own up to anything? Certainly not him.

C.A. Wright specialised in writing reviews for the travel section of a national newspaper and his brief included reviewing hotels, restaurants, and other attractions in the area in which he was staying.

This little hotel in Laura Place was a gem and anyone of a more honest disposition than him would have praised it to the skies. But C.A. Wright was not honest. Neither was he very nice. Even his own mother had called him a shit.

However, words were water off a duck's back to C.A. Wright. Words were also how he made his living and writing in glowing terms about small establishments ran by loving and hard-working couples wasn't the way he did things. Wright knew which side his bread was buttered.

His full name was Colin Alan Wright. Professionally he preferred to be called by his initials. Some people called him other names. Not that he was that bothered. He quite liked infamy. It suited him better than namby-pamby-lovey-dovey. Wright is always right! That was his motto.

C.A. Wright worked the world of review writing to suit himself and did it usually while under the influence of drink. Even the more accurate reviews were written in the company of a bottle of whisky and a sturdy glass tumbler.

He reworked the details on some others depending on who he was writing for and also what the kickback would be. Big hotels paid him to praise their premises. Small ones did not.

Although writing about travel and hotels were his mainstay, he also wrote articles about other aspects of service to the general public.

The tone of his articles made him come across as some kind of consumers' crusader. The truth was far from that. He loved what he did. He loved manipulating, cajoling, squeezing every pleasure possible from every assignment. At times he was almost close to admitting to himself that he loved feeling the power of criticism so much that he might consider writing the reviews for free — not that he really would. A line had to be drawn somewhere.

He liked the way small hoteliers jumped to attention when he played the role of awkward customer. He liked it even better when he told them who he was. They would do anything for a good review. He was OK with that and told them that he was always up for offers. He took all that came.

The trouble was that there had to be some balance in his work, i.e. bad reviews had to be balanced against good ones, mediocre good against mediocre bad. He couldn't write bad reviews about every hotel and there were very obvious exceptions.

Never in the world would he dare to write a bad review for a hotel belonging to one of the big groups. Big hotel groups were his bread and butter. After reading a favourable review, most of them sent him a cheque in a brown envelope. Sometimes they asked him to come in and have lunch with the manager. On those occasions the brown envelope held cash. The big groups had a contingency fund for that kind of thing and with that knowledge firmly in mind he went out of his way to be kind to them.

However, he'd been too kind and sugary of late, mostly due to the fact that he'd met his son for the first time in years. He'd split up with Warren's mother after going on one binge too many but on reuniting with Warren he'd made a great effort to stay on the wagon. It might have worked out if Warren hadn't decided to emigrate to Canada, where he had a girl and a great job waiting for him. C.A. had got angry. They'd rowed and Warren had stormed out, headed for the airport, and flew off without saying goodbye. 'And to think I stayed on the wagon for the ungrateful brat,' he snarled to himself, already reaching for the whisky.

As it turned out it seemed the whisky was the muse behind his articles. At least that was the conclusion he came to after getting a drubbing from one of his regular editors.

'Where's the cutting-edge criticism? Where are the dirty sheets, the grimy bath, and the cockroaches running through the foyer?'

This particular editor had once been a 'gore and guts' journalist. He'd been good at reporting the grisly details in murder cases. Sweetness and cute were not part of his creed.

'We're doing a feature in our weekend magazine. Get something a little spicier, more cutting-edge, more *critical*! OK?'

Wright, who was now firmly off the wagon and drinking like a fish, knew exactly where to go to get the quality accommodation and the vast range of small hotels and guesthouses that he could pull apart at will; something dirty and grimy, huh? The description was in place. Now all he had to do was find the hotel to suit it, not that it would really fit the bill, of course, otherwise he wouldn't damn well be staying in it. He wouldn't dream of staying in a downmarket dosshouse, a place that really did deserve a dressing down. Oh no. Not C.A. Wright. He had standards. He had taste.

Bath was a world heritage site and a great favourite with him, and he'd been here before, which meant he had to be careful not to check in to a place he'd already stayed in. If his name and the resultant review from his last stay were mentioned, he could be thrown out on his ear pronto. All he had to do was find the right place that suited all his needs. It shouldn't be too difficult.

He'd breathed a sigh of relief on finding the Laurel Tree Hotel, a little place with only eight bedrooms and run by well-meaning amateurs who wouldn't know anything about passing a bung.

Strictly speaking the place wasn't really big enough to call itself a hotel. For a start it had no proper bar, no barman dispensing cocktails with a simple flick of the wrist. But there was an honesty bar in the lounge as well as in his room which Wright had every intention of using — and bugger the honesty.

Mr and Mrs Dodd, the couple running it, were middle-aged. They'd retired from their former careers, him as a master builder and her as a secretary with Dorchester Town Council, in order to work for themselves.

'We thought it would suit us in retirement,' they'd said, beaming at him innocently as he checked himself in, not guessing for one minute what he was about to do to their reputation.

He'd asked them if they were enjoying the hard work.

'It's hard, but yes. We enjoy it.'

Their naivety was breathtaking. New to the trade, they were only just beginning to find out how much work was required catering for other people. They weren't ground down just yet. Give them two years and the Laurel Tree would be on the market.

He smiled and agreed with them how very nice it would all be and how lucky they were to own such a lovely place in such a lovely city.

Fools, he thought to himself, their enthusiasm filling him with disdain. They were amateurs in a professional world. In time they might get things right, not that it would make much difference to him. Whether it was now or later they were susceptible to the poison that dripped from his pen.

One side of his face lifted in a self-satisfied smile. Writing a bad review was so much more fun than writing a good one, though in all honesty this place was above average. The room was pretty and clean. Pale lemon-striped curtains hung at the window. The pillowcases were crisply white. An upholstered armchair sat in one corner, a stool that looked as though it had once accompanied a grand piano was pushed under the dressing table. The bathroom had a separate shower and bath and big fluffy towels were folded neatly on a towel radiator which was switched on.

The tea- and coffee-making facilities were well appointed, the teacups mismatched but purposely so. The Laurel Tree boasted a quirky though elegant shabby-chic style. Such a style was the worst mistake these people could make. Not everyone appreciated its quaint homespun charm. Keep it modern or keep it stately-home elegant — don't muddy the waters.

Folding his arms beneath his head and replete with sufficient booze, Wright sighed with satisfaction. Despite its many attributes, the Laurel Tree was about to get a drubbing. What fun!

He slept like a baby, happily contented with his surroundings and his plans.

When he awoke it was six o'clock and his mouth was as dry as the bottom of a birdcage. He needed a drink.

Not a man to drink his own supply when he could drink someone else's, he raided the small fridge, noted the honesty list complete with pen, but didn't bother to write anything down. The one thing he did do was to boil the kettle and make a pot of tea — not for drinking, of course. He would leave the tea to stand overnight. By morning it would be cold enough to pour into the empty whisky bottles and put them back in the fridge.

That night he went out. The hotel didn't do evening meals but that didn't matter; he had a little restaurant in mind, a new place where he'd make himself known and possibly get the meal for free. A few more drinks and he would turn in, though not before having a quick nightcap before bedtime.

At breakfast he ate half of the full-English — bacon, sausage, eggs etc. — then complained that he thought the oil his breakfast had been fried in might be a bit off. A pale-faced Mr Dodd apologised profusely and offered him a fresh plateful. Wright accepted.

By the time he'd finished he was set up for the day. After lunch he was off to Chepstow and Tetbury, Welsh and English towns respectively, where small hotels proliferated. Once again he had done his homework, researching online for those under new management.

Before and after breakfast he dictated notes on his digital voice recorder, relishing words like 'pathetic', 'calamitous', and 'amateurish'—that was besides imbibing his first drinks of the day.

Before leaving he transferred some of his remaining whisky supply into a plastic lemonade bottle which he secreted inside his jacket, though not before taking another nip.

Once his bag was packed he looked out of the window on to the fountain in the middle of Laura Place. All around Regency buildings and mansard roofs, landmarks of a cultured age, stretched into the distance. Beyond were the green hills.

It had been a while since his last visit here. He smiled at the thought of it. Gone but not forgotten. He'd stayed in another small hotel that had suited his needs; that was what was so special about the city of Bath. The big groups were represented but the smaller places were unusually good — despite what he wrote about them.

Like the Laurel Tree, that hotel he'd stayed in back then had also been run by a middle-aged couple. Apparently they'd sunk all their savings into it; that's what he was told by the man who'd phoned him, begging him to retract, screaming at him, 'Do you know what you've done? You've ruined us, bloody ruined us.'

'No,' he'd replied tersely. 'You've ruined yourself.' Then he'd put the phone down, picked up his keys, and gone for lunch.

Before leaving he opened his laptop, tapped in a few notes — enough from which to build a reasonable draft before embarking on the full thing. It was his experience that terse points led to a biting review and was his preferred way of working.

Before shutting down his laptop he checked his bank accounts. He had one for his business, one for domestic use from which he paid his utility bills, and another account, a savings account that only had money paid into it by those he fondly regarded as his 'clients'; rarely did he pay anything out. What the taxman didn't know, he couldn't grieve over.

Focusing his eyes on the last entry on the online statement, his thin features hardened. A large credit he'd been expecting had not been paid in. One of his clients had defaulted. He was not pleased. Small indentations beneath his cheekbones heaved in and out like the gills of a fish.

The client was relatively new and he'd only come across him by accident. His other clients were small fish in comparison with this one. Well, he thought, looks like I need to send a little reminder.

He phoned the number he'd been given — not a personal phone but one in an out-of-the-way place that was untraceable — he presumed a phone box, still around though less used than they used to be.

To his surprise an old-fashioned answerphone clicked in. So, it wasn't a phone box. But at least it wasn't a mobile phone. He trusted that it wasn't traceable. He didn't deal over traceable phone lines.

'You haven't paid me,' he said into the answerphone. 'You've got until six o'clock, and then, my friend, your neck is in the noose.'

Satisfied that all was well and that the problem with the missing credit was purely an oversight, he closed everything, stretched his arms above his head, and thought about what he would do today.

He was feeling good; the sky was blue and liberally decorated with powder puff clouds. Why not do the sightseeing, he thought to himself? How about playing at being a tourist and enjoying what the city had to offer?

Mr Dodd was manning Reception. His smile was broad.

Wright paid him with the credit card he used for his business expenses. The newspaper would ultimately pick up the tab.

'I trust you've enjoyed your stay?' Mr Dodd, the proprietor, smiled in the hopeful way of someone fishing for compliments.

Wright was not the man to dish out compliments *that* easily. Scrutinising the figures before pocketing the receipt, he noted with pleasure that the drinks he'd consumed had not been added to his account. The cold tea he'd poured into the whisky bottle had done the trick.

'It's a fine day,' Mr Dodd added when Wright failed to respond.

Now it was Wright who smiled. 'Yes. Very fine.'

Slinging his overnight bag over his shoulder, he left the hotel behind him and headed into the crowds, crossing Pulteney Bridge and heading in the general direction of Bath Abbey.

C.A. Wright could do smug big time. He wore it like a cloak around his shoulders. He beamed it from his thin-lipped mouth and it oozed like mildewed seaweed in his watery blue eyes. He'd hit the hotel for his booze and the suckers didn't even know it. He'd even managed to empty one of the ridiculously small sipping bottles before leaving. Soon he'd have to sip some more, but not just yet and anyway he carried his own personal supply with him; he always did.

The tourists were out in force and easy to recognise, a hindrance to his progress. He thought how wonderful it would be if he had the city entirely to himself — except for those who could aid his comfort, of course. Lackeys were in such short supply nowadays. They had to be found. They had to be worked on. Still, if there were no tourists he could live here like a lord.

One or two bumped into him. Tourists never looked where they were going. They strolled languorously as though the city was not a living, breathing thing where people went to work or school, or to shop and do their daily business. To them the city was like a theme park, a Disneyland constructed of wire mesh and stucco and built purely for their entertainment.

Wright, being a severely selfish man, wished that they'd all drop dead around him and not get in his way. Then, what with people bumping into him and the sun getting hotter, he began to feel thirsty.

Veering away to the right at the last minute he cut through the Corridor, glad of the shade though finding it too crowded for comfort. The Corridor was a popular shopping arcade where specialist shops, cafés, and the odd building society did business.

Reaching the end of the walk-through, he paused and considered his options. Shopping wasn't his thing; he could do that anywhere.

Taking another nip of whisky from his apple juice bottle, he considered his options. In his mind he reviewed the list of attractions he could visit. The first place a tourist would visit when in Bath was the Roman Baths.

The hot springs had always bubbled up through the earth. The Celts had thrown in offerings to the god of the steamy waters. The Romans had channelled the warm water into a pool, a lido where they could submerge their aching Italian bones, not used to the colder, damper climes of what they had then called Britannia.

It had become something of a holiday town, a spa where citizens and soldiers on leave from the army could take their ease. There was nothing else quite like it in the whole of Romanised Europe and besides, there were dark places in there, places where he could loiter and tip more drink into his throat.

C.A. liked the Romans; no-nonsense types who ruled with a rod of iron and took anything they fancied — a bit like he did really.

Oh yes, he thought with a sigh of selfish nostalgia, Ancient Rome and the Romans would have suited him fine.

As he walked with bottle in hand he thought about his stay at the Laurel Tree. The review would be printed. There'd been no chance of a trade-off. He might have propositioned Mrs Dodd, told her straight that he'd do a favour for her if she would do a favour for him. Unfortunately Mrs Dodd was one of those 'domestic goddesses' whose beautiful cooking is far removed from their physical attractiveness. It was amazing what people would do to make him change his mind. There hadn't even been a pretty daughter hanging around. Shame, he thought, as he surveyed the array of delectable flesh on Bath's busy shopping streets. Pretty girls in abundance. Well dressed, too, sporting fashions that ranged from way-out to high-street to international designer.

All facets of life, culture, and class rubbed shoulders in Bath. Girls, some bare-shouldered, in short summer dresses and showing plenty of leg. Despite the booze the thought of exploring that flesh further kindled a fire in his loins.

Drink had never curtailed either his sexual appetite or his performance, at least he'd never had any complaints.

Sunshine, ambience and atmosphere all played their part in raising his temperature. He fancied chancing his luck. It was just a case of picking on the right girl.

His eyes darted from one likely-looking damsel to another, trying to catch their eye, looking for a flicker of returned interest.

The day was young. He'd get one. Eventually.

He was passing through the arcade of columns dividing Abbey Churchyard from Stall Street when somebody jangled a yellow plastic pail of coins under his nose.

A mousy-haired girl wearing fingerless gloves thrust out her chin and asked him to give generously. 'A pound would be nice. Five if you're feeling generous.'

She was pretty, casually dressed in jeans and green waist-coat with fur fringing over a long-sleeved red T-shirt. Her eyes were blue and her fresh-faced complexion appealing. Her hair was long and straight, dark brown and glossy. Her figure was curvy, her T-shirt gaping wide enough to expose a creamy cleavage.

Wright stopped in his tracks. 'Is that so, darling? So what exactly am I to give you this money for?' he asked, making no effort to take his eyes from her bosoms.

'The Devlin Foundation. It's for disadvantaged kids mainly.' She hadn't noticed his lust — not at first.

'And what do I get out of it?' he asked, finally bringing his own glassy eyes up from her boobs and on to her face. 'Go on. Tempt me.'

She didn't hesitate, her expression bright with self-right-eous zeal. She was doing her bit for poverty and feeling good about it. What did it matter that he had whisky breath and had all the attraction of an emaciated leprechaun. He had money, didn't he?

She pasted on her best smile. 'Satisfaction that you're giving to the poor and destitute. But if that's not enough, you can have your photograph taken with Teddy Devlin.' She jerked her head to where a massive teddy bear at least a head taller than a human, was propped up between two columns.

C.A. Wright was far from being a charitable person. In fact he loathed circulars asking him to give money, he loathed television commercials asking him to give money; in effect he hated being asked to give money at all. On top of that he wasn't particularly keen on teddy bears.

His bottom lip curled in disdain at the same time as he tried to remain charming. 'Not my scene. I feel no satisfaction either from giving alms to the poor or being having my photo taken with a giant teddy bear. However being close to a lovely young lady, well, that's a very different matter . . .'

His smile sent a wreath of wrinkles around his mouth, pulling one side up and the other down.

The girl was streetwise. She saw the inference in that look and knew what was coming. All the same, she made one last effort.

'Giving to those in need is very satisfying,' she intoned. Being coached in the right things to say was part of the training she'd received before hitting the streets.

C.A. Wright was all sickly charm as he leaned forward until his lips were close to her ear.

'I bet you could satisfy me, darling. I'd even give you more than a fiver for that.'

His tongue flicked at her ear.

The girl stepped back. 'Sod off!'

'Now that's not very charitable, and why take umbrage, dear girl? The urban poor and destitute would be very grateful for your honestly-earned contribution.'

She gave him the finger, her lips forming silent words that no upright charity collector should really be saying.

Turning her back, she marched off shaking her bucket of coins.

Feeling slighted but certainly not dejected, C.A. watched as generous souls rummaged in their purses and pockets, some delving more deeply than others.

'Bloody fools,' he muttered. What was the point of giving money away and getting nothing in return?

He licked at the dryness forming around his mouth, took out his lemonade bottle, and sipped.

Never mind, the girl had been pretty but there were plenty more fish in the water. No doubt he would find a more gullible damsel in need of his undoubted charm and sexual prowess. In the meantime, it was lunchtime and crowded outside — quite warm too. People were making the most of the sunshine and the cut-price shopping. C.A. liked neither warm sunshine nor shopping. He headed for the shade of the Roman Baths where he could be sure of some respite from the hustle and bustle outside.

It had been a long time since he'd walked around the city's most famous attraction. He recalled the darkness, the smell of it, the sight of its waters tumbling rust-red and steaming, the air lightly tinged with sulphur. A hint of hell if there really was such a place, which he thought not. He'd chosen his time well. Hopefully he would have the place to himself. The water that bubbled up from deep within the earth was on sale, decanted in small plastic cups. C.A. Wright — who tried never to think of himself as Colin — wrinkled his nose. He'd tried the waters once and once was enough. OK, it was said to be packed full of minerals that could only do you good, but seeing as in his opinion it tasted like bad eggs, he'd stick to Highland malt, thank you very much.

'The guided tour has already left,' someone said to him. She further pointed out that he was left with the choice of waiting for the next one or going it alone.

'Well, that's no big surprise, and I don't need someone to tell me what I already know,' he said imperiously.

Snatching one of the brochures from a rack near the payment desk he examined it closely before buying a ticket to see around the baths.

The brochure was OK by local standards, he decided. Glancing through it he concluded that a top-flight London outfit could do far better. Nothing could be done better than the people he knew in London. In his view provincial towns just weren't in the running when it came to style.

He hung around to give the tour plenty of time to get ahead of him. The public might digest his reviews with trust and enthusiasm, but he certainly didn't feel the same about them. In any case, he preferred to peruse the site alone and without being rushed. He didn't want to be jostled. He didn't want anyone to interrupt his enjoyment.

Luck was on his side. There was a lull in ticket purchases; most people coming in were making their way into the Pump Room for lunch. He couldn't have timed it better.

Once he was sure he'd be on his own, he purchased his ticket and proceeded to follow the signposted route into the shade. Not that he would necessarily stick to the designated route. He'd been contrary all his life.

The interior of the Roman Baths had a ghostly quality. The lighting was low, the darkness aiding the imagination. History hung in the air.

Inside was cool, full of inscriptions, information, and artefacts. Bumping into people coming from other directions, he took it slowly past where the orange-coloured water poured from a slit in the rocks smelling of iron and sulphur, all things mineral. He breathed it in which in his opinion was far better than drinking it.

Close to where the water steamed hot and rust-coloured from the earth, he paused by the tomb of a child. According to the inscription the child had been British and had been adopted by a Roman couple. She'd died at three years old. How odd, he thought. What would possess a couple to do that? I mean, he thought to himself, some scruffy little kid smelling of mud and pigs living with a cultured pair of Romans. He didn't like kids himself. If drawn on the subject he'd testily reply that he preferred them roasted; his little joke and as nasty as he was.

Pausing next to a display of what remained of some Roman central heating, he brought himself to attention, saluting as though he were a centurion. He quite fancied himself in that role, telling others what to do, flogging the odd errant legionnaire or being bestial with a female slave.

Finding a comfortable corner with a convenient stone to sit on, he settled down, brought out the lemonade bottle, and proceeded to get well and truly drunk. The more he drank the more he fantasised. He was back in time, not here at all. The rumbling hum of conversation, kids shouting and footsteps sounded far away. Even the resident stonemasons who spouted bits of Latin were gone for lunch.

For a while he relished the feeling of isolation and being somewhere else. Unfortunately it didn't last. The sound of raucous voices came from behind him, tumbling like gravel and loose stones along the passageway.

'Damned tourists,' he hissed.

At first he saw only their shadows elongated and black, the light behind them.

Four young men swaggered into view, their loudness and size destroying the other world he'd been so comfortable in, their voices echoing off the ancient stones.

One of them was wearing a Bath University scarf. He was dark-haired, red-faced, and battled forwards like a full-back. The others too looked as though they were good at rugby; Bath did well at the game. C.A. had no time for games or sport of any kind — except war games, but they didn't count.

Colin scowled. He resented their intrusion. The acid rose on his tongue as much as from the booze as from the resentment.

They turned their cheery faces in his direction. He smelled the drink on them and guessed they'd had far more than a tipple. Funny that he could always tell when someone else had been drinking even though he himself was well-oiled.

One of them slapped his shoulder. 'All right, mate.'

Colin slapped his hand away in the same manner as he would a basking bluebottle.

'I am not your mate.'

'Ooow. Touchy.'

Wright scowled. These boys had been enjoying their drink, though in the company of others whereas he preferred to drink alone.

One side of his mouth curled upwards into a sneer. 'You know what mate as a verb means? Well, that's what I'm telling you to do. And the word that goes with it is "off".'

The four young men stopped, their grins frozen on their faces. One broke first.

'Are you telling me to eff off?' asked the guy with the pink cheeks and the dark hair.

'You've got it, Snow White,' he replied, turning his back.

Behind his turned back, the young man frowned. Wright was right about one thing. He had been drinking — quite a lot in fact. So much that he hadn't noticed the stink of drink on Wright's breath because it had been cloaked in his own. Not that it mattered that much whether this man who'd annoyed him was drunk or not. His anger had fuel to feed on. Booze and bad words. Like Wright his common sense was on hold, his anger hot.

'Snow White? What the bloody hell do you mean by that?'

'Let it be, Deke.'

One of his friends tried to lead him away, placing a hand on his shoulder, pulling him back.

Deke shrugged off the restraining hand, his eyes blazing.

'He's taking the fucking piss.'

His outburst reverberated off the subterranean roof and walls. Head down, shoulders braced, he charged forward. Luckily for Wright his friends grabbed him.

'I'm warning you,' he snarled, fronds of slicked black hair falling damply on to his forehead. 'Shut your stupid mouth or it gets filled with my fist.'

Fired up with booze and confident that Deke's friends could hold him back, Wright's verbal abuse was undiminished. Sober he wouldn't have dared. Courage didn't run in his veins but Scotch did. He was enjoying this.

'Animals are not allowed in here, certainly not without a leash or a keeper. Best make for the exit where some kind human might give you a bunch of bananas and a pat on the head — or a kick up the backside.' He pointed along the walkway.

The pink cheeks flushed to purple. The man named Deke leapt forward. 'You . . .!'

Three pairs of hands grappled to hold him back.

'Deke! Come on, you bloody fool. Let it be. He's as drunk as we are.'

Wright's snarling smile was undiminished.

* * *

As the four young men left one of them commented on Wright's breath.

'Phew! Did you smell that guy? He stunk like a Highland distillery.'

'I did.' The spokesman was Johan, a tall blond with the longest reach of the lot of them. It was his arm that remained around Deke's neck, frogmarching him all the way to the exit.

'Hey! We were supposed to be having a look round,' Deke complained once they'd reached the more brightly lit foyer. 'I haven't seen enough dead Romans yet.'

Johan, his arm still round Deke's neck, gave him a shake. 'There aren't any dead Romans, you prick.'

'So what were we s'pose to see?' Deke was as surly as his speech.

Johan shook him. 'Leave it out. Bits of stone. Artefacts.'

'Nothing dead in there — though there could have been,' said the fourth member of their group. Dominic was from Samoa, over six feet tall and weighty. The university had chosen him rather than the other way round; he was a brilliant scrum half. Bath was up for bringing in new blood for its top-quality rugby team.

The guided tour that had preceded them were milling around, some asking their guide for bits of information before filtering off.

Caught in the crowd, the young men, all university students, bided their time.

'Better now?' Johan asked Deke. Like the others, he'd joined the university to play rugby — as well as doing a little studying. Hailing from Johannesburg, his main love was rugby, his aim to play for the national side, the Springboks, one glorious day. Apart from his passion for sport he was a steady guy, the anchor of common sense to the rest of them.

At first Deke did not respond.

'Are you?' Johan asked again.

Deke gave a feeble nod and Johan released him. 'Good boy,' he said, patting Deke's shoulder.

'Hey!'

Before he could stop him, Deke shot off, straight back into the Roman Baths.

Johan swore under his breath. 'What the hell's got into him?'

Stefan, the Polish member of their little band, belched tellingly. 'Seven pints of premium lager.'

'Christ!' Johan tore back in after him. Shouts went up from those manning the ticket office as the others attempted to follow.

One of the attendants, thinking they were trying to get in without paying, raced in after them, her voice and her face ripe with alarm.

'Excuse me, but returns are not allowed! You've only paid to go round once.'

Dominic, his shoulders almost filling the gap, turned round to reassure her. 'It's all right, Miss. One of our mates had too much lunchtime. We lost him in one of those dark corners. Don't mind if we go in to fetch him, do you?'

The woman looked unsure at first, but he was young, had twinkling eyes and a ready smile. Besides that his broad shoulders filled the gap like a made to measure door. Blushing, she patted her hair just a little too self-consciously and lowered her voice.

'All right. But be quick.'

Led by Johan, the three of them rushed back in to find their friend. Retracing their steps over stones worn shiny from the footfall of nearly two thousand years they found Deke kneeling beside a body lying on the floor.

Deke was looking down at the flat-out figure as though not sure what either him or the guy who had given them grief was doing there.

Thinking the worst, Stefan muttered another expletive, only this time in Polish.

'I think he's dead.'

Johan said what they were all thinking out loud. 'Oh Christ. You'll go down for this, Deke, you drunken sod.'

Deke looked up at him, a confused look in his eyes. 'I found him like it. Honest.'

Stefan bent his knees and peered closer. 'Is he dead?'

Deke shook his head. 'Of course he fucking ain't. He's pissed. I can smell it from up here. He smells like a bloody brewery — correction, a distillery.'

'He may have slipped and bumped his head,' Stefan added.

Deke grunted. 'Serves the old bugger right.'

Johan was used to taking charge of situations and of people. It was the way he'd been brought up.

'Well we can't leave him here. The old biddy outside is sure to call the police if we don't get our asses out of here and him too. Here. Help me get him up.'

C.A. Wright groaned as they hitched his arms around their shoulders so he could hang there between them. He muttered something as they carried him along, his feet dragging at times between a few unsteady steps.

'What's he say?' said Johan.

'Not a clue.' Deke was annoyed.

'Bollocks,' Wright muttered. 'Fucking perverts. Pansies, the lot of you.' He slumped a bit, his feet beginning to drag.

Stefan yanked Wright's arm and none too gently. This guy didn't know when to quit, the ungrateful bastard.

'Did he just call us what I think he called us?'

'Chuck him in the water. That should sober him up,' said Deke, accompanying his statement with a scowl.

'Are you sure you didn't hit him?' Johan sounded alarmed.

'No. But I was tempted.'

Another mumbled expletive.

Johan leaned him against a wall, cupped Wright's jaw with his hands, and shouted into his face. 'Look mate, we're trying to help you.'

'Piss off.'

'Friendly sort of bloke,' murmured Stefan.

Eventually they were out of the Baths, through the Pump Room entrance, and heading towards the shade of the colonnade between Abbey Square and Stall Street.

The girl Wright had propositioned earlier saw them coming and recognised who they were carrying.

Her bottom lip curled as she looked Wright over. 'What happened to him?'

Stefan locked eyes with her. 'Do you know him?'

'No. And I don't want to.' The interest she saw in Stefan's eyes wasn't unwelcome. She told it as it was, rattling her collection bucket as she did so. 'I asked him for money but he wanted a lot more than charity in return.'

'What a creep.'

She jerked her chin in a resolute nod. 'The worst kind. A drunken creep!'

In a bid to impress her, Stefan rattled off the info. 'And now he's out cold. At first we thought he'd slipped and bumped his head. He might have done. First and last his liver's had one hell of a hiding. Not a bloke likely to make old bones. Dead by the time he's fifty-five, I shouldn't wonder.'

'Couldn't happen to a better bloke,' grumbled Deke.

'Well, you lot got a cheek calling him a drunken bum. You've been drinking yourselves?' asked the girl.

Stefan grinned. 'We're students. What do you think?'

'I think you've been drinking.'

'Wanna come for a drink with us?'

'Possibly.' She grinned. 'So what are you going to do with him?'

Deke shook his head. 'Well we can't take him with us. Wouldn't want to. We experienced instant dislike when we met.'

'Me too,' said the girl. 'So what do you do with a drunk you don't want to go drinking with?'

'A bit of a lesson wouldn't come amiss. Would it?' Deke's eyes travelled to the gigantic teddy bear. A wicked grin spread across his face. 'Is that teddy bear hollow?'

The girl eyed him quizzically. 'Yes.'

The others, knowing Deke was a great one for cracking practical jokes, laughed and joked as they tried to read what was on his mind.

Deke's grin widened. 'Lads. I have a dastardly plan; something we wouldn't do if we were cold sober.' He paused. 'Well. Perhaps I would.'

By the time they'd finished and to the amusement of a few passers-by who noticed, they had stuffed C.A. Wright inside the giant teddy bear. Laughing and looking pleased with themselves, they brushed off their hands. Someone suggested they head for the nearest pub.

'He won't suffocate in there will he?'

'Course not.'

Stefan was looking at the girl.

'Are you up for coming with us?'

'I might be.'

'Are you alone?'

Her sidelong glance met his. Her lips were pale pink and smiling. 'Yes. Everyone else has gone off for lunch.'

'What's your name?'

'Tracey Maplin.'

He bowed and clicked his heels together. 'Tracey, would you care to join our merry band for a sub and coffee, the latter liberally laced with best quality Courvoisier?'

Tracey Maplin had dated quite a few students in her time. Most of them were stony broke. A student who offered her coffee laced with brandy wasn't short of cash. 'You sound flush.'

'Won a bit spread betting online,' he replied.

It was good enough for her. Smiling she hooked her arm through his. 'I think that's the best suggestion I've had all day. It beats keeping company with a teddy bear. Anyway, Teddy Devlin is quite capable of taking care of himself.'

CHAPTER FOUR

Honey looked up at the sound of the applause coming from the conference room and smiled. Doherty's ordeal was finally over.

'He's done it,' she breathed, sounding as though she'd had no doubt that he'd sail through his talk.

Lindsey chuckled. 'That brave policeman looked as though he were about to confront a pride of lions, not a group of literature enthusiasts from Somerset. But then, that sort of crowd can be very intimidating.'

Honey was inclined to agree with her. 'I'll buy him lunch. That should make up for it.'

'He could probably do with a cuddle or two.'

Honey found herself blushing like a sixteen-year-old schoolgirl.

'Lindsey!'

Her daughter grinned up at her from beneath the triangular-shaped fringe that covered one side of her face. The geometric style was coloured a fetching shade of light orange, Lindsey's colour of the month.

'Relax, Mother. You were a woman before you became my mum, and you're still a woman now. Plus you're single, plus you could do with some male company now and again.'

It was hard not to blush. This was her daughter offering to keep her on track in the modern world of relationships.

'I'll bear that in mind,' she murmured, her pink cheeks hidden behind her flopped-forward hair.

Honey had always held the belief that there were few secrets between her and her daughter, though actually it seemed like one-way traffic of late. Lindsey was as outspoken as ever about her love life; the latest in a long series of boyfriends was named Archie.

'The last of the Goths,' Lindsey had told her mother before bringing him home for coffee.

There was no need for her to explain further. Archie, who bore a glancing resemblance to Johnny Depp and his character in *Sleepy Hollow*, had not shaken off the black clothes, silver studs, and ring-through-the-nose fashion first introduced in the eighties. Back then Honey had taken the view that the Gothic punk phase was a natural reaction to the sleek looks and sweet harmonies of Abba. She'd been keen on the darker look herself but that was years ago. Bearing in mind the generation gap, she had not expected ever to see the like again. Now there was Archie: black clothes, black hair, black eyeliner, and what looked like a small bedspring inserted into his right ear. Another one hung from his nose.

Lindsey was cool about Archie. 'It's just a phase. I'm intrigued as to how he'll come out of it and what he'll turn into, so for now I'll hang in there, just to see what develops.'

Her mother wasn't at all sure what Archie would turn into, and whether she would find out was up to Lindsey having the patience and curiosity to hang on in there.

As far as her own relationship was concerned, she couldn't be cool about Doherty, at least not in front of her daughter. 'I'm just sensitive,' she'd said to her friend Rachel who she'd had lunch with the day before.

'You're old-fashioned, Honey. Do you remember Pauline Palmer? She's had at least four live-in lovers since divorcing good old Dave the builder. And that's a woman with three kids.'

'And you?'

Rachel had paused. 'Justin is at college. I mostly confine my liaisons to the times when he's away, but things have gone a little awry. He caught me unawares. Came home unexpectedly.'

'And?'

Again there'd been a pregnant pause. 'He pointed out that chlamydia is very prevalent among the over-fifties. I was livid! I'm only forty-six!'

Old friends were not the best people to talk to about relationships. Rachel was a case in point. She couldn't stand the course — and she couldn't be faithful.

'I get bored easily,' she stated whilst stuffing a spoonful of clotted cream and rum and raisin cheesecake into her mouth.

Lunching with Rachel more than once a month was hazardous to the waistline; on the advisory, agony aunt front, it was a dead loss.

Sighing, Honey cupped her face in her hands and went back to scrutinising the marketing plan for the coming year.

An instantly recognisable voice came winging through the air. 'Good morning, everyone.'

Mary Jane, a permanent resident of the Green River Hotel, was floating down the stairs and would have looked like some ancient apparition if it hadn't been for the clothes she was wearing. She was tall, thin, and had pale blue eyes that could fix you with a frightening stare when she got intense about something — and she got intense a lot.

Her fashion sense was stuck in a time warp and on two favourite colours — pistachio green and shocking pink. Today she was wearing a tracksuit made of some shiny velvet kind of material that had been the in thing along with platform shoes and fluffed-up hairdos several years ago. Though dated, the upside of wearing luminescent outfits was that she was never likely to get run over by a bus on a moonless night.

Taking great strides with her overlong legs, she almost seemed to float across the room. She was on them before they expected her. Despite the avalanche of face powder and as many wrinkles as you'd find on a shrivelled apple, there was an intensity to those sharp blue eyes that couldn't be ignored.

Her voice was hushed as though she didn't want anyone else to hear.

'I had a dream,' she said breathlessly, her long, skinny fingers gripping the reception counter. 'I dreamed I was flying over the rooftops in my car and finally came down to earth in the middle of the Royal Crescent. Unfortunately, the car landed on a passer-by. I think it was that Casper fellow friend of yours. I must say I sincerely hope it doesn't happen. I wouldn't want to be locked up for manslaughter. Do you think it possible?'

Honey patted her hand. 'Did you have blue cheese for supper last night?'

Mary Jane nodded. 'I only had fish for main course so had cheese and biscuits afterwards to fill me up.'

'Then that's the cause of your dream.'

'Ah,' said Mary Jane, holding erect one thin, pointed finger. 'I was just wondering about that old saying, *a Friday-night dream on a Saturday told, will come true be it never so old.*'

Mother and daughter froze — mother more so. Bearing Mary Jane's driving in mind, it wasn't beyond belief that this particular dream might come true.

However, nothing much got past Lindsey and her sharp-eyed observation that it was Tuesday and she probably had no need to worry.

Mary Jane's narrow chest heaved as she sighed with relief. 'I'm really glad about that. At my age I couldn't cope with a careless driver cutting me up in their car.'

'That would be worrying,' said Honey, wearing her sweetest smile. The fact of the matter was that Mary Jane had to be the worst driver in Bath. If anyone was going to be careless and cut other drivers up, it was her.

Honey shook her head in exasperation. Some days the Green River seemed more like an asylum than a hotel. But never mind. Keep your head and soldier on.

'Just to be on the safe side perhaps you'd care to stick to walking today — just long enough to settle your nerves,' said Lindsey, eyeing Mary Jane from beneath the fringe of her carrot-coloured hair. Lindsey adopted a different colour for every season, sometimes for every week.

'That's a very good idea. Why didn't I think of that?' The answer was obvious; Lindsey was a very rational person. Honey was more 'seat of the pants' kind of thinking. However, Honey was proud of her daughter's logical mindset. She was the anchor to her gas-filled balloon of a brain.

'So what are you up to today, Mary Jane?' Honey asked her.

'I'm off to the country. I want to find somewhere tranquil to be buried once I've crossed over. Bearing in mind that I'm an ethereal creature in touch with her earth as well as her air side, I'm off to see this place called Memory Meadow. It's environmentally friendly, and I'm all for that.'

Lindsey pointed out that she'd said her spirit would roam the Green River along with Sir Cedric, her long-dead ancestor.

Mary Jane agreed that this was true. She had indeed suggested that her spirit would forever haunt the Green River Hotel. It was a family tradition to haunt the place and she intended upholding that tradition.

'However,' she went on. 'My spirit will be resident here most of the time, but the rest of the time it'll be moseying around wherever my earthly remains are interred.'

To Honey's ears it sounded like some kind of dead souls' retreat, a place where they could lie around a swimming pool, play poker with friends, and have all the time in the world to complete *The Times* crossword.

'Is it really possible that when you cross over you can book in and out of a place at will?' she asked.

Mary Jane looked affronted. 'Of course it's possible. In fact it's perfectly logical. You send messages from your phone, don't you? The message goes out there, but the phone is still in your pocket. Right?'

Honey felt a silly smile creep on to her lips, disrupting the professional stance she daily fought hard to maintain.

Lindsey had sucked in her breath. If she didn't let it out pretty soon she was liable to pass out. But if she did exhale, she'd probably burst out laughing.

Mother and daughter therefore made the effort to look as though messages from the 'other side' were not that much different to your average phone call. Dealing with Mary Jane had never been easy. She had an "otherworldly" logic which sometimes bordered on cuckoo. But Mary Jane was a guest at the Green River and the customer is always right. It was Mary Jane's logic so they had to accept it.

With a sweeping movement of her very long right arm, Mary Jane threw a soft pink pashmina around her scrawny neck.

'Right. I'm off to pick up your mother. It was her that thought this Memory Meadow place was right up my street,' she declared with an air of self-importance. 'Gloria is expecting me at twelve. Toodle-oo!'

Mary Jane swept through the first people emerging from the conference room.

Lindsey shook her head despairingly. 'I really don't know what's happening to the older generation. What happened to the little old grannies baking cakes and knitting oversize sweaters?'

'They're all dead.'

The thought of her mother, Gloria Cross, knitting or baking anything was totally off the wall. She didn't do either. She shopped if she wanted warm woollen sweaters and ate out if she wanted a decent piece of cake. Much the same applied to Mary Jane but for different reasons.

The revolving doors swung into action. In the process they belched out the head chef, Smudger Smith, a dab hand with a meat cleaver and a pretty good one with a frying pan too.

Without glancing to either side, fists clenched tightly, he ploughed through Reception with rounded shoulders and a severe frown on his face. He glowered just in time for Honey to notice and worry that she may have done something wrong before he disappeared through the double doors leading to the kitchen. Chefs were prickly and arrogant, but if they were good, you did your damnedest to hold on to them. Honey had every intention of doing that.

She opened her mouth to ask him what was wrong.

'Don't ask,' he snapped.

She thought about it but decided that she was the employer, he was the employee and she had every right to ask.

'I take it the salamander wasn't up to much.'

'Don't. Ask,' he snapped again, and headed off to the kitchen.

Lindsey pressed the button on the Dragon voice recorder she was only just getting used to. The unit would record and could be transferred on to the computer. It was really for taking verbal bookings. Lindsey was testing it out.

Smudger's words were repeated.

'Oh dear. I'm afraid harmony is going to be in short supply in the kitchen today,' she remarked.

Honey had to agree with her. 'And all over a salamander.' She pulled a face. 'I wonder what went wrong? I'd better ask him, when he's calmed down a bit.'

Charles Sheet of the North Somerset and West Wiltshire Agatha Christie Association came up to confirm that an extra place had been set for Doherty for lunch. Honey said that it had not and apologised for the oversight.

'I'm sure he'd love to join you.'

She wasn't really sure about that at all, but as a seasoned hotelier she knew that the first rule of thumb was to tell the guest what he or she wanted to hear. For a time at least, everything would be fine.

Lindsey was nothing if not a seasoned co-conspirator. 'I'll make sure it's done,' she said with the kind of sincerity that becomes part of the professional persona.

Neither hoteliers nor chairmen of fan clubs could account for the unexpected. Honey espied Doherty coming out of the conference room. He was wearing a serious expression and had his phone flat against his ear.

'Well, he looks relieved,' Honey remarked. 'Though engaged.'

Lindsey eyed him too. 'You can say that again. Before he went in he looked as though he'd seen a ghost.'

'One ghost around here is quite enough,' Honey said, thinking of Sir Cedric.

'I'd like to see him sometime,' said Lindsey, whilst thoughtfully nibbling the tip of her pen.

'So would I.' Honey's remark piggybacked on a deep sigh.

'Are you talking about Doherty. I was talking about Sir Cedric.'

'Yep! I'll be right there,' Doherty was saying as Honey watched him.

He sounded serious and he certainly looked serious, but Honey had known him long enough to know the truth. She could tell when he was bluffing. Where was that tiny tic he tended to get beneath his right eye when something big was going down, i.e. murder most foul?

Looping her arm through his, she held him tight against her. With her free hand she stroked his face as she smiled up at him in such a way as to lull him into a false sense of security.

He smiled back at her, his voice softening as he did so.

'I won't be long. Just a personal matter to attend to and I'll be right there . . .'

'Personal matter, my foot,' she said quietly.

'Well . . . yes . . .'

His words were aimless and he hadn't the bird of prey look in his eyes. That was how she'd likened his look; when there was a job to be done, a killer to apprehend, his eyes took on the look of an eagle, the colour intensifying, the look sharp and far-reaching before getting his talons into the killer.

At present she didn't believe he was anything of the sort. His mind certainly wasn't on work. Neither was the phone call but it wouldn't hurt to get it confirmed.

'Now tell me, sweet thing,' she said in her sweetest, sexiest voice. 'Are you really speaking to somebody on the other end of that thing or are you trying to avoid having lunch with the Agatha Christie enthusiasts?'

'Excuse me a moment,' he said before taking the phone away from his face. 'There's been an emergency,' he said to her.

'Of course, darling.' Her fingers traced the edge of his jaw.

'Look, I have to . . .'

He couldn't help tripping over his words though he only admitted to himself that he was putty in her hands. It happened only rarely and usually following some serious sensuality. On this occasion she'd only implied sexuality, acting sensual, acting as though every wish was her command. The subterfuge was enough for him to loosen his grip on the phone.

Honey grabbed it, turned it over and looked at the screen. She pointed. 'The screen's dead. It's not even switched on.'

He snatched it back. 'Bear with me on this. Please.'

He went back to what he'd been doing, pretending to be on the phone. He paced purposefully to the other side of Reception. Honey went back behind the reception desk.

'What's he up to?' asked Lindsey.

'He's taking evasive action.' She nudged her daughter with her elbow. Lindsey took in the scene outside the conference room. The reasons for his behaviour were spilling out of the door to the conference room and flocking like pigeons. Most of them were heading for lunch in the restaurant. Three ladies were hanging back, politely waiting for him to finish his call.

One of them, a lady in a floral dress with a matching band holding back a square-shaped bob, tottered across to the reception desk and whispered behind a cupped hand, 'We insist he sits on our table for lunch. We want to get hold of him before anyone else does.'

So do I, Honey thought, but no worries. I'm OK to stand in line.

Her smile was broad and beaming. 'The company of three ladies for lunch. How wonderful. He won't believe his luck.'

'Fame at last,' murmured Lindsey. 'Doherty has his own team of groupies.'

'He'll be thrilled,' Honey murmured back.

The moment he'd finished the call, the women were upon him. The likeness to pigeons went out of the window. It was now like seeing a flock of hyenas circling a wounded buffalo.

'We insist you have lunch with us,' cried one in a high-pitched voice.

'We absolutely insist,' said another.

'We won't take no for an answer,' trilled the third.

Doherty shook his head sadly. 'Sorry, ladies. Duty calls.'

Honey watched impassively, her elbow sliding slightly on the polished reception countertop, hand across her mouth so that no one could see her smile.

They accepted his declining of their invitation stoically though she fancied she saw their eyes fluttering and the odd blush spreading over their silky soft faces. Old memories never die, she thought, and neither do old passions.

Their expressions were full of disappointment.

'What a shame. We could have given you the benefit of our experience,' said the first, who wore a beret and had wrinkles as deep as tramlines.

'No doubt you could,' Doherty said gallantly.

'We've read all of Agatha's books,' said the second. 'We know how to look out for bits of cloth left on bushes and footprints in the rose beds.'

'Great,' said Doherty, maintaining a smile on his lips though his eyes said: 'Get me out of here.'

The three ladies began heading for the restaurant, but paused before they got there and turned to face him. 'Just you remember that if you ever need us to help you with one of your cases, feel free to get in touch.'

Doherty forced a final smile. 'I will.'

Lindsey folded her arms on the counter and dropped her head on to them, her shoulders shaking with laughter.

Doherty's smile dropped. 'Very funny.'

Honey cocked an eyebrow. 'You passed up on a date with three women? They were gasping for your company. You must have seriously impressed them.'

Heaving a deep sigh, he looked skywards. 'Quit the funnies. I did what you asked me to do.'

'They loved it?'

'Thoroughly,' he said, not without some smugness. 'They enjoyed it but they asked a lot of questions.'

'What's wrong with that?'

He threw her a hard look. 'Once the professional questions were over, they moved on to the personal ones. They wanted to know if I was married.'

'Looks like you've got the beginnings of a harem,' Lindsey sniggered.

Honey jammed an elbow in her daughter's side. Her own lips were doing a kind of soft-shoe shuffle as she tried to stifle her own amusement.

'OK, OK. It's not that funny,' said Doherty, sounding a little off. 'And there actually was a phone call at first. Not a big case. Just something of an emergency. I just hung it out a bit. I have to get away.'

'OK,' said Honey, straightening both her navy-blue shirt and her expression at the same time. 'So! What's the emergency? Anyone got murdered?'

'Sorry to disappoint you, but no, they have not. It's a case of kidnap.'

Honey frowned. He sounded terribly light-hearted about it, but surely kidnap was a serious offence.

'Anyone we know?' asked Lindsey.

'You might do. Apparently, Teddy Devlin's gone missing.'

'Who?'

Both women said it in unison.

'Girls, you are so ill-informed,' he said, looking at them with amusement. 'Teddy Devlin is the eight-foot-high mascot of the Devlin Community Project. They use him for fund-raising events. You may have seen him propped up near the abbey with people milling around him collecting money for good causes.'

Lindsey clicked her fingers. 'I've got it. He's a teddy bear! You've been called in on a case of a missing teddy bear — correction, a *kidnapped* teddy bear.'

Doherty grinned and his eyes twinkled. 'My dates for lunch were charming, but a teddy bear? I just cannot resist.'

CHAPTER FIVE

The dreaded day had dawned when Sean O'Brian, beloved of many of the SASAs of the city (as in senior and sexually active), was being planted in fertile earth. It was a Friday and the funeral was to take place in the pretty country church next door to Memory Meadow, the modern and ecologically friendly way to be buried. On top of that it was raining.

Dressed head to toe in black though far from feeling grief, Honey sighed.

'The great outdoors, mud and rain. Now isn't that just my luck?'

'Sometimes I think you've got your own personal rain cloud following you around,' Lindsey remarked. 'Hope I haven't inherited it.'

'I don't think you have,' Honey replied, thinking of her daughter's life. The sun shone when Lindsey went for a day out. If she went skiing the snow was always the right depth. If she went abroad for a holiday in the off-season the sunshine was guaranteed to be as bright as on a summer's day.

Honey sighed into her morning coffee. There'd been no chance of getting out of the funeral though God knows she'd tried, but here she was, suitably geared out in black, hanging around until the last possible minute. She'd phoned her mother the night before in an effort to wriggle out of her promise. Citing illness, lack of staff, and dying from some dreadful disease had cut no ice. Her mother was adamant.

'Hannah! You promised.'

The phone rang. Lindsey took the call.

She could tell from what Lindsey was saying that her mother was on the other end of the phone.

'Why didn't I offer to pay for a taxi?' she groaned.

Lindsey put down the phone. 'She says to remind you.'

Honey sighed.

Lindsey went back to her computer screen. 'Mother, it's water under the bridge.'

'You're right there,' Honey remarked gloomily. 'It's raining cats and dogs.'

Lindsey's attention was fixed on the computer screen. She seemed far more enthralled with that than with her mother's reservations and moans about attending a funeral.

Her eyes were bright with interest. 'Hey, look at this lot.'

Honey watched as her daughter deleted a series of emails with a swiftly moving finger.

Suddenly she was gripped in a moment of unexpected nostalgia remembering the first time she'd held that tiny finger one of four and a thumb on her newborn's hand. She'd counted all her daughter's fingers and toes, marvelling at how perfectly formed they were. She'd wanted to share that joy, but had no one to share it with, certainly not the other person who had contributed to her daughter's existence. On the day Lindsey was born her father was away sailing and Honey was alone. She'd never forgiven Carl for that. He should have been there, if not for her then at least for their daughter.

Absorbed in what she was doing, Lindsey didn't see the look on her mother's face, her attention riveted on trawling and deleting.

'Look at some of this rubbish. Shall I read it to you?' Her voice was full of contempt.

'Sure. Maybe just one,' said Honey, still warm from the memory of her baby daughter.

Lindsey chose a message. 'This one should hit the spot.' She went on to read the email purporting to be from the brother of an assassinated African politician with money in a bank account who would share the proceeds if you would use your bank account to get around some legal wrangle.

'Then they've got your bank account details and clear out your money,' Lindsey went on.

'Or in my case they get my overdraft and a warning letter of closure from the bank,' Honey commented wryly.

'You're not the ideal victim, Mother. They try and target people with actual money in the bank. Sometimes they go amiss. They get away with it because most of the time, the banks cover the loss. The banks get stuffed.'

The thought of stuffing her bank — and more specifically her bank manager — was intriguing. She peered more closely at the screen just in case one of these scams had found money in her account that she didn't know she had.

'So what's that one about?' She pointed at an email that Lindsey was about to delete. The subject was listed as 'Save for your Grave. Your Plot Number 172341.' The deal was that you paid for a plot online at a graveyard of your choice. All you had to do was pay a £300 deposit. '*Your last wishes observed putting your mind and your family at ease.*'

'Hmm!' exclaimed Lindsey, sitting upright and viewing the message with downright scepticism. 'You pay £300 and that's the last you see of your money. There's no plot. No such company. Nice deal, huh?'

'Well, it is for the recipient of the money,' said Honey. 'What's commonly called a nice little earner.'

Her gaze and her thoughts wandered away from the computer screen to this damned funeral she had to go to. How the hell could she get out of it?

Propped up on one elbow over the reception desk, her mind was ticking with possibilities even at this late stage. 'I mean if I could come up with a good enough excuse . . .'

Lindsey's face burst into a big grin. 'You're incorrigible.'

'Just reluctant,' Honey responded.

Lindsey shook her head disapprovingly. 'I know what you're thinking, a whole day with a group of old ladies and you're thinking of saying, "Mother, I can't possibly leave Lindsey alone to manage this place by herself." Well, cut it out. You know damned well I can manage.'

Honey considered other excuses. 'Perhaps if you said you were ill . . .'

Lindsey shook her head. 'Now, now, Mother. I'm not going to pretend to be ill. I'm not going to pretend to be incapable. If you really didn't want to go you should have let Mary Jane take them in your car.'

Honey gasped. 'I couldn't! You've seen the way she drives.'

'The car would have survived.'

'But would your grandmother have survived? Would her friends? God knows but they're pretty decrepit as it is without travelling with Mary Jane.'

'Well, there you go. It's no good. It's too late to back out now. You should have been thinking on your feet.'

Honey heaved a heavy sigh. 'Are you sure you don't want to take my place?'

Lindsey shook her head. 'No. Anyway, I know you've got ulterior motives. There's a great auction going down at Bonhams and you'd prefer to be there.'

'But I've got a hole in my umbrella.' She held it up tellingly, wriggling her finger through the said hole like an agitated earthworm.

Lindsey pointed out that even Smudger, head chef and one-time all-in-one wrestler, had total faith in her capabilities. According to him Lindsey could run the place standing on her head — and had, many times.

Heaving another elephantine sigh did nothing whatsoever to attract her daughter's pity or spur her into changing places. Children could be so exasperating at times.

'I suppose I'd better be off.'

'I suppose you'd better.' Lindsey grinned.

Using both hands, Honey pulled her hat firmly down on to her head and left the hotel feeling beaten and bettered.

Once outside neither the hat nor the umbrella was equal to the pouring rain. Water dripped through the hole in the umbrella all the way to the car park. Wearing a broad-brimmed hat didn't help matters because the broad brim kept connecting with the umbrella spokes. It was a job to keep it on and gradually, very gradually, the sweeping brim was becoming waterlogged and starting to flop.

Getting into the car was some respite. The car was in the multi-storey, dry and protected from the rain — unlike herself who'd got sopping wet on her way here. Once the heater was switched on and directed at her feet she felt a hell of a lot better.

Traffic beetled its way through the inclement weather. Tourists huddled in shop doorways along with the policeman who should have been on traffic duty. Progress was slow but Honey didn't feel much like rushing anyway.

The building where her mother lived came into view, splendidly archaic and hinting at the elegance of a bygone age. Unlike some of her friends, Gloria Cross had not moved into a flat for the over-fifty-fives, preferring something more traditional, more elegant, and a lot more expensive.

Built around 1800, the building had at one time housed a lord and his family, their second home which they used when accompanying the Prince Regent to Bath. The conversion to luxury apartments had taken place in the eighties, but the elaborate ironwork balconies — reminiscent of those in New Orleans — were still *in situ* and combined favourably with the modern interiors. The flats having such balconies were more expensive than others in the building.

Hanging baskets bright with scarlet geraniums, trailing aubrietia, and variegated ivy hung from the ironwork and greenery planted in pots peered over the balustrade.

As though trading on instinct, her mother's head bobbed over the balcony of her flat. 'Ah. You're here at last. You're cutting it a bit fine, you know.' The voice was ripe with reprimand.

'The traffic was heavy because of the rain,' Honey shouted back. The excuse sounded lame but on this occasion was the absolute truth.

'Dora's coming down in the lift with us but she'll need some assistance getting into the car.'

Typical. A good excuse and it was totally ignored. It just didn't pay to tell the truth.

'OK.'

But her mother had already disappeared, no doubt gone inside to inform everyone that her daughter was late, but there, it was only to be expected. She never could be on time. Never could be as perfect as she had wanted her to be.

Honey glowered up at the sky. The rain had eased but still threatened. Getting another soaking should be avoided at all costs and the only way to do that — besides purchasing a new umbrella — was making a direct appeal to the powers that be.

'God, would you please hold off until I get Dora into the car. It could take some time and I don't want this hat brim to get any floppier than it already is.'

Dora was plump and walked with two sticks and owned a Norfolk terrier named Bobo that wasn't properly house-trained. Bobo was of the persuasion that if you gotta go, you gotta go. And she did. Often.

The lift doors opened, revealing four women all dressed in black. Even the horrendous Bobo sported a black bow tied to her collar.

On sight of Honey, the little dog wagged from head to tail. Unfortunately its warm welcome had a downside. As it wagged it trickled urine all over the marble tiles of the foyer.

'Bobo is *so* excited to see you,' trilled Dora, seemingly unaware of the dog's lack of good manners.

Feeling she should appear delighted to see the dog even though she was not, Honey gave the little bitch a cursory pat and a few words of endearment.

'Bobo. How lovely to see you.' Once she was out of Dora's earshot her tone changed. 'If you pee in my car you'll be running behind, at the end of a very long leash.'

Umbrellas went up the moment the gang of four hit the outside air. The rain was back with a vengeance and their feet sloshed over the wet pavement as they scuttled to the car.

Honey was lumbered with the task of getting Dora and her dog into the front passenger seat. Being of medium size or smaller, the other three piled into the back, their umbrellas sticking out through the back doors like porcupine quills as they shook rainwater all over the place.

Dora, being of copious proportions, squeezed herself into the front, the very excitable Bobo on her lap.

The French are not known for making limousines; Honey's Citroën was spacious enough for five normal-sized people. Dora was not normal-sized. Her lap was copious and her whole body was big. Bobo was perched on Dora's belly, her front paws resting on the dashboard.

Feeling the rain soaking into her back, Honey took Dora's walking sticks and put them in the boot along with her umbrella, there being no room at the front.

Her black hat, a nice felt trilby style with a black ribbon around the crown, was getting distinctly droopy. So was the black dress she was wearing. Luckily she'd opted for boots, a little over the top perhaps in the middle of June, but she'd never trusted the weather gods since a sailing trip with Carl from the Isles of Scilly to South Wales. Her ex-husband, now deceased following over-confidence while sailing in the teeth of a North Atlantic gale, had assured her that everything would be all right because all the weather forecasts on his electronic gizmos had said it would be so. It hadn't been. Far from it, in fact. Unluckily for him he'd drowned. Luckily for her she hadn't been with him.

The windscreen wipers swished all the way to Much Maryleigh. It was as though somebody was throwing buckets of water at the screen.

Oblivious to the weather, the girls in the back and Dora in the front were discussing the attributes of the deceased. It was unanimously agreed that Sean O'Brian had loved the ladies — a lot!

'He knew how to give a girl a good time,' said her mother. 'Money was no object.'

Sean had been a retired bank official operating on an international level and was known to be wealthy.

'His pension alone was six figures a year,' said Amber. Amber sported an orange wig beneath her cloche-style hat. The hat was purple but Amber had become eccentric with age. She didn't believe in conforming. Her real name wasn't Amber at all, but Millicent. She'd decided at seventy to change her image and her name. The sparse grey hair had been hidden beneath a wig and her name had gone west too.

There was something to be said for sporting a wig, thought Honey. Having glanced in her mirror she'd noticed that Amber's hair was still dry and shiny, its nylon content leaving it untouched by the dampness. The purple hat had a feather in it.

'He also had a very large stock market investment portfolio,' Edith, the fourth of their party, added.

'According to rumours, that's not all that was large,' sniggered Dora.

The others joined her. They sounded like schoolgirls. Honey found herself rolling her eyes.

'Arlene Tipping was always very lucky. I knew her when we were at school together,' said Edith, a lithe woman with pursed lips and big earrings.

Honey recalled Arlene as being tanned with striking blonde hair and two-inch long fingernails. Why anyone, least of all somebody of her age, would want fingernails like that, she didn't know. It brought too many difficulties to mind.

'Of course, my Hannah had her chance with Sean,' declared Gloria Cross.

Honey cringed. 'Mother!'

'He offered to partner her on a Saga cruise. It was obvious he was interested. I tried to persuade her, but she wouldn't listen to me. Children never do, do they?'

The others shook their heads in sombre agreement and murmured exactly what Honey's mother wanted to hear.

'That's kids for you.'

Honey gritted her teeth. Best not to make comment that Sean was years older than her with a body that had seen better days. On top of that she was not a child. Best not prolong the agony.

Then the subject of conversation altered to the subject of coffins though for no particular reason as far as Honey could work out.

'My money's on a walnut casket with solid brass handles,' Dora declared. 'Don't you think so, Bobo?' she added in a high voice, chucking the little creature under the chin.

Bobo wagged her tail, tongue hanging out as she looked up into the fat face of her mistress.

Honey thought of her car seat. Hopefully any wetness would be absorbed by Dora's dress. Besides, it could never get through that enormous lap, could it?

St Luke's church loomed up before them through a curtain of pouring rain. Umbrellas mushroomed around the church door, everyone trying to push through into the dry.

Bobo bared her teeth when Honey tried to help Dora out of the car.

'She's just being playful,' trilled Dora when Bobo snapped her jaws less than an inch from Honey's fingers.

'Of course she is.' Honey gritted her teeth. Bobo, she decided, was living on borrowed time.

By the time she'd got them all out her hat brim was flopping over her face. It was just at that point that the sun decided to come out. A rainbow arched over the rear of the church. All eyes looked skyward, smiles and satisfaction out in bucketfuls.

'Sean would have liked that,' her mother commented. 'He always did like the sun on his skin.'

Bobo tiddled all up the church path.

Gloria Cross lingered looking up at the sky. Honey was bringing up the rear — after all, she wasn't really a mourner. She could even stay outside the church if she wanted to.

She paused by her mother.

'Did that dog leave any puddles in your place?' she whispered to her mother.

'Certainly not,' she whispered back. 'I put her in the janitor's closet out on the landing. I didn't tell Dora that.'

'Obviously not,' murmured Honey.

The church was crowded, mostly with women. The reason for that could have been that women outlive men anyway, though the women attending might also have been members of the Sean O'Brian fan club.

She noted that most of them had been sensible enough to bring umbrellas without holes in. Their clothes were still pristine while her clothes were steaming. I must look like a half-baked jacket potato, she thought.

Despite their age and their joints, the fearsome four she'd brought here marched off down the aisle, letting nothing get in their way.

Old ladies, in fact old folk in general, have angular, bony elbows, lethal weapons they use indiscriminately if you happen to stray unknowingly into their path. The girls had arrived and were out to get a good view of what was going on.

Heads down, elbows sticking out at lethal angles, they pushed their way through. A few scuffles cleared the way. Some others knew better than to get in the way. Eventually Gloria and her friends managed to get a pew halfway down and with a good view of the altar and the vicar officiating. Honey followed, suddenly glad that her hat brim was flopping over her face; it hid her embarrassment.

Her mother gave her a push. 'You get in first. I want to be on the end so I can see what's going on.'

The old ladies stood back whilst Honey eased herself along the pew until she was pressed up against the whitewashed wall.

Some of those who'd been dug in the ribs or had their toes mangled beneath a purposeful footstep threw venomous looks their way, not that the old girls noticed or, if they did, they were big enough to ignore it. Their bickering among themselves was loud — too loud for attending church anyway.

Honey rolled her eyes heavenwards. The hammer beams overhead were suddenly of infinite interest. She wished she was up there, perched like a pigeon while the service went on beneath her.

At last they were all settled and getting ready to pay homage at the funeral of a man they'd much admired, perhaps even lusted after. Dora got out a box of paper tissues and blew her nose. The box was quite large. Honey couldn't make up her mind whether the tissues were to mop up their tears or one of Bobo's 'little accidents'.

Never mind. The flagstone floor was easily cleaned. The old girls were in their element. They didn't need her now. They could enjoy the service in peace — even in enjoyment, if that was the right word.

For the first time since collecting them the tension left Honey's shoulders and the knot in her stomach slowly began to unravel. Closing her eyes she bowed her head as though in prayer, though to be quite honest it wouldn't take much and she would be dozing. She was drained, but at least she was through the worst of it. Now all she had to do was get through the sermon, the burial, and the wake, then get them home again. Simple! Given half a chance she'd doze off between now and then.

Suddenly, a voice that could only be described as disturbingly resonant burst into song.

Honey, whose eyelids had been feeling heavy, sat bolt upright. Had she missed something? She certainly hadn't heard any introduction. *Because you were dozing*, she told herself.

No chance of that now, she decided.

The voice stirred to the rafters.

Instead of an organ a young woman in a clingy silk dress with a low-cut neckline had burst into the first verse of 'Simply the Best'. Tina Turner she was not. Nevertheless, the song choice came as something of a surprise. Honey had been expecting 'All Things Bright and Beautiful' or, more fittingly, 'The Day Thou Gavest Lord Has Ended'.

Honey looked around her. With the exception of her immediate companions, the congregation was looking stiffly at the altar. Her mother and the others were tapping their feet and fingers and humming along. At the same time, their necks were craned, heads turned towards the aisle and the Norman arch through which Sean O'Brian would take his final promenade.

Mother and friends were determined not to miss a thing, principally checking what the coffin was made of. Dora had bet ten pounds on walnut. They'd all taken sides so there was no way they were going to miss getting a last shifty at Sean O'Brian, a man of legendary proportions if gossip was anything to go by. They still couldn't quite take on board that environmentally friendly meant something far less than oak, ash, mahogany, or walnut.

The whisper ran from one end of the pew to the other and from the front pews all the way to the back.

Honey raised her eyes to heaven again — not in prayer, merely in forbearance. From gazing at the rafters, which didn't seem half so interesting as before, she let her gaze wander to some members of the congregation. Short, fat, skinny, tall, and all the shapes and sizes in between.

Not everyone was dressed in black. There was a surprising amount of green being worn. Some of the younger women were wearing garlands around their heads, summer solstice types who looked as though they would be travelling on to Glastonbury for the festival after the service was over. Some of the men had dreadlocks the colour of straw and tangled like horsehair from an overstuffed sofa.

'I'm betting on mahogany,' her mother murmured. 'I can't believe he'd go for anything less than that despite this environmental lark.'

But Dora stuck to her guns. Her money was still on walnut.

The four of them turned their heads, waiting for the coffin to make its dignified progress down the aisle. Honey wished she could shrink to three inches high and make a dash for the exit. Old ladies could be so embarrassing; she vowed she would never end up that way.

It struck her suddenly that Bobo was incredibly quiet. The little terrier was usually vocal as well as excitable. A quick glance ascertained that the black bow had been removed from Bobo's collar and tied around her muzzle.

Poor thing. OK, she wasn't the best behaved of dogs, but funerals were no place to take them. She'd have been better left musing and messing around her own garden leaving the adults to get on with things.

It was whilst Honey was coming to that conclusion that the coffin passed. Her money was on pine or even matchwood, something stiff but recycled from old orange boxes perhaps. Whatever the coffin was made of it was expected to be a departure from the norm. Those of a more traditional nature were bound to be shocked.

I'm right, she thought, on hearing a great intake of breath plus gasps of astonishment. She couldn't see the looks on the faces of her mother and her companions, but she could see their heads mutely following the coffin, their shoulders stiff as though they'd suddenly turned to stone.

It wasn't until the coffin had reached its allotted place before the altar that she saw the reason for their shock. Sean's coffin was not made of any endangered hardwood. In fact it wasn't made of wood at all but cardboard, and not any old cardboard. The coffin was brightly coloured, printed with an effigy that even from this distance she thought she recognised.

Well, she thought to herself, that explains the dreadlocks, the hippy-style songstress, and the predominance of green clothes as opposed to black. Good old Sean had been very committed to preservation of the environment. He'd picked Memory Meadow in the full knowledge of the nature of its burials. Not for him a shiny hardwood coffin with brass handles.

However, she just had to get the details verified; was that printed effigy on the coffin really what she thought it was?

Stretching her neck she stood on tiptoe, one hand resting on the pew in front for support. She wasn't the only one standing up and craning their neck to get a better view.

Whispers of amazement echoed from the ancient stonework. Like her there were others stretching their necks, wanting confirmation, too impatient to wait until they got outside to where old Sean was to be buried.

Thankfully, the vicar spoke only a few words, followed by Arlene, the widow who spoke even fewer.

'This was the funeral that Sean wanted. This is the poem he wrote.'

She unfolded a piece of paper, cleared her throat and read it out.

'I'm not in the earth,
I'm not into dying,
If you want to see me,
Look up, 'cause I'm flying.'

Nobody had a clue what was meant, but one or two, including Honey glanced up at the rafters. They were empty except for a few flitting pigeons. Was one of them Sean?

Like the others, she had to wait to properly see the coffin, but the wait was worth it. Two black clad undertakers pushed the trolley carrying Sean's coffin towards the exit to the strains of 'Hi Ho Silver Lining' where four pallbearers took over.

Leaning forward she finally got confirmation of what Sean had requested to be buried in. Her jaw dropped, but she also smiled. Sean O'Brian had indeed chosen one of the new cardboard coffins, not dissimilar to though larger than the sort of box the groceries arrive in.

But there the similarity ended big time. Sean's cardboard coffin was decorated with a picture of Superman. Superman's side view decorated the sides; Superman full frontal, complete with blue outfit and red underpants, was printed on the lid.

Loud whispers ran between one old lady and another, rippling like an incoming tide along every pew. They were shocked to the core. Wealthy men did not get buried in a cardboard box with printed exterior.

'It's like a wine carrier from a supermarket,' breathed Dora and sounded horrified.

Heads turned. Most people looked amused. Older people looked shocked. Younger people were completely unfazed.

A line of words printed along the side caught Honey's eye.

'Did you see what that said?'

She wasn't really asking anyone. It was a spontaneous outburst but once it had sunk in, she began to giggle.

Her mother heard, bent from the waist and glared at her from the end of the pew.

'Honey. Remember where you are,' she hissed.

Edith nudged her. 'What's so funny?' she whispered.

Honey tried stuffing her fist into her mouth, but still couldn't stop.

Edith nudged her harder.

'Honey. You're making a spectacle of yourself. What's so funny?'

'I can't . . .' she giggled, 'help it,' she managed to whisper back.

Edith rummaged in her bag, brought out a small bottle, opened the top, and shoved it under Honey's nose.

Smelling salts! They smelled disgusting!

Honey gasped and the giggles stopped.

The last notes of 'Hi Ho Silver Lining' tinkled on the air. The vicar followed the coffin, rearranging his vestments like a model on the runway.

Edith looked at her, half smiling as she silently mouthed, 'What is it you're laughing at?'

Honey clapped her hand over her mouth. If she told Edith what she'd seen she'd start giggling again.

'Tell me,' said Edith.

'It's . . . it's what's printed just below the flying Superman on the side of the coffin.'

Edith raised her eyebrows. 'Go on.'

The others were also now tuned in, their faces turned expectantly in her direction.

She gulped back her laughter, cleared her throat, and told them what was written on the side in small but sharp lettering.

'Suitable for recycling. It said suitable for recycling!'

The service, sermon, and reminiscing over, the coffin finished its journey up the aisle and out into the rain. The congregation followed on behind. Old Sean was about to get buried.

Keeping her head down whilst trying to banish her smile, Honey moved with the rest of them. Getting the vision of Sean O'Brian being recycled out of her mind was almost impossible. It was the funniest thing that had happened all day — that and the notorious Bobo watering the vicar's shoes!

Held aloft on the shoulders of three hefty men and one slightly shorter one, the sides of the cardboard coffin flexed a little. On seeing this, the pallbearers linked arms beneath it.

Noting the disproportionate heights of the four men carrying the coffin, Honey remarked of the disparity in size to her mother and said that she hoped nobody stumbled.

'Well, that's Arlene for you. No sense of proportion,' snapped her mother.

Honey had no real idea of what that meant and trusted, like everyone else, that things would go smoothly. However, the grass was slippery underfoot and the short man stumbled, which sent the corner of the coffin scraping against the wall.

'That's a bad omen,' whispered her mother.

'I don't think Sean will worry about that.' In Honey's opinion, Sean O'Brian was beyond concerning himself with omens.

The corner of the coffin lid was now rumpled however and likely to be letting in rain.

'At least he won't be needing an umbrella,' Honey murmured to herself.

'It's like one of them cardboard wine carriers,' murmured Amber as she adjusted her wig. 'They're not strong enough. I lost six bottles of bubbly when I trusted one of them things.'

'You're right, Amber,' said Dora, shaking her head. She frowned on the coffin as it proceeded down the church path to the lychgate over the wet grass to Sean's final resting place. 'Fancy not having a nice bit of walnut.'

'Or mahogany,' Honey's mother added a little sadly, and dabbed at her eyes with a tissue.

As it was, nothing seemed unduly amiss as the throng of umbrellas burst like mushrooms over the heads of the mourners whilst the rain pattered on the coffin lid and trickled down inside the damaged corner.

The route they took was down the church path, out on to the pavement, and then into what had once been a field where grazing cows had eaten grass and nurtured the soil.

Honey's mother caught hold of her arm. 'This is slippery.' Her mother was muttering beneath her breath, angry that her pretty little kitten heels were spearing clods of mud. She looped her arm more tightly through Honey's. 'Hold on to me.'

Dora passed Bobo to Edith and used her sticks. Amber grabbed Honey's other arm. 'I don't want to fall. Might go sliding into an open grave by mistake.'

Beneath their feet the sodden grass and soft earth of Memory Meadow was becoming as mushy as a paddy field.

Suddenly forgetting that the grass was slippery, Amber and her mother let go of her arms and headed for the graveside. 'I've got to get another look at that casket,' muttered Amber. Even Dora got a spurt on.

Honey sighed, glad to be unburdened and having no wish to take another look at Sean O'Brian's coffin.

Slowing her footsteps, she fell in with the stragglers at the back of the crowd.

'Hi. Did you know the deceased?'

The young man walking next to her had a hippy look about him; long hair, crumpled green shirt, and jeans.

'Not intimately,' Honey replied. 'The decoration on the coffin came as something of a surprise.'

His face brightened. 'Cool, don't you dig it? We don't just do off-the-shelf designs. We do custom.'

'You make them?'

'Too right we do. Innovative, yeah?'

'That's as good a description as any.'

'Here. Take my card. Joel Jackson's the name. And remember I can print anything you like on your casket. Anything at all.' He beamed.

'I'll bear that in mind.' She thought of the reference to recycling. 'Can I have one saying, "please resuscitate"?'

He laughed. 'If you want.'

'I'm not in the market for one just yet though,' she told him. She was speaking of course from a personal point of view.

'Elderly parents?' he asked hopefully.

'Perish the thought. If I buried my mother in anything less than hardwood, she'd come back to haunt me.'

'Well, perhaps something pre-ordered for yourself. You never know. Here today, gone tomorrow. Gather ye rosebuds and all that . . .'

'I'll bear you in mind.'

The young man was garrulous and although he must take his business very seriously, for him it was all about making figures, not being fearful. Death for him was a long way off, barring anything accidental.

He went off circulating amongst the other mourners gathering feedback and handing out cards, noticeably paying more attention to those on sticks or thin enough to be in danger of the wind whipping them off to the Land of Oz.

Led by the coffin and the vicar, the crowd had come to a halt. Honey brought up the rear with some confidence, deciding that wearing boots with flat heels had been a good decision.

Perhaps the worst-case scenario wouldn't have happened if the heavens hadn't opened and the grass hadn't been saturated. And if that one man hadn't been six inches shorter than his pall-bearing companions.

The open grave and the piles of earth each side was at the bottom of a slight slope. If the ground had been dry, it wouldn't have made any difference, but it wasn't dry and the slope was slippery. Most people stayed on top of the slope. A few ventured down, the vicar first followed by the coffin.

The front right-hand pallbearer slipped. The coffin tilted forwards, front down, the back springing up into the air.

The shortest pallbearer was one of those at the rear. He did his best to hang on as the coffin tilted, the rear end rising beyond his reach.

The man who had slipped on the wet grass slipped again. The coffin tilted almost upright and escaped their grasp, sliding down the slope like a toboggan on ice.

The pallbearers ran after it.

The mourners gasped. The widow shrieked.

'Sean must be in a hurry,' Honey muttered to herself.

The coffin ended up where it was supposed to. Unfortunately it went in feet first, standing upright in the hole.

The sound of rain pitter-pattering on umbrellas was loud, but the outraged gasps and shocked exclamations drowned it out.

In an effort to see what had happened, everybody pushed forward, sending those at the front of the crush down the slope. Some slithered down on legs that were fighting to stay upright, but some went down on their backsides and slid down ending up with their legs hanging over the side of the grave.

The pallbearers muscled forward and grabbed the end.

'All together now,' shouted the biggest bearer, who also had the biggest voice.

'Heave!'

The coffin, the cardboard now looking decidedly soggy, was pulled back out, the men leaving it resting on the grass while they got their breath. Everyone attending took the opportunity to survey the printed image of Superman again.

At last, in unison, the pallbearers jerked the coffin back on to their shoulders.

Dora shook her head.

Amber mumbled something else about her experiences with a cardboard wine carrier . . . 'If it gets soggy . . . wham! Everything falls out the bottom.'

Things would have been all right, Honey was sure they would have been, if it hadn't been raining, if the coffin hadn't fallen into the muddy abyss of its final resting place; if the grass they'd rested it on hadn't been soaking wet. Anyway, the coffin was reacting in exactly the same way as Amber's supermarket wine holder. Sogginess was taking away its strength.

The pallbearers heaved the cardboard box on to their shoulders so it could be more easily placed in the straps that would lower it into Sean's final resting place. Another shout of 'Heave!' and the straps were underneath and readjusted when the middle bit of the casket gave way. Sean O'Brian's bottom, clad it seemed in scarlet underpants, was on show to the world.

More gasps of shock alarmed the crows in the trees and sent them flying and cawing.

The church deacon, a spirited man in black robes, eased himself into position and tried to push Sean's red rump back into place.

'Get him into the ground quick,' said the young man Honey had been talking to who was now looking worried, no doubt concerned that all his best marketing efforts had been in vain.

The vicar had taken his place at the head of the grave, eyes heavenward; probably praying that this will soon be over, thought Honey.

Clearing his throat and opening his book, the vicar looked down into the grave, waiting for the pallbearers and funeral directors to get the show on the road and for the mourners to stop eyeballing the coffin and gather back around the grave or at the top of the slope where they'd been earlier.

Honey began to hiccup. She held her breath, she held her nose, she closed her eyes, but nothing would stop it.

'*Hannah*, do control yourself,' snapped her mother, eyes beetle-hard. 'I wish I hadn't asked you to come with us.'

'Oh, but I'm glad I did.' She hiccupped. 'I wouldn't have missed it for the world.' Another hiccup. She knew if she wasn't hiccupping she'd be laughing. Of the two the hiccups best suited a funeral, though only just.

Suddenly the bottom of the cardboard coffin gave out altogether and Sean O'Brian flopped out onto the grass.

A gasp of surprise ran through those who saw what he was wearing. Those that hadn't seen pushed forward, unwilling to miss the thrill of having something to talk about at the next Senior Citizens' meeting.

Some giggled. Some gasped.

Honey's hiccups stopped immediately. She hid her face and her laughter with both hands. She just couldn't believe what she was seeing.

Some folk insist on being buried in their best clothes. Military types prefer the uniform they wore when serving their country. In Sean's case he'd selected his own uniform — of sorts. Just like the printed effigy on his coffin he was wearing the unmistakable blue and red of Superman. Without the physique to fill it of course; his legs were skinny. His pants were large. His hair was tucked like a pillow beneath his head.

Honey pulled her hat down over her eyes and did her best to stifle her laughter, though she was far from the only one who found this amusing. Gasps and giggles of surprise were erupting with abandon. The widow had smothered her mouth with her handkerchief and was blushing profusely. Obviously, he'd made stipulations in his will about what he wanted to be buried in. Judging by the widow's blushes the outfit had been worn in life too, possibly in the bedroom.

'I've got some tape,' said the man representing the makers of the cardboard coffins as he rushed forward.

He proceeded to tape the bottom of the coffin back together.

'Ease him gently in,' he said to the pallbearers.

Tears were streaming down Honey's face. She held a balled-up tissue tight against her mouth. No TV comedy show could rival this!

Her mother's elbow dug into her ribs. 'Hannah! Show some respect.'

Fat chance. Or it would have been if she hadn't caught sight of the look of horror on the vicar's face.

His eyes were big and round and he was looking down into the grave. His long white fingers were splayed over his wide-open mouth.

'There's someone down there already.' His comment was directed at the church warden who, it seemed, was working on the side for the people who owned Memory Meadow.

A blast of wind blew water from the nearby trees. Honey felt the full blast of it sprinkling her face, but she didn't move. Something was wrong.

The warden knelt at the graveside, finally going on all fours so he could peer into the grave without falling in himself.

Getting back on to his knees, face pale and confused, he looked up at the vicar.

'It looks like a . . . gorilla,' he said.

Taking off his spectacles he gave them a wipe with a cloth.

Someone else, another mourner of fewer years and clearer eyesight, peered down too.

'It does look kind of furry.'

Intrigued as to what or who might be in the hole and with a sense of foreboding, Honey edged her way forward and took a look.

'It's not an ape. It's a teddy bear. It's Teddy Devlin.'

Those gathered looked at her as thought she'd taken leave of her senses.

'It's a teddy bear,' she explained. 'I'm pretty sure it's the one that's missing from the Devlin Foundation. It's a charity. They use the teddy bear for fundraising. You must have seen it in Bath if you've been shopping there.'

The vicar looked perplexed. 'But what's it doing in there?' His question was aimed at the church warden.

Feeling a great weight of responsibility on his shoulders, the church warden sighed.

'I don't know, your reverence.'

'Then you'd better get down and find out. Get it out, in fact. It shouldn't be down there.'

The vicar's eyes were on him and speaking volumes. Fair enough, the plot had been reserved by Sean O'Brian and the teddy bear had no business being in there.

The church warden knew what he had to do. When it came to job description, he didn't really have one. Whatever needs doing was his job in the absence of there being anyone else to do it.

With a heavy sigh, the middle-aged man took off his shoes and socks, rolled up his trouser legs, and tied his black robe between his legs.

The crowd, rabid with curiosity, ignored the action of the pallbearers stuffing Sean back into his coffin and peered into the hole.

The warden was helped down in order to carry out a closer examination of the teddy bear.

He looked at the bear then looked up.

'She's right. It is a teddy bear. A giant teddy bear.'

Honey bent closer. The bottom of the hole was awash with soft mud. The teddy bear would be pretty heavy to lift out. She pointed the facts out to them.

'He'll be heavy. It may take more than one man to get him out.'

'Well. We'd better get it shifted,' said Joss, the representative from the Cardboard Coffin Company. 'Can someone give me a hand?'

A strong-looking girl in green leapt down into the hole with Joss and the church warden. She was wearing a pair of stout Doc Martens beneath her ankle-length skirt.

Between them they bent to take a grip. They barely moved him, silently straightening as though unsure what they were seeing or what to do next.

The church warden looked up, his face paler than when he'd gone into the hole. Raindrops spattered his glasses. Trickles of water ran down the sides of his face and a droplet hung from the end of his nose.

Honey felt that tinge of foreboding again.

'Vicar. We can't move him.' His voice was shaky. 'I think we'd better call the police.'

Honey straightened. The church warden had called the teddy bear 'him' not 'it' as she would have expected.

'Only a teddy bear?'

He looked up at her, his face white and rain soaked. 'I think there's a man inside.'

There was a man down there. A body.

Honey opened her mobile phone and pressed a memory key. Doherty answered on the third ring.

'Honey! Having fun at the funeral?'

She cut him off.

'Steve. I think we just found Teddy Devlin — and he's not alone.'

CHAPTER SIX

Honey pulled off her hat. The brim had got so sodden that it had flopped around her head like a mildewed mushroom. Keeping it on would have meant cutting slits in it for her eyes.

She was still standing in the rain. The young man from the Cardboard Coffin Company was standing beneath an ancient tree which occupied a spot among the graves in the churchyard next door. Its branches overhung the wall which formed the boundary to the burial plots of Memory Meadow.

The young man was smoking. The vicar and the church warden had opted to stand in the church porch. Honey had explained her affiliation to the police via the Hotels Association.

'Call me an amateur sleuth and formally appointed police consultant,' she said rather boldly, suddenly feeling quite proud of the description.

The vicar looked relieved. 'Good. If you're a crime madam you can take charge and tell the police where we are in case they need to question us. I want nothing to do with dead bodies unless in my official capacity.' He glanced at his watch. 'And they'd better hurry up. I've got a christening at four.'

So Honey opted to stay put on the slope at the top of the grave. Number one, she thought it her duty and, number two, although the oak under which Joss stood gave shelter from the elements, she didn't want to put up with a smoker.

The mourners, including the widow, had gone off to the Poacher where the wake was being held.

Honey had expected Arlene, Sean's widow, to be upset but actually she turned out to be quite pragmatic about the whole affair.

'There's a hole in the ground reserved for Sean. He'll get in it eventually. I can't neglect my guests. It wouldn't be right.' So off she went to the Poacher to preside over her late husband's wake.

Honey felt it a little selfish of the woman, but under the circumstances the fewer people treading around the crime scene the better.

There was time to study the scene before the heavy mob arrived — that is, Doherty and his cohorts.

The biggest victim, poor old Sean O'Brian, was left inside his soggy cardboard casket getting steadily soggier, though the church warden had borrowed one of the scouts' tents to throw over it. Despite rejecting Sean's advances, Honey couldn't help feeling sorry for the poor old chap. He'd been abandoned at his own funeral, even by his wife.

Feeling a bit of a crime madam, which seemed quite a fun term to her mind, Honey had taken charge. The church warden, who acted as custodian of both the church graveyard and the ecologically acceptable, had been intent on getting the teddy bear-covered victim out of the hole so that the burial could go ahead. Honey had stopped him. 'The crime scene must not be disturbed. You'll contaminate the evidence. Detective Chief Inspector Doherty is on his way. Do nothing until he gets here.'

It sounded funny saying that. Detective *Chief* Inspector Doherty. Steve had finally got the promotion he'd never wanted, foisted on him due to the lack of other candidates, or so he'd informed her. She didn't believe that. Doherty liked to go his own way and without interference. A bit of a loner, he'd never liked having a sidekick trailing round with him either — except her, but that was different. It was only occasional. So far, he'd avoided the sidekick thing, but it couldn't last.

She was thinking all this as she gazed down into the hole. Teddy Devlin's black button eyes reflected the glassy gleam of the sky and droplets of rain glistened like teardrops. Poor old Teddy Devlin. Stuffed with a corpse.

Screeching car tyres heralded the arrival of the cavalry. Four police vehicles arrived in quick succession, sirens blaring, their occupants spilling out on to the verge on the other side of the wall.

Doherty was the first to come striding across, his feet sensibly clad in green wellies. The rest lingered on the other side, some changing into waterproofs, others into the white jumpsuits of their trade.

A smile lurked around his mouth though he shook his head as though in reprimand. 'What's with you and dead people? Are you in communication with the afterlife or something?'

She stood with folded arms, hat in one hand, hair running with water.

'I'll run that one past Mary Jane. Anyway, Teddy Devlin is down there.' She pointed at the hole.

Bending down and resting his hands on his knees, he peered in. His toes were close to the edge, pressing water out of the mud.

Honey waited.

Still bent low, he nodded grimly.

'Well he definitely fits the description.'

'Definitely a teddy bear.'

'More to the point, it's definitely Teddy Devlin. Right,' he said straightening. 'I suppose we'd better see what Teddy Devlin is made of.'

'Well, it certainly isn't kapok.'

He jumped into the grave and bent over the body. Carefully, so as not to disturb anything too much, Doherty pulled at the costume. The head, made of something solid, came forward. He pulled it down thus exposing a face.

'Poor sod,'

Honey's jaw dropped. 'I know who that is.'

Doherty looked up at her. 'You do?'

'C.A. Wright. And he's not a poor sod. He's a rat. Put me down on the list of suspects.'

'That bad?'

'Very.'pShe'd had a run-in with Wright some time ago. It had been an experience best forgotten. He'd wanted a price for giving her a glowing review, but that would depend on her taking up one half of the double bed in his room. She'd declined. What was more, she'd thrown him out and told him never to darken her door again.

She gave him a hand getting back up. Beyond him she saw the church warden skirt the incident tape and walk hurriedly over the grass, the hem of his black robe splattered with mud.

'Inspector . . .'

'*Chief* Inspector . . .'

The warden, still polishing the drops of water from his glasses, asked when he might expect use of the grave. 'After all,' he pointed out imperiously, 'we have a body for burial. The vicar, our eco-interment officer, Joss, and I are quite concerned. We cannot guarantee how long we can keep the deceased decently covered.'

The young man who'd given Honey his card and had stood smoking beneath the tree joined the church warden. This was Joss.

'The casket is meant to decompose pretty quickly,' added Joss. 'We're going to have a body lying here with nothing protecting it. I cannot guarantee how long the casket will last before disintegrating. I've put him in the tent for now.'

Doherty took a peek beneath the soaking wet tent which was imprinted with the logo of the local scouts group. 'I shouldn't think he's going to worry too much about being decent. Is that the coffin?' He sounded surprised.

Joss volleyed forth with his lengthy sales pitch about earth to earth, wastage of hardwood on coffins being unnecessary, and the planting of trees. He also added the bit about how you could have your cardboard coffin printed to order.

'In your case you could have a policeman in full uniform,' he said cheerily.

'I'll bear that in mind,' Doherty said neutrally, scrutinising the coffin. He kept a straight face, though his facial muscles were quivering under the strain.

'Superman! Well, that's original.'

'He's dressed like Superman too,' Honey informed him. 'I think he may have made a habit of it — you know — in the bedroom.'

'Is that so? Never done that one myself. Still,' he glanced at her, 'there's always a first time.'

One side of his mouth threatened to smile, but this was a serious incident and good for him, he managed to keep it under control.

'Sean had something of a reputation with the ladies,' Honey explained, ignoring the suggestion in his voice.

Doherty's eyes met hers. 'I get your meaning. Superman. Right.'

He turned to the church warden and Joss, the self-styled eco-interment officer.

'How about digging a fresh grave away from the crime scene? Down the bottom there against the wall?'

He pointed to the wall skirting the road.

The warden and the young man looked at each other as though a one-hundred-watt electric light bulb had just been switched on — or at least an energy-efficient alternative.

The church warden shook his head. 'I can't get a gravedigger out to dig at the drop of a hat. These things have to be planned.'

'We've got a digger. I'll do it,' said Joss. 'I think over there by the wall should be OK. It's a bit near the road but I do know that there's no bodies buried there.'

Doherty nodded slowly. 'Great. That works for me.'

His eyes followed them all the way to an old stone barn in the corner of the field where Joss unfastened and opened one side of the big double doors. A puff of smoke, the sound of an engine, and a mechanical digger emerged.

As he helped Honey down the slope, he told her the good news. 'They're going to dig a new grave. I didn't expect them to be mechanised. Will you look at that?'

'I am looking. Not exactly hard labour; not exactly eco-friendly labour either.'

His hand brushed her elbow. It was nothing to an observer; nothing in the great scheme of sexual fantasy, but it still made her tingle.

'I like your touch, DCI Doherty, but I'm afraid I have to leave you to it. Duty calls.'

'Back to the hotel?'

She shook her head. 'I'm off across the road to the Poacher.'

He nodded casually, his eyes still following the progress of the mechanical digger. 'Lucky you.'

'Would you like me to have a word with the widow?'

Doherty shrugged. 'She's not likely to know much about the bear or the victim, is she?'

'I meant offer her commiserations and inform her that Mr O'Brian is being interred in another part of Memory Meadow.'

'Oh, I see. Yes, you do that. I'll hang around here and ask this guy what he knows about it. He dug the hole. I have to ask the question, did they also throw in a stiff?'

'Or even a Steiff.'

'Pardon?'

Honey rolled her eyes. 'They're famous teddy bears. Made in Germany.'

'Not this one. He was made for a stage production of *The Three Bears*. The charity bought him once the theatre had finished with it. That's why he's so big.'

'You are so well informed.'

His eyes twinkled when he grinned at her. 'I try to keep abreast of things.'

* * *

The wake at the Poacher was in full swing by the time Honey got there.

Honey scanned the crowded bar, finally finding Mrs Arlene O'Brian sitting in a window seat, a gin and tonic in one hand and a chicken leg in the other. If she was grieving it didn't show. Her cheeks were pink, her eyes were merry, and she was laughing at a rude joke somebody had just told.

'Do you mind if I sit here?' Honey asked the winsome widow. She didn't wait for an answer.

'Cheers!' Arlene O'Brian, formerly Mrs Donald Tipping, swigged back the not inconsiderable contents of her glass.

Clearing her throat and taking a small sip of vodka and tonic gave Honey enough time to consider her words. The widow was here for the funeral. She and Doherty had agreed that Arlene couldn't possibly know anything about the stolen teddy bear and its grisly contents.

'I thought you'd like to know that they're digging a fresh grave for Sean. I'm afraid it could be some time before the police are finished with the present grave.'

'As long as he's where he wished to be interred,' said Arlene with a nod of her neatly-coiffured head, hair-dyed beige blonde with a hint of pale pink.

'The policeman in charge asked me to convey his condolences,' Honey added.

Arlene looked at her with shiny bright eyes and blinked. 'Is that the one you're sleeping with? I hear you met him on the rebound when Sean dumped you.'

Honey felt her face going red. 'Excuse me?'

'Your mother told me,' said Arlene with a surly curling of scarlet lips. 'She said that there was interest between the two of you. I bet there was. I bet you wanted him to put some money into that business of yours. I bet that was all you wanted him for. Well, my Sean saw through you. He knew a gold digger when he saw one, mark my words. Well, I got him! I got him!'

Hoteliers were tolerant by virtue of the fact that they had to deal with some right idiots at times. But this was too much. Whatever gaskets Honey possessed blew left right and centre.

'You stupid bitch.' It wasn't often that she lost her temper but Arlene had bugged her good and proper. She pointed a rigid finger to within an inch of Arlene's upturned nose. 'Let's get this straight,' she growled. 'I wouldn't have gone out with your old man if he'd been the last man on earth. I don't do geriatrics. I like them young, virile, and hot to go. So don't kid yourself that he was Prince Charming and that you're the bloody Fairy Princess. I didn't come here to talk about your husband and him fancying his chances with younger women . . .'

'Just hang on there, you policeman's Jezebel!' Arlene snapped, meeting Honey's anger with her own. 'Just 'cause I'm a bit older than you don't mean to say that I'm past it. You know the old saying, just because there's snow on the roof doesn't mean to say that there's not a fire in the grate. And there was plenty of fire in Sean's grate, I can tell you.' Her eyes glittered and her voice was shrill enough to strip wallpaper.

'Then it was two old grates together,' said Honey, sick and tired of hearing that same old saying about snow and fire grates. 'And you were well and truly welcome to each other. I've never been keen on role play in the bedroom and Sean in a Superman costume would have made me puke. I've seen better muscle on the legs of an earwig!'

Arlene tossed her blonde-haired head, the veneer of respectable wife superseded by the old brass she really was.

'You're only saying that because you didn't nab him! I did. Me and old Sean were made for each other.'

'You bet,' Honey snapped back. 'Two old antiques together.'

Arlene's face reddened, but she wasn't out for the count just yet.

'You're frigid then. My Sean was probably too fruity for you!'

'On the contrary, Mrs O'Brian. Your husband was over-ripe. Time to be turned into mush!' Honey shouted. The words came out before she could stop them. And everyone in the room stopped talking. She heard a breathless gasp from those who had heard. A few titters also.

'Whoops!'

Arlene was glaring at her.

But Honey was unrepentant. She'd sounded callous but try as she might there was no way she was about to apologise.

Arlene spoke first. 'Cow.'

'Bitch!'

Her mother's perfume fell over her in a suffocating haze. 'Hannah! That is so insensitive. Arlene has just been widowed, in case you've forgotten.'

Honey rolled her eyes. Old ladies stuck together.

'My fault,' she said. In a way it was true. She'd got so riled thinking of her name being linked with Sean's that she'd forgotten where she was and who she was with. 'I'm sorry. I really shouldn't have said that.'

Arlene went from fishwife to wounded wife in one swift move. Tears had replaced red-faced anger. She dabbed at the corners of her eyes with the corner of a lace-edged handkerchief.

'I'm quite upset,' mewed Arlene, playing to her audience for the sympathy vote.

'You weren't just now. In fact, I would say that you were coping extremely well.'

'I am now. Grief is like that. It hits when you least expect it.'

It could be so. Honey gave her the benefit of the doubt and shook her head. 'I suppose that was rude of me. I shouldn't have said it. I'll make it up in any way I can.'

Arlene O'Brian's face froze as though someone had pressed the pause button on a remote control. Her tears evaporated in double-quick time.

'Well you can make a start by getting me a double gin, ice, lemon, and not too much tonic. And get one for your mother. She deserves one having a daughter like you.'

CHAPTER SEVEN

Teddy Devlin made the six o'clock news. Or rather, that a man had been found dead stuffed inside a giant teddy bear made the six o'clock news.

Honey was watching the television with her eyes closed — listening to it but only vaguely. Bundling old ladies in and out of taxis was extremely tiring. And watching them enjoy themselves at a funeral was more so seeing as they'd been drinking and she could not.

Jealously she'd watched them downing their gins, their whiskies, and the glass of champagne specially laid on by Sean's middle-aged son who was something in the wine trade — she hadn't caught what. Being designated driver she'd held off the booze, having slowly sipped her way through a single vodka and tonic. After that it was pure tonic water — grieving when everyone else was indulging big time.

She made up for lost time once her mother, her mother's cronies, and Bobo the dog were all dropped off, the car was in the car park, and she was finally sat down.

The restaurant was heavily booked tonight and owning a hotel meant when it called for all hands to the pumps, there were no exceptions.

Just one glass of wine before I go on duty, she told herself. Accordingly Honey poured herself a glass of Australian Shiraz, knocked that back, then poured herself another. The wine was accompanied by a few chocolates left over from Christmas plus a wedge of very gooey Camembert — delicious for dipping when left out of the fridge for a few days. The crackers she'd found had gone soft so she opted for sucking the cheese off her finger.

The news over, she turned the television off. Quality time for at least an hour before re-entering the fray. First, get comfortable. The chair cushions were old-fashioned springs and horsehair beneath tan-coloured velour. Sinking into the soft cushions was like being swallowed by a marshmallow.

Using her toe, she prised off one shoe then the other and wriggled her toes. She followed this with another plump chocolate and a sip of red wine.

Bliss!

Comfort eating and comfort for the body; it didn't get any better than this.

The phone began ringing just as she'd selected her second chocolate — a Brazil nut, one of her favourites.

'Hellope.'

'Hellope? That's not the name I want. I'm sorry but I appear to have the wrong number.'

Shoving the chocolate to one side of her mouth. Honey sat bolt upright. 'Casper?'

'Ah! Honey. I take it you're eating something.'

Honey sucked in her lips. Why did Casper always make her feel she'd been caught doing something she shouldn't — like making chasseur sauce with red wine instead of white or wiping her nose on her sleeve? Or eating chocolates . . .

'I've just come back from a funeral.'

'Have you heard the news?' He failed to offer his deepest sympathy; neither did he ask who had died. Casper was not naturally sympathetic. But if something happened to him, that was a different matter; he expected sympathy. It was giving it out that was a problem.

Honey sighed. 'Of course I have. I was there when they found Teddy Devlin.'

'Teddy Devlin? I've never heard of him,' he said dismissively. 'I'm talking about C.A. Wright. He's been found murdered — stuffed inside some outlandish costume and thrown into an open grave, so I hear.'

The chocolate swallowed, Honey took the opportunity to explain the identity of Teddy Devlin and his link with the victim. Casper St John Gervais was chairman of the Bath Hotels Association. For Bath, he wore his heart on his sleeve. Crime made him shudder. It shouldn't be happening in a place he considered to be God's little acre. Casper was the person who had pressurised her into being Bath Hotels Association Crime Liaison Officer.

Explaining what was going on in the crime sector was all part of her remit, though for the most part she preferred to keep Casper in the dark. He got too uptight about things. OK, murder was something to get uptight about, but she was on the case. So were the police.

She went over the day's events.

'Teddy Devlin is a very large teddy bear used by the Devlin Foundation for fundraising activities. I was there when C.A. Wright's body was found stuffed inside him.'

'Honey! You didn't hear me. C.A. Wright. Are you hearing me now?'

Honey put down her glass, closed her eyes and blinked them swiftly open again.

'I thought I'd just explained that. He's the big bug who writes reviews for the national newspapers.'

'Of course for the nationals. He certainly wouldn't be doing it for the *regional* press, would he?' Casper sounded totally disgusted that she would even suggest such a thing.

Just for once Honey was having none of it. Perhaps the wine had gone to her head.

'Now listen carefully to what I'm saying, Casper,' she said fiercely. 'C.A. Wright was *inside* that bloody bear. Personally I feel sorry for the bear. Wright was a right shit. In fact, I suggested to Doherty that my name should be on the list of suspects — along with half the hoteliers and restaurant owners in Bath.'

She said it with vehemence and for her pains perceived an unequivocal silence on the other end of the phone. Casper was obviously considering what she had said. He'd had to have had a run-in with Wright himself.

C.A. Wright had come close to having his ears chopped off in her own establishment following his criticism of Smudger's sticky toffee pudding. This occurred just after C.A. had got Honey alone and offered to give her a glowing review. All she had to do was accompany him inside the walk-in closet in his room, with the doors closed, in the dark —naked!

Following her rebuttal — which consisted mainly of terms not resorted to by well-mannered hoteliers — he'd put his venomous revenge into action. Unfortunately he hadn't taken on board that the head chef at the Green River Hotel ran a tight ship on a short fuse. C.A. enjoyed making hotel staff squirm. Following Smudger's threat to do something very nasty with the rough end of a pineapple, the famous, ill-respected and well-disliked reviewer took a sharp exit. He never did write the bad review, mainly because he'd left behind a very brief leather thong that hadn't been there before he'd taken the room. Honey had threatened to expose him. 'With your thong rather than without,' she'd informed him.

'I suppose you have a point,' said Casper at last after he'd given what she'd said due consideration.

Honey reached for another chocolate — a soft one that could be swiftly despatched without curtailing her speech.

'A very valid point. He was a well-hated man.'

'That's beside the point. We don't want this crime hanging around. We want it solved. See to it, Honey. See to it very quickly. I shall expect there to be a list of suspects very shortly.'

'You can bet on that. In fact I'll have a queue forming. Those that didn't get a bad review had to have given in to blackmail.'

'I have heard rumours,' said Casper in a muted tone.

His tone made her wonder whether Casper wasn't keeping his own dealings with the man to himself. 'He seemed to home in on certain people,' Casper added in a manner that made her think Casper himself was not one of them; that Wright wouldn't dare.

She slumped back into her chair and prepared to confess. 'I think it depended on whether you had a walk-in closet and were up for standing around in the dark with no clothes on.'

'I see.' So non-committal! 'I think we need to close ranks on this.'

Honey's eyebrows shot up. 'In what way?'

'We have to protect each other's backs.'

'We do?' She thought about it. Hoteliers plus highly-disliked reviewer plus bad publicity equals murdered reviewer. She'd cottoned on to where he was coming from. 'You're right, Casper. Every hotelier in Bath is a suspect, but more so those whose businesses he ruined, and I understand he ruined quite a few.'

'Precisely,' Casper said chillingly.

Doherty rang just as she'd crushed the empty chocolate box and was fighting to do up the zip on her skirt.

'We've located where Wright was staying. A Mr Dodd at the Laurel Tree Hotel stated that he left there alive and well yesterday morning. My sidekick went round to get a statement. Only thing is we can't find any luggage. It's not at the hotel and it wasn't down the hole with Wright.'

'How about our eco-friendly gravedigger and the church warden? Did they see anyone hanging around?'

'No.'

The way he said "no" was slow and thoughtful. Something was bugging him.

'What are you thinking?'

'There's a cesspit just back from the grave that used to serve the church. It's not used any longer since they got connected to the main drain, in fact it's in the process of being broken apart and filled in. One of the men is a local bloke named Ned Shaw. He's got a criminal record.'

'For violence?'

'And rape.'

CHAPTER EIGHT

Death for C.A. Wright had come by virtue of a meat skewer through the neck, justly deserved if Smudger's reaction was anything to go by.

'But it wasn't me,' he'd added.

Doherty had promised to keep her informed, so Honey put the matter to the back of her mind and went all out to concentrate on her guests and them alone. Tonight the Green River Hotel would have her undivided attention.

Mary Jane, she of the paranormal persuasion, had acquired certain habits since living in Bath. Number one habit was that she frequented Sally Lunn's coffee shop quite a lot. Smiling benignly at everyone, she easily got into discussions with strangers from all over the world. In the twinkling of an eye the strangers became friends and were invited back for tea and crumpets or carrot juice and swordfish soup.

Tonight her guests were proving to be rowdier than the norm. Today she'd picked up half a dozen young people. Declining her offer of tea and crumpets, they'd purchased bottles of wine — quite a few bottles of wine as it happened.

Using the excuse of clearing wine glasses from the table, Honey took the opportunity to look them over.

They looked like students, the girls lithesome and fresh-faced, the young men broad-shouldered and looking ready for a scrum — on the rugby pitch of course, not with the girls, though on second thoughts . . .

Mary Jane looked up at Honey as though everything was fine, no different than if she were surrounded by people of her own age, which was quite considerable.

'I was telling these good folk about Sir Cedric and the fact that he lives in the closet in my room and how he talks to me and tells me things.'

To Honey's mind the little group looked as though they'd been drinking all day; either that or their heads were made of cast iron and thus too heavy for their necks. Their chins were making little elliptical movements as their balance took time out to readjust.

One of the young men looked up at Honey with what could only be described as lust in his eyes. His smile was toothpaste white and his face well-scrubbed, though a five o'clock shadow was threatening his jaw line.

'You're nice,' he said. He smiled stupidly before his chin sunk on to his folded arms.

Honey grabbed what was left of the wine from the table. 'And you're drunk.'

She threw Mary Jane an accusing look.

Mary Jane bit her bottom lip. They were friends and she kind of had free rein about the place, but she knew when she'd reached her limit.

'I'm sorry,' she whispered. 'But they're great guys really. Honest they are.'

One of the students tugged at Honey's arm. 'Do you know that my friend here does table tapping?' he said, nodding in the direction of Mary Jane. 'She reckons she can reach people on the other side. Isn't that incredible?'

'I would never have guessed.'

Honey couldn't help the vinegar-laced response and the sour look. She was still wearing it when she went through the door into the kitchen. Lindsey was heading in the opposite direction.

'I suppose you know that our dear Mary Jane has found some more friends,' said Honey, her face set firm as she marched towards the kitchen. 'They're all drunk. I think I'm going to have to get you to throw them out, Smudger.'

Lindsey took a glimpse through one of the round portholes in the double doors. 'Have they paid their bill?'

'They have. Their great day and early evening with Mary Jane has left them potless.'

'Right,' Lindsey said with an air of confidence that only the young can contemplate. 'Leave it to me to get rid of them.'

'I think Smudger would be best . . .'

Bouncing along on the balls of her feet, Lindsey swung out into the restaurant with a smile on her face and a wiggle on her hips.

'My daughter is so cute,' said Honey, shaking her head in disbelief.

'And plucky,' Smudger added.

They held the door open ever so slightly so they could hear what was being said.

'OK guys,' they heard her say. 'Would anybody like to go outside with me?'

The response was overwhelming. All four guys struggled to their feet, swaying like willows in the wind once they'd got there.

Surprised that all four guys were following Lindsey outside, their female companions sprang to their feet too, possessiveness lighting their eyes.

'Hey! Wait for us.'

Honey could see their point. After all, wasn't one guy enough for each girl?

The guys went out. The girls went out. Lindsey came swinging back through the revolving door.

'They're gone. Simple.'

Honey shook her head. 'Are you sure of your age?'

Dimples appeared at the sides of Lindsey's mouth when she smiled.

'I'm reliably informed that I'm nineteen.'

If ever an old head had got placed on young shoulders, then Lindsey had it. 'Darn. Could have sworn you were forty-seven.'

'Those guys are a hoot,' said Mary Jane who had got to her feet, meaning to aim for the stairs and her bed as quickly as she could without facing the music she knew was coming.

'They're drunk, is what they are,' Honey reiterated. Sometimes it seemed that Mary Jane just didn't hear or didn't remember what had been said. Possibly both. She also got over being told off as though there'd never been a problem in the first place.

'They were telling me about what the other day,' chuckled Mary Jane. 'This guy was giving them some real stick in the Roman Baths. He was drunk as a skunk and passed out because of it, so they stuffed him . . .'

'OK, OK,' Lindsey murmured. 'Let me get you up to bed, Mary Jane. If you're good I might read you a bedtime story.'

'Hold it right there.' Honey was all ears. 'What was that you said?'

Mary Jane threw back her head and laughed. The veins and tendons of her neck were like fine twigs poking through her skin.

'Oh my dear. I do so love young people.' Then Mary Jane looked at her blankly. 'What was what I said, my dear?' she said in that soft Californian drawl she used when she wanted to be forgiven.

Placing both hands on Mary Jane's shoulders, Honey turned her round so they were eyeball to eyeball.

'You said something about a man they'd met in the Roman Baths. You said something about him being stuffed in somewhere. Was it inside of a giant teddy bear, Mary Jane? Think. Think carefully about this.'

A pair of pale blue eyes widened, staring at her as though this was some kind of quiz and she wouldn't offer an answer until she knew what the prize was.

'I need to know,' Honey said reassuringly, purposely distressing her voice. Mary Jane, the sensitive soul she was, didn't respond well to shrieking.

Nothing in Mary Jane's face diminished as she nodded slowly. She was all eyes and awestruck puzzlement.

'They said it was just a joke.'

'Right.' Honey found herself mentally counting to ten. 'Now. Do you recall the names of your friends?'

Mary Jane opened her mouth as if to speak.

Honey held her breath and prayed.

Mary Jane shut it again.

'I can't remember.'

'Not even one name?'

'John — I think. And Emma. I think there was an Emma. Yes,' she said, nodding vigorously. 'There was definitely an Emma.'

She went on to ask Mary Jane if she recalled them being students.

'They were here studying something, that's for sure.'

'Great.' Honey could feel her excitement rising. If she could at least point Doherty in the right direction . . .

'They all went for a drink afterwards,' Mary Jane went on. 'When they got back the teddy bear was gone.'

'How do we know that for sure?'

Mary Jane sucked in her lips. 'Is there something going on here?'

Honey sank down into a chair, put down the glasses she'd gathered and stroked her hair back behind her ears.

'The man inside the teddy bear was found dead.'

'Oh my!'

'He was found at the bottom of a grave where someone was about to be buried. I was there. I saw it all.'

'Oh my!'

Mary Jane's eyes were now almost popping out of her head.

'So who did it?'

Honey looked back at her, speechless. Mary Jane hadn't grasped that her newly-acquired friends may very well have had something to do with it. Friends of hers just couldn't do things like that.

'They're suspects, Mary Jane. How long have you known them? Not long I bet.'

'I know good people when I meet them,' Mary Jane replied hotly. 'I can tell whether they're the sort to go around killing people and they're not that sort. Trust me on this.'

Exasperated, Honey buried her face in her hands.

'I'll see you in the morning,' Mary Jane continued. 'Everything will look better in the morning. You just see if it doesn't.'

There was no point in trying to get Mary Jane to see reason. She saw the world her way and that was all there was to it.

Peering out from between a gap in her fingers, Honey's gaze dropped to the quarter bottle of wine remaining. Reaching for a clean glass she poured until it was skimming the brim. Then she drank it. Alcohol cures nothing, but then neither did trying to reason with Mary Jane. And both could give her a severe headache.

CHAPTER NINE

Lindsey helped her to clear away the detritus.

'Then I'm out clubbing,' said Lindsey, flicking her hair back from her eyes. 'I've got a hot date.'

The clubbing was expected; the hot date was not. This was the first Honey had heard of it.

'With Archie?'

Lindsey went on clearing up at a rate of knots not looking likely to divulge anything interesting.

'No.'

'Oh. Anyone I know?' She said it casually.

'Of course not. I wouldn't go out with anyone you knew. You're not quite up there with my grandmother's taste, but I prefer to feel my way with a guy — not literally of course. Well, not yet' she added with a wicked grin. 'I take it you're off to meet your devil-may-care policeman.'

'I'm saying nothing.'

'You don't need to.'

Lindsey paused. She was wearing that certain look, the one that made Honey feel as though her daughter was older than she was.

'He's shy. You know that don't you?' Lindsey said.

'Pah! Of course he's not. He's anything but.'

Of course Doherty wasn't shy. She'd know it, wouldn't she?

'He's shy about me being your daughter, about me knowing that he's sleeping with my mother — well not exactly *sleeping* — I've seen that cat that got the cream look in your eyes the morning after. It embarrasses him that I know what you two get up to. Old-fashioned, isn't it? Quaint in fact. Quite endearing.'

'I'll tell him that.'

'Don't!' Lindsey laughed. 'He'll curl up with embarrassment.'

She wouldn't have told him anyway but it was all she could think of to say.

Doherty phoned her just before ten to confirm.

'Look sexy for me.'

The request brought a smile to her face. 'I'll do my best. I take it you've had a hard day.'

'Not good. Wright's death seems to have caught the headlines. There's an endless list of who would have wanted to kill him, though I suppose that doesn't surprise you.'

Honey grimaced. 'I have total empathy with my associates in the hospitality trade. Did you get my email?'

In the email she'd outlined as much as she knew about the students stuffing Wright inside what turned out to be his shroud.

'I did. I've interviewed the people at the Devlin Foundation including the girl collecting for money. She confirms going off with the students to the pub but swears she only knew their first names. She was adamant that Wright had been alive when he got stuffed inside the teddy bear and the post-mortem bears that out. I got the impression she was hiding something but wasn't about to tell me.'

'She doesn't trust policemen?' Honey suggested.

'That's the way it goes.'

After lunch she took a stroll to her favourite auction house where they were holding a preview of lots for the next day's sale of collectibles. There was no mention of collectible clothes or underwear, but she loitered anyway. There were so many different things going on in her life at present and an hour loitering amongst old items would give her something to think about.

'Are you coming in or what, hen?'

She smiled at the sound of Alistair's familiar voice from behind the cashier and collection counter.

'Is there anything in there for me?'

He winked one bright blue eye at the same time as stroking his copper-coloured beard.

''Tis mostly collectible coins and weaponry, but there is one particular item that might take your fancy.'

She followed his crooked finger into the cool interior that was Bonhams Auction Rooms. Prospective bidders browsed amongst the locked glass cases displaying the more valuable items. Those of a more bloodthirsty persuasion slid daggers in and out of ancient leather or metal sheaths. In quick succession two men who might have fancied themselves as William Wallace balanced a claymore across their fingertips. Others who preferred percussion rather than cold steel cocked pistols over their forearms. One over-enthusiastic soul shouted, 'Stand and deliver,' which sent every person in the room freezing on the spot or ducking for cover.

'This way,' said Alistair, after threatening the would-be Dick Turpin with immediate expulsion from the premises if he did not desist. The threat was rendered with undisguised amusement and received in the same vein by the man it was said to. A known antique pistol dealer, he knew Alistair was only having fun and vice versa.

The item Alistair had referred to was balanced on top of something round and wooden.

'It's a rum cask,' said Alistair on seeing her puzzled expression. 'But this,' he said. 'Am I right in thinking what I'm thinking?'

It was similar in shape to an apron and just like an apron had strings to tie it around the waist. The rest of it was covered with frills and it was padded — quite heavily padded.

'A bustle! And I don't have one like this!'

'That's what I thought. You could get it cheap. It's the only item of ladies' attire here. Do you want it?' He said it with a twinkle in his eye. It sometimes occurred to Honey that Alistair could be more than a friend if she wanted him to be. So far they'd never crossed that bridge and she couldn't ever see it happening. They enjoyed being friends; they enjoyed the banter and all the innuendo they sometimes threw at each other. Things were good as they were. She wasn't going there unless Alistair mentioned it, and he never mentioned it. Besides, she had Steve now.

The bustle was made of linen and in good condition. On top of that it was doubtful whether there would be any other bidder seeing as it was a one-off item of clothing. Clothes dealers would only attend the auction if there were more than a single collectible. Honey's mind was made up.

'I'll leave a bid.'

'Fine by me, hen.'

The atmosphere of the auction house was calming. She found herself looking around, not wanting to leave just yet but merely to browse.

Alistair picked up on her mood.

'Wander at will. It'll do your blood pressure the world of good.'

'Wander with me. Tell me what's been going on. Any good gossip?'

Alistair knew everything that went on locally in the antique world. He knew who was buying, who was selling, and who was trying to pull a fast one.

'Business is up and down, but then, what's new? There's a lot of stuff coming in from Russia, some of it a bit dubious. Difficult to prove whether it's legally acquired by the owners, but we're getting there. I blame it on metal detectors. Every shade of villain from here to Vladivostok can buy one on eBay.'

'Best to stick to the home-grown stuff then?'

Alistair made a clicking sound with his teeth. 'We have to have a care there too. The metal detector is more widespread in the British Isles than anywhere else in the world, and to be fair, I can understand that. We have more precious metals buried in the earth than most countries. Take these, for instance . . .'

He stopped at a glass cabinet in which ancient silver and gold coins were displayed on a background of dark blue velvet.

Her eyes flickered over the coins of varying age, size and colour. 'They're very old.'

'Roman. I'm just waiting for them to be picked up and taken to a museum. They're part of a cache found in a field near Cirencester. A bloke with a metal detector went wandering in a ploughed field one morning and came up with this lot and some jewellery. The theory is that the people who hid them were Romano-British round about the time the Romans were scurrying back from whence they came. In the meantime the Sassenachs —begging your pardon—the Anglo-Saxons, the English, were coming. People were hiding their loot in the hope that the Romans would come back to protect them. Unfortunately they had a long wait. It never happened.'

'Hmm,' Honey murmured, her breath misting the cold glass as she peered closer. 'I thought it was only the Vikings who came pillaging and raping.'

'Not so, but mind you, they were famous for it. If you or I should ever be so lucky as to find buried treasure, we're not likely to receive the full benefit. The treasure trove, as it's called, must be proven to have been buried by owners who can't come back to dig it up.'

'Dead for over a thousand years being a pretty good reason . . .'

'Correct.'

They came to an empty display cabinet, the velvet within rumpled and wearing thin in places.

'Somebody nick the contents?' Honey asked.

'You could say that. They made the mistake of counterfeiting the provenance in order to avoid declaring the treasure trove to the Crown. We employ someone to check up. The whole lot got confiscated.'

Honey pursed her lips and nodded. 'Oh well,' she said. 'Time to get going.'

Alistair winked. 'I'll keep an eye on your bustle.'

Honey smiled. 'I'm counting on it.'

CHAPTER TEN

Doherty had requested that she look sexy, so she went all out to knock him dead.

The skirt was tight, the heels were high, and the white open-necked shirt was only buttoned as far as decency allowed. She was particularly careful to wear her best brassiere — the uplift and push-them-together type. That alone should boost Doherty's spirits.

On the walk through the cooling streets to meet her 'sleeping partner', she thought about what Lindsey had said. Beneath Doherty's hard, streetwise surface lurked a squashy marshmallow of a man.

She was also thinking about Mary Jane's friends, the students she'd invited back for a meal and a drink. Students were famous for living on baked beans and beer. They must have thought Christmas had come early with Mary Jane's offer of a meal and a bottle or two of wine.

Stuffing Wright, injured as he was, into the teddy bear was a typically student thing to do and she didn't doubt it had only been done in fun. Even when the teddy bear had gone missing, it hadn't fazed them that much — not until the body was found. No doubt they'd presumed that Wright had walked off with the teddy in revenge for what they'd done to him — which was why they hadn't owned up to the joke in the first place. Owning up to it now, they could well be charged with murder.

It was close to midnight and the Zodiac Club was jam-packed with members of the hospitality trade. Hoteliers, pub landlords, and restaurant managers were pressed up against the bar, dining on steaks the size of the plates they were being served on, and gossiping and moaning about every aspect of their respective trades.

Money, mostly the lack of it in sufficient amounts, was the chief topic of conversation. Hotel guests and restaurant diners rated highly too.

The place didn't get lively until after eleven o'clock at night, when sensible tourists were tucked up in bed and pubs were closing, except for those catering for the young, but that was mainly at weekends, and besides, they were run by junior managers not yet jaded by the trade.

Those who frequented the Zodiac on a regular basis revelled in its dark smoky atmosphere and the strong smell of steaks cooking and garlic prawns oozing with butter. On many an occasion Honey had come out smelling like a garlic prawn, but nobody minded that too much. Once the smell hit, sticking to a diet was a non-event.

One trick Honey adopted to prevent her instantly devouring one of the huge plates of food was to hold her breath. Another was to eat before coming, then order a drink at the bar and content herself with devouring the little dishes of nuts placed there.

She was currently on her third bowl of cashew nuts thanks to a friendly barman who kept replenishing them for her. The barman knew her, knew she'd been working her ass off all day, and kind of fancied her. Not that he was likely to make a move; gossip had it that she was currently in a relationship with Detective Chief Inspector Doherty.

Detective *Chief* Inspector Doherty.

Honey smiled at the memory of when Doherty had told her of his promotion. He'd been so curmudgeonly about it, as though he wasn't glowing with satisfaction inside — which she knew he was. They'd pressurised him into taking promotion; how noble was that?

It was shortly before midnight when Doherty entered bringing just a hint of the fresher air outside.

Rodney Eastwood, Honey's occasional washer-up, was on the door. Rodney was better known as Clint — for obvious reasons. His looks were a far cry from the *real* Clint Eastwood's, though. For a start, he was nowhere near six feet, let alone a few inches over it. He also shaved his head and polished it. Having tattoos all over his skull helped alleviate the glare that might have been there without the spider's web, the matt-black tarantula, and the tip of a rattlesnake's tail.

For once, Clint didn't make a smart remark to Doherty; he must still have been wary following his recent run-in with the Mafia. On seeing Doherty enter Honey immediately ordered a drink — a double gin and tonic. He looked as though he could do with it. Without saying a word he slumped on to the bar stool, grabbed the glass, and knocked half of it back.

'I was right in thinking you needed that,' she said to him.

'Your consideration is appreciated.'

Once the gin was in his system, his eyes raked her over before settling on the inch of cleavage she was flashing.

'You look sexy.'

'I dress to order.'

He downed the rest of his drink, set the glass back on the bar, and ordered another. Then he sat there with his eyes closed.

'I take it you don't want to kiss me or anything?'

His eyes flashed open. 'Damn it. I knew there was something I'd forgotten to do.'

His kiss was quick. They were in public after all.

Doherty stroked his brow. 'This promotion has turned out exactly the way I thought it would. Less contact, more paperwork.'

'How will you deal with that?'

The corners of his eyes crinkled with amusement. 'My assistant's a degree entrant. She's used to paperwork.'

This was the first time he'd mentioned that his new assistant was female. He must have seen the look on her face and read what she was thinking.

'She's all spectacles and wrinkled brow, very academic. Bound to make Chief Constable in no time at all.'

He gave a little grin that was meant to reassure and she was reassured, though she had every intention of checking the competition out when the occasion presented itself.

'I was disappointed in the manner of Wright's death. I'd fully expected you to say that he'd been done to death with his own poisoned pen.'

'I keep asking myself whether there was something symbolic about the meat skewer.'

'He deserved a roasting?'

'A nasty way to die. Whoever did it was behind him and took full advantage of his inebriated condition.'

'He was drunk?'

'As a lord.'

Honey rested her chin on her clenched fist, a faraway look in her eyes. 'He deserved being spit-roasted.'

He stopped talking and looked at her. 'I hear your tone and from my enquiries I understand that Mr Wright wasn't exactly Mr Popularity with the hoteliers and restauranteurs of this fair city. The feedback received consists mostly of certain expletives that I won't use and certain accusations that I will. Blackmailer and lecher come top of the list. Dare I ask you about your first-hand experience and which of these terms best describes said experience?'

'Easy! Lecher. It went something like this: I'll give you a good review and you can give me . . . fill in the rest of the suggestion yourself.'

Doherty's face hardened. 'A meat skewer was too good for him then.' His voice was cold. 'I take it from that look on your face that you refused his advances and that Mr Wright never dared cross your threshold ever again.'

'That look means that C.A. Wright was about as popular as a boil on the bum. Think Dracula with a pen instead of a pair of big teeth. His favourite tipple was the blood of hard-working members of the catering and hospitality trade.'

'So his pieces weren't always favourable and when they were they came at a price.'

She eyed him sidelong. 'That depended on the trade-off.'

'You scratch my back, I'll scratch yours?'

'I've already told you he was a lecher. So not his back as such, but I think you get my drift.'

Doherty fell to silence and looked down at his drink. She could guess what he was thinking.

'OK, he tried it on with me, but I had a knight wearing chef's whites and brandishing a carving knife. Smudger overheard.'

Doherty nodded slowly as he let the information sink in. Smudger Smith, Honey's sometimes errant and irascible chef, was volatile but likeable, a no-nonsense guy with his own code of chivalry. He also had a short fuse and a wide variety of kitchen knives at his disposal. Steve Doherty had learned long ago that upsetting certain chefs could be bad for one's health. Obviously C.A. Wright, the dead man, hadn't cottoned on to that simple truth. Strange, he thought, considering he specialised in articles about the hospitality industry.

'I didn't do it,' said Honey. 'But whoever did so deserves a mention in the Queen's Birthday Honours list.'

'Sorry to butt in . . .'

A shiny head replete with spider's web butted in between them. It wasn't common for Clint to interrupt their evenings at the Zodiac unless it was something serious.

Honey checked his outfit. Just for once he wasn't wearing fancy dress — the Zodiac seemed to have quite a lot of fancy-dress evenings.

'What's the problem, Clint?' asked Doherty.

'It's about Teddy Devlin. Any idea when the trust can have him back?'

Honey eyed him quizzically.

Clint saw her look and went on to explain.

'I do a bit for them now and again — collecting money on the streets, assisting with sorting out donations, old clothes and stuff like that. You can get a packet for recycling nowadays. I told them the copper in charge came in here with his bit of . . . sorry . . . his lady friend, so told them I would ask.'

The subject of recycling brought the cardboard coffin to mind, and not just because Memory Meadow was now an official burial site for the ecologically motivated. A fit of the giggles threatened.

Doherty shook his head. 'I'm sorry, Clint. Teddy Devlin is impounded as evidence. Whoever put him in there might have left some important clues behind. Forensic are on the job. I'm afraid your friends at the charity won't be getting him back in a hurry.'

Clint pulled a face, at the same time sucking in his bottom lip as though there were more to say, more that he didn't really want to say but couldn't help saying.

'It couldn't have happened on the street though. It must have happened when it got nicked — by the geezer who did the job — who killed the bloke inside I mean.'

Clint was shuffling from one foot to another. He shuffled like that whenever there was something he didn't want to divulge. He'd done it when he'd bent a stainless-steel ladle — ostensibly competing with another of the hired helps as to who was the strongest. The ladle was never the same again. It still had a kink in it and soup was as likely to end up over the floor as it was in the dish.

'Is there something you're not saying?' Doherty asked him.

It sounded as though Clint might know something of the case and as such this totally changed Doherty's demeanour. To describe him as a coiled spring wasn't far off the mark. Honey sensed he was ready to grab Clint if he dared move away before giving an adequate response.

Clint continued his soft-shoe shuffle. 'Umm. There could be. It's just a teeny-weeny bit of info from a friend.

She had nothing to do with it really—she was just out there collecting . . . It was just a laugh, you know how young folk are . . .'

Doherty rose off his seat. Honey was all ears.

'The young folk. Who were they?'

Clint shrugged. 'I don't know the names of the students. Just her.'

'A name,' Doherty was saying. 'Give me a name.'

'Tracey Maplin.'

CHAPTER ELEVEN

It wasn't the best location in the world, seeing as the traffic on the A36 never let up until late at night and thundered anew around six in the morning. But the noise and smell of diesel had never bothered Agnes Morden, who watched from the pavement as a giant 'SOLD' sign was pasted across the auction notice. At least it covered the sign beneath, the one she found both embarrassing and terribly hurtful.

'Bank Acquisition', it said on the sign. The sad fact of the matter was that the bank had pulled the rug from under their feet. Agnes and her husband, Walter, had worked hard to get their little hotel going. It had only had nine rooms, so was small by hotel standards, but quite large if termed a guest house.

They'd steadily gone from strength to strength, working on the building as well as in it, replacing the old-fashioned decoration with something light, bright, and attractive. Throwing out old furniture, they'd replaced it with antiques purchased at a reasonable price from local auction houses.

The old place had looked a treat when they'd finished. It was cosy and traditionally furnished. Most people had found its quaint décor appealing; very few had not. For a while they'd made a good profit, enough to keep themselves living well and send their son to study Economics at university. Everything had been going swimmingly until one night in June.

Agnes scowled at the thought of the person who had gone out of his way to destroy them. C.A. Wright had been cutting and contemptuous. What right had he had to run them down so badly? It wasn't as though he hadn't been well taken care of. She'd gone out of her way to look after him. 'Perhaps,' Walter had said, 'that is exactly why he did what he did.'

C.A. Wright had liked people to fawn over him. Some people were like that. They weren't out for good honest service; they wanted servility and the lower you bowed and scraped the better they liked it. She pursed her lips at the thought of his imperious attitude. She'd done her best to cater for him, even staying up half the night to wash and iron some clothes he said he desperately needed for the following day.

The following day had not been half so sunny as the day before. He'd laughed in their faces; told them they were a couple of amateurs who had no idea how "the game" worked. You only got a good review if you paid for it. That was what he'd told them.

Agnes had burst into tears. Her husband Walter, an extremely honest and upright man, had been furious and refused bluntly to pay him anything. Then he'd made a pass at their daughter. Only sixteen, barely out of school, Cathy had been flattered. Strong-minded and intrigued, she'd encouraged his attention despite her parents' opposition.

The incident had brought on Walter's first heart attack. He'd never been the same after that. Then the recession; changes in the exchange rate meant people from abroad just weren't staying. Everything coincided to destroy them, but the trigger for it, in her mind at least, was C.A. Wright.

The fact that he was dead actually brought a smile to her face despite the pain she was feeling. It saddened her to see the old place being sold for conversion to luxury apartments, but at least she had some vestige of revenge. C.A. Wright was dead. May he rot in hell!

'There's some justice after all, Walter,' she said out loud. Nobody was listening, of course. Devastated at losing all that they'd worked for, Walter had died of a heart attack two months ago. Her world was shattered.

C.A. Wright had persisted with his pursuit of their daughter, Cathy, until Walter had lost his rag and landed him a right hook. The man had backed off, then laughed. That's when he really began to needle them. Calls followed from Health and Safety Officers, the planning department, even the Inland Revenue. Wright stirred them all up. Walter had recovered only slowly from the first heart attack. The business had gone downhill from then on. There was nothing that could be done. Tending Walter had been more important than business. She'd let things slide. Guests no longer came. Money became scarce. By the time Walter had suffered the second heart attack that had taken him off, there was little business left and little she could do. She certainly hadn't wanted to keep the place: too many memories of working together, too many late nights worrying about how to cope with their growing debt.

Sighing, she turned away. It was all water under the bridge now.

After a few footsteps her phone rang. She fumbled in her bag and got it out, checked the number, and smiled.

'He's dead then,' said the voice on the other end.

'Yes,' she said, the smile widening. 'He's dead. There's some justice in this world after all. God bless whoever did it.'

* * *

Doherty was told there was a woman to see him.

'She reckons it's relevant to the murder case, guv,' said Samantha, his latest uniformed assistant.

Doherty grunted. The usual collection of nuts seeking their fifteen minutes of fame had been in to say they knew who did it. Some owned up to the crime themselves, lured by the prospect of a warm bed and food for the night. Once their stories were checked out they'd be let loose on the streets again — until the next murder likely to make the newspaper headlines.

'She states that Colin Wright ran off with her daughter.'

Doherty stopped filling in his expenses sheet, pen dangling over one of the inevitable boxes waiting to be ticked.

'How does she look?'

Samantha smiled. 'Clean and tidy. Respectable in fact.'

Doherty sighed with relief. He couldn't take interviewing yet another down-and-out desperate for a mug of hot tea, shepherd's pie, and apple dumpling and custard.

'Bring her in.'

The woman ushered into his office had tired eyes that might better be described as searching. Her hair was pulled back into what used to be called a French pleat. He wasn't sure what it was called now, but he remembered his mother wearing the same style.

'Mrs Morden,' said Samantha as she pulled out the chair on the opposite side of the desk to where Doherty was sitting.

Doherty welcomed her and told her his name.

She was wearing a trench coat with the collar pulled up. It wasn't raining outside so he took it she was cold. Either that or she wished to hide behind it.

Hands forward, fingers interlocked, he leaned forward across the desk, making sure his expression was pleasant.

'So, Mrs Morden. You told my sergeant that your daughter ran away with Colin Wright, the man who was recently murdered. Is that true?'

The woman on the other side of the desk seemed to swell up with the depth of her sigh.

'He was staying with us. He wouldn't leave her alone.' Her hooded eyes, up until now downcast, flashed wide to look at him. 'She was sixteen, Mr Doherty. Sixteen!'

The writing pad on which he made notes during interviews or doodled if he was bored had been half hidden beneath the folder containing blank expense sheets. Mrs Morden had mentioned that Colin Wright had stayed with her. Just in case this proved useful, he pulled the pad in front of him and reached for a ballpoint pen.

'You say he stayed with you. Was that at your private residence?'

She shook her head. 'We used to own a small hotel. My husband and I. Our daughter lived with us. Mr Wright stayed with us for a few days. He told us he would write a very favourable review about our hotel. Walter and I were over the moon about it. That's before we discovered what he was like and what his motives really were.'

'What was the name of your hotel?'

'Twin Turrets. It was one of those Victorian places with a turret at each corner, a bit like a castle built in the Gothic manner. He pursued our daughter, Mr Doherty, and persuaded her to go off with him.'

All Doherty had written on the pad so far was Mrs Morden's name and the name of her hotel. He couldn't see himself adding anything more because he couldn't see where this was going. Far from assisting in capturing the murderer, as an ex-hotelier, Mrs Morden was likely to end up as a suspect herself.

He felt it only proper to point this out to her.

'Did you feel like killing him?'

His eyes looked deeply into hers as much as for any sign of guilt as well as putting her on the spot, making her understand that she could quite easily incriminate herself.

Mrs Morden, it turned out, was no fool.

Her eyes blazed with the intensity of a tigress seeking her young.

'Don't mock me, Mr Doherty. That man killed my husband without using a weapon. He broke his heart, Mr Doherty. He destroyed our business and enticed our daughter away. I would have killed him with my bare hands myself if the opportunity had been presented. However, it wasn't me that killed him. All I came here for is to ask that you bear my daughter in mind. She might have moved in with him. She might have gone abroad.' She shook her head forlornly, her eyes getting moister by the minute. 'We've heard nothing at all from her since he took her away. All I ask is that when you investigate this case you bear my Cathy in mind and find her if you can.'

CHAPTER TWELVE

The old saying 'it never rains but it pours' came to Honey's mind as she tried to cope with more than one job and more than one piece of news at a time.

Anna, her best chambermaid, was heading back to Poland with her baby, Casper was pressing her for details of Wright's murder, and her mother had left messages regarding some kind of emergency she needed help with.

So far she'd only managed to wish Anna all the best and phone Casper to tell him as much as she knew, which, so far, wasn't very much.

'He got skewered through the neck. As you can imagine, the suspect list is likely to be very long.'

Casper had tutted. 'And it would have to happen here. How very unfortunate. So inconsiderate. Why couldn't it have happened when he was staying somewhere less prominent like Brighton or Bournemouth?'

There was no answer to Casper's callous single-mindedness and Honey had no intention of trying to find one. In Casper's book the reputation of Bath superseded sympathy for the deceased or for the reputation of Brighton or Bournemouth, or any other place for that matter.

Not that he had any empathy with C.A. Wright, or didn't seem to, but she really couldn't tell. Casper was closed-mouthed about his dealings with the man, but Honey did detect a slight change in his tone of voice when Wright was mentioned.

All this plus the everyday running of the Green River Hotel was playing on her mind.

'You're stressed,' Lindsey said to her.

'Nonsense. I'm just engrossed in my work.'

'No, you're not. You're stressed.'

It wasn't until Lindsey had gone to the bathroom and she'd taken payment from Mr and Mrs Aicher, a nice Austrian couple in room six that she realised just how stressed out and busy she was.

The invoice was located on the computer system and printed off, payment was made by debit card, and Honey wished them both a very good day.

'You wash dishes too?' asked the wife, an amused smile playing around her mouth.

'I help out wherever I'm needed,' Honey responded chirpily, not too sure what the woman was getting at.

'So we see,' said the Austrian woman, exchanging yet another wry smile with her equally smiling husband.

She smiled and waved at them as they left.

'I wonder how they knew that I've been washing dishes?' she asked with a sigh of satisfaction.

'Easy,' said Lindsey. She nodded down at her mother's hands. 'I think the yellow rubber gloves are a definite giveaway.'

'Ah!'

The guests were next to make the day wobble, more particularly the Fans of Agatha Christie Association, North Somerset and Wiltshire branch. They'd been away for a few days in Dartmouth where they'd done the tour of Agatha Christie's house. Now they were back for their bi-monthly meeting. Tucking the yellow gloves beneath her arm, Honey was on her way to the kitchen when a small group of them spilled out of the lounge, their faces rapt with the enthusiasm of those who spend most of their time living in a dream world or crocheting for charity.

One of the members was a little woman Honey knew as Miss Sofia Clacton. The beaming little figure approached on stick-thin legs which ended in feet encased in lace-up brown shoes.

'Mrs Driver. My friends and I have been talking and well, this conference is turning out to be far superior to any other we've ever had. We have been inspired. Indeed, we feel fired up with enthusiasm and sharper of mind that we've been for absolutely ages.'

Thinking that hotel ambience had something to do with it, Honey beamed expectantly. Good feedback was always welcome.

She gushed the usual platitudes. 'I'm so very glad you're enjoying your days here. If there's anything else we can do please say so.'

Sofia Clacton clasped her little hands together, her eyes shining with gratitude.

'Oh, Mrs Driver! We think you've done enough. Having a murder happen while we're here was more than we could have hoped for.'

Now this was nothing like what Honey had been primed for. She'd been prepared for praise of the hotel's good food and a well-stocked bar. Laying on a real murder wasn't on the list. She felt a need to explain.

'You do realise it was a *real* murder. I didn't lay it on as such. A man is *really* dead.' She spoke slowly, stressing the fact so that Sofia Clacton was under no illusion that murder was not part of the service.

She wasn't entirely sure that what she'd said had sunk in. Ms Clacton and her entourage of Agatha Christie fans nodded appreciatively.

'We feel sorry for the man of course, but it does give us the chance to do a spot of detective work — you know, just like Miss Marple. We can help. We're sure we can. Being versed in criminology, we have a measured advantage to the everyday policeman.'

The speaker was a tiny little old lady with a chirpy expression — another spinster, a Miss Fox. Ferret would have been a better name. She did resemble a ferret, though the fact that she was wearing bright red lipstick made the allusion a little surreal. Splashes of the lipstick were smudged on her face at cheekbone height and she was hugging a spiral notebook to her chest. A pencil perched behind one ear jiggled each time she opened her mouth to speak. All she needed was the knitting and Miss Marple was alive and kicking if this old dear was anything to go by.

Honey gave her what shouldn't have been — but was — a condescending smile.

'I'm sorry?'

'Our association. We can help solve the crime. We would *love* to help, in fact. And I'm sure that nice policeman who gave us the talk the other day would appreciate having us add our expertise. We saw the news on television. That nice policeman was holding a press conference asking for help and we're offering our resources.'

Honey stood gaping.

Miss Fox must have been ninety if she was a day and had been brought up in India just before it gained independence. There was something of the old school about her, the sort of aura that comes from growing up in a fading empire, in a world within a world, closeted from reality in a house full of servants. It was Honey's opinion that Miss Fox's thinking was a little off-kilter and not all of it was down to ageing.

Assuming that Honey hadn't seen the broadcast, Miss Fox explained what was required in measured tones. 'That nice policeman was asking for help from anybody with any information regarding the murderer or anyone making off with a giant teddy bear.'

Other members of the Fans of Agatha Christie Association came out to join Miss Vincent, their faces beaming with zealous interest. Enthusiasm glowed from their faces, not at all like professional policemen. Unlike poor old Doherty, these detectives were not snowed under with paperwork. They were up for old-fashioned detective work, the parlour game sort that only happened in books where there was murder in the library and the butler was always a possible suspect.

Having such a crowd pressing around her was slightly unnerving, but Honey had held business conventions where the delegates had paid more attention to their alcohol consumption than they had to their spreadsheets. Maintaining a cool outer façade, she took small backward steps towards the kitchen.

'I'm afraid you'll have to excuse me,' she said cheerily, thinking that today had been strange and couldn't possibly get any stranger.

A sudden draft accompanied the squeaking of the revolving doors. In a haze of perfume and wearing a rust-coloured linen suit from Max Mara, her mother wafted into the reception area. Everyone noticed. Everyone was meant to notice. Her mother dressed to attract attention and she usually got it. Everything about her, from her coiffured hair to her polished patent shoes, was immaculately chosen and immaculately presented.

Sometimes she resented her mother appearing like a genie from Aladdin's magic lamp. Today she took immediate advantage of her arrival.

'My mother,' she exclaimed with gushing affection, much more than she usually showed for her mother's unheralded arrival. 'Do excuse me.'

A gap appeared in the encirclement and Honey slipped through, quick marching it to her mother, taking her arm and guiding her behind the reception desk and into her office.

'Entertain them,' she hissed to Lindsey on her way past. 'Talk to them about the Romans.'

'A Roman detective?'

'Do you know one?'

'Yes, actually . . .'

Honey didn't catch the name.

Once the office door was shut, she took a deep breath and leaned against it just in case the old ladies decided to attack *en masse.*

'Would you like coffee?' she asked her mother.

'What are you up to?'

Gloria Cross eyed her daughter quizzically until her attention was drawn to the rumpled sleeve she had hold of. 'Hannah! You're ruining my favourite Irish linen.'

'Sorry.'

Honey removed her hand.

Frowning enough to send her brows tumbling on to her nose, her mother smoothed a softly scented hand over the wrinkled sleeve, determined to it press it down into obedient flatness.

'Do you know how much this cost?' she grumbled, her attention still focused on the sleeve.

Honey didn't ask how much, concentrating instead on pouring the coffee. She handed a cup to her mother.

'So. What brings you here?'

'Does there have to be an excuse? Can't I just visit my only daughter?'

There was something about her tone, something about the look in her eyes that put Honey on her guard. There was always a reason for whatever her mother did. Today was no exception.

'There is usually an ulterior motive.'

Her mother sipped the coffee, her pink lips leaving an immaculate imprint on the cup. She swallowed and seemed to be gathering daisies before voicing whatever it was she'd come to say.

Honey considered making a swift exit. Something about this visit was disturbing; bad vibes as Mary Jane would say.

She decided it was the pause that was worrying. Her mother rarely minced words, immediately declaring the reason for her visit before a morsel passed her lips. Usually she started off with demands, or at least, observations; things like 'you're putting on weight', 'when was the last time you had a decent facial?' and 'isn't it time you found a man who shaved at least once a day?'

All these things when added together really did equal bad vibes. Honey smelled a rat.

'Dora's dead.'

It was said in a single breath. Her mother's shoulders heaved with a heartfelt sigh. 'Another of my friends has crossed over.'

Regretting her suspicion, Honey bit her lip.

'I'm so sorry to hear that.'

Her mother sighed again. 'Another funeral. Funerals form the backbone of my social life nowadays.'

Another funeral. The words rang like a dinner gong inside Honey's head. Hopefully she wouldn't be expected to provide the transport yet again, but it wouldn't help to offer a little prayer to the powers that be: Dear Lord, please ensure a plentiful supply of taxis.

On the other hand, providing sympathy was no problem.

As befitting the occasion, she sat down far more sedately than she usually did and spoke very softly.

'So how did it happen?'

'She was found dead in the bath, a truly horrible occurrence. The paramedics had to drain the water and get the fire brigade to cut the bath with a cutting torch to get her out. She was wedged in that tightly.'

'How dreadful. I'm so sorry to hear that.'

She was not surprised. Dora had been grossly overweight. She'd been a great lover of chocolate, cream cakes, and rum truffles dipped in Cornish cream.

Honey reached over and patted her mother's hand. 'What a terrible thing to happen. I'm so sorry.'

'They said she died from a heart attack. I really don't think she should have taken a bath that soon after her midday meal. She'd been warned by her doctor that her arteries were clogged up and that she should leave dairy products alone. She did cut down from full cream to semi-skimmed milk at least.'

'How about chocolate?'

Her mother shook her head and made a whooshing sound through her pouting mouth. 'Oh no. Dora thought that would be taking things a bit too far. She didn't want to overdo it. No, she shouldn't have taken that bath.'

'Neither should she have eaten a large midday meal,' Honey murmured. 'Dora always did things large and the stuff clogging her arteries was probably Cornish cream.'

The pause happened again, an odd silence when Honey could almost hear the cogs in her mother's brain making distinct and well-planned manoeuvres.

'The trouble is,' said her mother, choosing her words carefully and speaking very slowly, 'she had no relatives. She left her estate to Bath Dogs' Home.'

'Ah yes. She would,' said Honey nodding agreeably. 'Dora was fond of dogs. Especially Bobo.'

She noticed her mother's eyelids flicker at mention of the widdling dog. It was as though a ton of grit had fallen on to her pupils and her eyelids were working overtime to get rid of it.

An alarm bell rang in Honey's brain. And then it happened. The truth finally hit her. Her mother did have a reason for visiting.

'Bobo is the problem,' she explained, her eyes downcast whilst still maintaining their shiftiness. 'She's left her to one of her friends. We don't know which one yet, not until probate is settled. In the meantime . . .'

Without her needing to say anything, Honey knew her mother was hoping she wasn't the chosen one.

She was thinking along the same lines herself, for one dreadful minute anticipating the dog having been left to her.

'It's very sad, but they're very good at the Dogs' Home. She'll be fine there until everything is sorted out.'

She should have known better. Today had been a pressurised kind of day and her mother was nothing if not a pressurising kind of person.

Patting her blonde bob, Gloria Cross made a big thing of clearing her throat. 'I'm afraid it's not as simple as that. Dora stipulated that Bobo should never see the inside of such a place. I promised her at Sean O'Brian's funeral that I would look after the little creature until things were settled should anything happen to her. She took me at my word, so I have to keep that promise, Hannah.'

Honey was still hoping that her suspicions were wrong. She was blowing hot and cold on the issue. Though she nodded approvingly, a big question mark flashed red inside Honey's head.

What her mother said next sent her suspicions soaring like skyrockets.

'I should never have been so accommodating. The trouble was that I'd had a few sherries and didn't know what I was saying. I really think I should go back to being teetotal,' she said shaking her head. 'I blame Mary Jane.'

Honey kept her eyes fixed on her mother. Something was going down here. Something she really didn't want to face but had a feeling she couldn't avoid. She was sure of it.

In the next breath the excuse she'd feared and its likely consequence came tumbling out.

'The problem is that I don't have a garden,' her mother began. 'As you know, I live on the third storey, besides which I lead such a busy life . . .'

'With all those funerals you have to go to . . .' Honey began feeling her throat tightening at the prospect of what might be coming.

'And Secondhand Sheila, and the literary society, and the dramatic society, and the lunch club. Also, I'm not one of those people who goes for walks in the park. Neither am I in need of exercise like those people who are always scuttling around indoors . . . like you. So I thought . . .'

Honey could feel the blood draining from her face. 'I don't have a garden.'

Setting teacup and saucer on the table, her mother sat ramrod straight. 'But you have a courtyard. And you live on the ground floor. Plus, of course, you need fresh air and exercise. I've made my mind up. Bobo will do you good.'

Honey was speechless. *Why me?* Why do I always end up drawing the short straw when my mother's about?

She tensed her shoulders and clenched her fists. She was all set. Defying her mother wasn't that dissimilar to a bout in the boxing ring. Her mother was stubborn. Her mother was a street fighter though she'd be appalled that anyone — especially her daughter — would think her so.

'Mother, it may have escaped your notice but I too lead a busy life. I run a hotel, for Chrissakes! I cannot possibly spare the time to feed it and take it for walkies, besides which it isn't properly toilet trained. I'm sorry. No. I do not have the time.'

'You've got staff.'

Honey barely restrained a deep-throated response that was close to a growl.

'They're here for the benefit of guests, not a dog!' she explained through clenched teeth. Her teeth ached with the effort of self-control. If she wasn't careful she'd start gnashing them to breaking point.

Her mother sprang to her feet, full to the brim with righteous indignation and about to throw a tantrum. Gloria Cross was good at tantrums.

Tossing her head, her little chin quivering, away she went.

'Hannah! How can you be so selfish? I have lost a dear friend. I have yet another diary date with a funeral, and now you're preventing me from keeping a promise to that dear friend to look after her beloved little dog!'

Honey couldn't believe this was happening. She shook her head. 'But I'm not the one who promised to look after him when Dora died. You are.'

Her mother began to wail.

'Hannah! How could you be so insensitive?'

Honey narrowed her eyes. 'This is ridiculous,' she muttered.

Sometimes, just sometimes, she could quite easily cross the thin line between solving a murder and committing one.

The lace-frilled handkerchief came out to be dabbed alternately at nose and eyes. Most people had long ago resorted to paper tissues for such a purpose. But her mother had standards, high standards. There was no way she was going to swipe at her countenance with anything like the paper used in toilet rolls.

Honey looked up at the ceiling wishing she could fly up there and barge straight through the plaster and up into the sky. It wasn't going to happen so instead she mouthed, 'Heaven help us.'

However, since there was not a heaven-sent angel in sight on that ceiling, nothing except a cobweb missed by the extendable duster, the matter remained the same and unresolved.

Her mother was weeping buckets. Half of her wanted to give her a damned good shake and tell her that crocodile tears would do no good. The other wanted to apologise for being so insensitive.

Because Honey was basically too soft-hearted for her own good, the second alternative seemed to be winning through. Her weeping mother made her feel guilty. It wasn't often she saw her mother distressed and looking small and old, though she wouldn't dare say that to her face — at least not the looking small and old bit.

But it was one of those days; there was nothing she could do but capitulate purely for the sake of peace on earth.

'OK. Have it your way. I'll take her, but you must understand that it's only temporary. Is that clear?'

Her mother shot up from her seat, weepy face no more. 'I am so grateful, my darling,' she cooed, the tears drying up as fast as they had appeared. She patted her daughter's face. 'You'll get points in heaven for this. I imagine that Dora is looking down at this very moment, flapping her angel wings with delight.'

'They'd have to be pretty big wings,' said Honey.

'That's my darling daughter,' said her mother, her face wreathed in smiles, her hands, the fingers sparkling with gems, clasping her daughter's shoulders.

She was ebullient. Honey was far from that. As a precaution against strangling somebody, she tucked her hands beneath her armpits.

'Cheer up,' said her mother. 'Bobo is a sweetie,'

Her daughter glared at her, wanting to say, 'Well why don't you have her, then?' but the words stuck in her throat. She couldn't believe this was happening to her. In order to hang on to her self-control no smile dared mar her expression of reluctant surrender. If she forced a smile it would look like a sneer.

'So when do I get the pleasure of welcoming Bobo into the Green River Hotel?' she asked, her jaw clenched.

Her mother gave a nervous laugh. A suspiciously nervous laugh.

'Well, actually she's already here. I left her outside attached to the door handle. I thought it only fair that I asked you first before bringing her in.'

Ask was hardly the right verb, but Honey jerked her head in an understanding, though as it transpired, a rather naïve nod. She didn't trust herself to speak.

She followed her mother out of the office, wondering how she was going to cope, where the creature would sleep and how often it needed to go for a walk. Top of the list was how she could avoid little puddles appearing all over the hotel.

Double doors opening immediately into the reception area of the Green River, beyond that was a set of revolving doors of chocolate brown mahogany with shiny brass handles. The revolving doors were divided into four equal quarters; a person entered, pushed, and the door went round, leaving an empty quarter for the next person to enter.

Honey could hardly believe her eyes. Her mother had fastened Bobo's leash to one of the brass door handles. Someone at some point had entered without noticing that the little dog was there. Bobo had somehow slipped from the quarter where Honey's mother had left her and become entrapped in the one behind.

Honey dashed forward. 'The poor thing. It could have been strangled.'

Restricted by the leash, Bobo's nose was pressed flat against the door, the length of its leash stretched across the preceding quarter. The little dog couldn't move.

'Now how did that happen?' Honey's mother queried as Lindsey appeared next to them and fought to untie the poor creature. 'Is she hurt? I hope she isn't hurt. Dora would never forgive me. Never mind. I'll leave you to it. I must go to the little girls' room and powder my nose.'

Lindsey tucked the wagging little dog beneath her arm. 'Hi there, sweetie,' she said, tickling the little dog under the chin.

The dog was ecstatic, eyes bright and tongue drooling from an open mouth.

'Now what's there not to love about a little mite like you,' Lindsey went on.

'The fact that she has a bladder problem,' Honey said with a grimace.

Lindsey put the dog down and dragged it outside so it could pee in the gutter. By the time Bobo had finished her business, Gloria Cross had emerged from the powder room, her tears dried and her make-up replenished.

Honey knew better than to check for any signs of distress, but just on the off-chance . . .

There were none. Her mother was bright as a button, far brighter than when she'd arrived.

'Now I must be going, dear,' she said to Honey, offering her cheek for a kiss. 'Do look after Bobo, won't you? I've left her things in there somewhere.'

She pointed in a vague direction to somewhere in Reception. 'I'll be in touch.'

'I'll let you know how she gets on, Gran — sorry — Gloria,' said Lindsey.

'No need. I know she's in safe hands.'

'Thought you might say that.' Honey glared at her mother disapprovingly though she knew full well it was water off a duck's back. An old duck. A clever old duck.

With a wave and the swiftest footsteps this side of the London Marathon, her mother tottered purposefully off. Within seconds she was gone, lost amongst a crowd of American tourists trooping along behind a guide who was holding a pink umbrella aloft.

'Follow me, follow me,' the guide was shouting out. The tourists did just that, fearful of getting lost in an alien city where nothing was very far from anything else and their hotel was most likely just around the corner.

The reception was new territory for the little terrier and Bobo reacted accordingly. True to form, she got overexcited, standing on her hind legs, little pink tongue flicking out in the direction of Lindsey's face. The excitement at one end was duplicated at the other.

Honey groaned in despair. 'She's leaking again.'

'Just overexcited,' said Lindsey, plucking the little dog from the pavement and holding her out from the door so that her tinkling fell on to the pavement.

'We're going to spend a bomb on disinfectant and air freshener.' Honey couldn't help sounding exasperated. Having Bobo come to stay was both annoying and unexpected. She didn't want her here. She had other things with which to exercise her body — one thing in particular.

'I've got work to do,' she grumbled, stomping back inside.

Lindsey followed her, holding the little dog out at arm's length with both hands.

'Oh what a nice little dog,' said Mary Jane, who was just on her way out, dressed in something stripey and pink which made her resemble a stick of rock.

'No. It isn't a nice little dog,' Honey snapped back.

Mary Jane looked shocked, though not for long. She shrugged her shoulders. 'No need to snap. Is it the time of year or the time of the month?'

'Have a nice day, Mary Jane.'

'You too, Lindsey.'

The polished wood of the reception desk was cool beneath Honey's forehead. She made a wish. Please make that dog disappear. If there are any magical spirits in this hotel, please make that blasted dog disappear.

She didn't hear anything, not even the panting little mouth of the mutt she'd been landed with. It occurred to her that it might have run away before Lindsey could bring it back in.

Suddenly she heard a bark. Her spirits sank back to somewhere around her ankles — as if they weren't swollen enough!

She sighed and looked up at her daughter. 'How about you tell me that it ran away like Little Bo Peep's sheep and we don't know where to find her.'

'No such luck.'

Honey sank her forehead into her hands. 'How am I going to cope with this creature?'

'It'll be fine.'

'And the toilet problem?'

'Don't worry, Mother. I have a plan. Everything will be hunky-dory.' She nuzzled the little dog's head. 'Won't it, Bobo?'

CHAPTER THIRTEEN

Doherty's plan was to interview Tracey Maplin, the fund-raiser who happened to be the last person to see the giant teddy bear before it had gone missing. She had also made the acquaintance of the students who'd stuffed Wright inside the teddy bear, thinking it great fun.

Seeing as Wright had hit his head, the actions of the young men had to be condemned. He could have been suffocated, though the post-mortem had stated otherwise: C.A. Wright had been skewered through the neck. The young men would have noticed that.

An appeal had been made for them to come into the station to help with police enquiries. No one had turned up. Doherty had even interviewed Mary Jane, hoping she'd remember something more about them. She proved just as unhelpful as the media appeals except that she'd insisted they were very nice and that her psychic powers judged them to be above reproach.

Blissfully unaware of his scepticism, she'd breezed into his office and declined coffee, saying it clogged the psychic corridors. She'd nabbed the best chair in the office and fixed him with her unblinking eyes.

'Have you got a resident hypnotherapist?' she'd asked in the spirit of helpfulness. He'd replied that this particular police force didn't hold with stuff like that.

'Not even on a casual basis?'

He'd wanted to say, 'we're talking weirdness here, not sex', the words 'casual' and 'sex' seemed to invite the comment, but he didn't go there.

'Not even on a casual basis,' he'd stated emphatically, settling himself as comfortably as he could on the corner of the desk.

'Well, I won't pretend that it's easy, but if that's the case I'll have to do it myself. If there is any chance at all of me remembering something, we might as well go for it.'

Mary Jane had the sort of eyes that never seemed to blink but fixed on you as though you were a rodent momentarily cornered but just aching to get away. She was eccentric, and getting on in years, but Doherty knew better than to underestimate anything she did.

Scratching at two days' growth of stubble had helped him consider whether he really wanted to go down this route. Stopping her would be easy. He could just get her driven home, but what the hell did it matter? The four young men were bound to show up eventually. If Mary Jane brought that moment a little nearer, then he'd live with it.

But his reservations had kicked in right away. Mary Jane was tall, bony, and colourfully dressed. She dominated his office, her bright colours lording it over the metal filing cabinets and the grey blandness of a wooden desk and a two-year-old computer.

He'd felt like Alice in Wonderland, shrinking in size and not likely to get back to normal until Mary Jane had gone home.

'First I have to make myself comfortable. I have to relax. Can you please close the door?'

While Mary Jane had made herself comfortable in a red plastic chair, he'd shut out the sound of police officers walking past, rustling paper and talking.

Doherty was cool enough not to appear uncomfortable with what she was doing. It paid to have an open mind in today's police force, plus a good understanding of body language. Her head was back, her mouth was open, and her eyes were shut. For a moment it looked as though she were about to slide off the chair. The only thing that stopped her was the size of the room, her feet had jammed up against the side of the desk.

Opening one eye she'd asked him if he had a pocket watch.

Doherty shook his head. 'I'm all digital.'

She'd pointed to his wristwatch, a nice stainless-steel number that showed the date as well as the time.

'Well, wave that around in front of my eyes. Dangle it from one of your fingers. It might work.'

Confessing he had no faith in this exercise whatsoever might have upset the old girl so he'd gone along with it. The wrist strap wasn't the open-ended sort but he waved what he could in front of her eyes.

'You have to say the words.'

'The words?'

'You know the ones.'

Sure. He knew the ones and steeled himself for what he had to do.

'Right. You are feeling tired. You are falling asleep.'

He wasn't sure that he was and did consider abandoning the scenario then and there. Still, it wouldn't hurt. Mary Jane was only trying to help and hypnotism seemed to float the old girl's boat. Her faded blue eyes were flicking backwards and forwards with the motion of the watch.

'Your eyelids are getting heavier and heavier. You are now falling asleep.'

Her eyes had closed. It looked like it was working — something of a surprise seeing as he didn't have faith in all this mumbo-jumbo.

Still, there was such a thing as beginner's luck, or even inherited skill. Hadn't one of his family been a bit that way inclined, swearing they had a gift for it?

Whatever. He didn't know for sure, but hey, he congratulated himself that he'd seen all the right movies and observed how this way-out stuff was done.

Then it was time for the questions.

'Now think back to the other day when you met four young students. You picked them up at Sally Lunn's, then what happened?'

He'd kept his voice steady.

Mary Jane frowned. Her hypnotised state seemed real enough. 'I'm not sure . . .'

'Think carefully. Think about their names . . .'

Christ, he'd thought. If I do get a result, how the hell do I explain it to the Crown Prosecution Service? *Hey, there was this weird American woman who agreed to be hypnotised in order to make identification of suspects.* Was a traditional line-up not possible, some Tricky Dicky would ask? The recently earned promotion could soon go due west if he didn't watch it.

Her eyes had suddenly flashed open. 'I didn't go to Sally Lunn's. I met them at the Poacher in Much Maryleigh. It was a nice day so I thought I would have a change. I drove there. I had a very nice portion of venison pie followed by gooseberry fool. It was crowded so I had to share a table with them. They didn't mind at all and I gave them a lift back. Then we got talking. They'd Greyhounded around the States for three weeks in order to see as much as they could, which wasn't much, but hey, they were happy. For some reason the trip back into Bath got to them a little. They said they needed a drink after that so I offered to buy them one. That's what happened.'

Doherty had nodded and looked down at his folded arms. Most people needed something to calm their nerves following being a passenger in Mary Jane's car.

'And their names?' he'd asked hopefully.

The painted wooden parrot earrings rattled as she shook her head. 'Not a clue.'

So there was only one thing for it. Clint had given him the name and address of Tracey Maplin. She was the main path to these guys and Mary Jane's intrusion and insistence on being hypnotised had only slowed him up. He could have sent a subordinate to interview Tracey, but he preferred to do the job himself. Besides, she wasn't going anywhere in a hurry; she was ill, wasn't she? She'd declined his request for her to come into the station stating that she'd fallen and sprained her ankle that morning so it was more convenient for him to visit her.

'She'd better be bloody ill,' he muttered under his breath.

'Say something, guv?'

He shook his head. 'No. Nothing.'

His assistant was still ploughing her way through the backlog of filing, plus entering the details of the present case on to the computer database. There should have been more civilian clerical help, but due to cutbacks jobs were being doubled up.

Guessing that Casper was on Honey's back about the case, it seemed sensible to invite her along. Besides, he was getting used to having her around and it wasn't just because she was becoming his right-hand man. Things had moved on.

He caught her at the hotel.

'Are you available?'

'I bet you say that to all the girls. You've caught me wearing rubber gloves and carrying a sink plunger.'

'My kind of outfit.'

'You have a fetish for sink plungers?'

He laughed then told her what was on his mind. She told him to come on over. She'd be waiting outside. 'I might not be alone though,' she added.

'Are you two-timing me?'

'Far from it. I'm bringing a friend — sort of.'

He'd caught the laughter in her voice, the kind of restrained laughter people have when the joke is as much on them as on anyone else.

He hadn't known what to expect but hey, he was cool with Lindsey or Smudger the chef tagging along, no problem.

She was waiting for him outside the hotel entrance and waved as he brought the Toyota MR2 to a halt. The two-seater had grey bodywork and a black interior. It was cosy, the modern equivalent of a bicycle made for two.

'You look good,' he said to Honey as she slid into the passenger seat.

She was dressed in a black sweater, faded jeans, and trainers with flashing blue lights in the heels. She said she felt like a mobile Christmas tree. There were reasons for her choice of clothes: number one, the black sweater made at least the top half of her body look slimmer. Number two, the jeans clung nicely in all the right places. Number three, the lit-up running shoes brightened the denseness of black and ordinary-looking jeans. She hadn't bothered with jewellery so the shoes made up for that; not that she explained any of this to Doherty. Such details would be lost on him.

Doherty's attention had shifted to what he had first thought was a bundled-up cardigan sitting on her lap. No cardigan he'd ever seen had beady eyes and a black button nose. He eyed Bobo with something akin to alarm in his eyes. The kiss he gave Honey landed on the tip of her nose mainly because he was taking in the details of the dog. He wasn't usually so distracted when he kissed her.

'That's a dog.'

'There's no fooling you, is there?' she said, rubbing at the tickling sensation his kiss had left on her nose.

'I wasn't expecting a dog.'

The truth of the matter was that he hadn't expected the dog to look like it did. Steve Doherty wasn't often lost for words. He prided himself on being a man of few words — after all, why use a long word or sentence when a short expletive did the job? But he was rarely, if ever, speechless. It took a great deal of searching to find his voice.

Bobo, the excitable little terrier, was sporting a Huggies disposable nappy.

'Is that some kind of fashion item for dogs?'

'They're supposed to be for babies. It was Lindsey's idea. Anna left a few behind when she went back to Poland. Bobo has a little bladder weakness. Lindsey cut a hole for the tail and hey presto! Bobo's little problem is sorted — or at least not trickling over my top quality, as in megabucks per square yard, seagrass carpet.'

The reception area of the Green River Hotel had been revamped a little while back. The job had not been without drama, the number one drama having been that Honey's interior designer had got himself murdered. Though she'd been saddened by the demise of the designer, the hold-up in her renovation plans had been even more annoying. Everything was now looking smart and she sure as hell wasn't having some little whippersnapper of a dog doing its business everywhere.

'Is Bobo likely to be a permanent fixture in the Green River Hotel?' Doherty asked.

'Over my dead body.'

'That bad, huh?'

'That bad.'

He suddenly got out of the car, went to the boot, and took out a black plastic rubbish bag. He placed it on the floor at Honey's feet.

'Put her on that.'

Honey had half expected this kind of treatment. Doherty had as passionate a relationship with his car as he had with her. There was no way he would allow the Toyota MR2 to be stained by an excitable Norfolk terrier.

Tracey Maplin lived in a flat in Walcot Street, a Bohemian area of the city where shops selling moth-eaten Oxford bags and straw boaters rubbed shoulders with stores selling second-hand musical instruments. There were also natural food shops with sacks of spices dumped on rickety shelving outside. Inside they smelled of dried nuts and ground ginger.

The top floor flat Tracey lived in was situated above a shop selling pre-owned goth and punk clothing of which black was the dominant colour.

Before they left the car, they sat, each looking sidelong at each other and then at the dog.

'I'm not leaving her in here.'

Honey eyed the nearest lamppost. It was tempting to leave Bobo tied up there until they were finished. However, there were concerns; someone might steal her, or she might get loose. She pointed that out to Doherty.

'I wouldn't mind that much,' she added, 'but I would then have to face my mother. And so would you.'

Doherty did not believe in facing her mother unless it was absolutely necessary. If there was a compromise he'd take it and in this instance he did.

He sighed. 'We'll have to take her with us.'

Doherty pressed the intercom. A girlish voice answered. Tracey Maplin was still at home.

'Come on up. I'm at the top of the house, up here with the cobwebs and spiders.'

The hall was communal and well-used. A bicycle was propped up against one wall. The hallway smelt of mud and tomato ketchup.

The stairs were narrow and carpeted with something that might have been described as cream when new but was now struggling to make beige. It looked very much as though it had not been cleaned since the day it was laid.

They still had some breath left when they finally got to the top floor flat, though only just enough to press the doorbell.

'It's not locked. Give it a push,' shouted the same voice that had spoken to them on the intercom.

Tracey Maplin was lying full stretch on an ancient sofa of chocolate brown velvet. A multi-coloured shawl was thrown over the back of the sofa, and the cushions were multi-coloured and trimmed with sequins, purple tassels, and ribbons. She was wearing a handmade woollen cardigan with huge buttons. Honey guessed it was second-hand. Whoever it had originally been made for must have been six sizes bigger than Tracey. The neckline was huge and hanging halfway down one arm, exposing her naked shoulder.

Four or five scatter rugs were thrown over bare wooden floorboards that looked as though they'd only recently been varnished. Tracey's flat being at the top of the house, the ceilings sloped beneath the eaves and the windows were small, though they had the benefit of great views.

'Do you mind us bringing in the dog?' Doherty asked.

'I can leave it outside on the landing tied to the banister if you like,' Honey added, but Tracey wouldn't hear of it. Her face was wreathed with smiles, one hand already held out in Bobo's direction, beckoning the little dog to come hither.

'What a cute little critter. Bring him in.'

'It's her,' Honey explained as Bobo went into doggy wag overdrive from her skull to the tip of her tail. Luckily the Huggies stopped her spraying the flat's varnished wooden floorboards.

'Love the outfit, dude,' Tracey said to the little dog.

Said 'dude' wagged uncontrollably.

Tracey continued to make a fuss of the 'little critter' or 'little dude', the two names she seemed to favour for the excitable Bobo. The dog seemed to be as keen on Tracey as Tracey was on her.

They took the seats that were offered, an antique nursing chair with low legs and a spoon-shaped back, which was instantly grabbed by Doherty, and a blow-up sixties plastic chair — great design perhaps, but not the most comfortable of chairs to sit in. Honey sank into it, her chin just about level with her knees, over which she threw Doherty slitty-eyed threats.

'So,' said Doherty, his hands folded in front of one knee. 'You think you may have some information?'

The merry interchange between her and Bobo lessened. She looked worried.

'Look, it was only a joke. Apparently that bloke had been giving the lads some stick. They'd found him lying flat out on the ground, absolutely paralytic. He stunk of whisky and although he was out of it when they brought him out, he certainly wasn't dead. Honest he wasn't.'

'Did he say anything?' Honey asked.

Tracey's face soured. 'Too right he did. A load of abuse. A right nasty piece of work and off his face. His breath would have ignited a gas stove. Anyway, the guys thought it would be funny to stuff him inside Teddy Devlin. So that's what they did.' She giggled, then bit her lip as though suddenly remembering that this was a serious matter. 'They thought it would be funny if he woke up and started staggering about in the teddy bear suit. It would raise a laugh with people passing by if nothing else. And it might make them reach deeper into their pockets.'

A pink balloon chose that moment to drift past the window. Honey followed it with her eyes. What with Bobo wearing a disposable nappy, Tracey referring to a teddy bear with a personalised name, and now a pink balloon floating past the window, everything seemed a little surreal today. Alice in Wonderland had fallen down a well. Honey, Doherty, and Bobo had climbed up into something that wasn't exactly an ivory tower but was high up in the air.

'Can you give me their names?' Doherty asked the girl.

'Only first names — Stefan, Johann, Colin, and Deke.'

'No last names.'

'No.' She shrugged her narrow shoulders. 'They were just guys I bumped into. Students, so they said. One of them was a medical student though basically they were all into rugby.'

'So what happened then, after they'd stuffed this man into the teddy bear?'

'We went for a drink. I should have stayed put really, but I was pissed off. People just weren't giving that day.'

'Can you tell me where you went for a drink?'

'The Saracen's Head.'

Doherty made a note to call in on the pub on his way back to Manvers Street. It was a vain hope that the landlord might remember them but what was more crucial, if they were regulars then he might know their names. It would certainly be a stroke of luck if they were.

Bobo squealed and yapped with excitement once they were back in the car.

'I think she likes your car,' Honey said. 'It is kind of kennel-sized, I suppose.'

Doherty didn't rise to the bait. 'Isn't it amazing; you'd think people would notice someone making off with a giant teddy bear slung over their shoulder? Nobody seemed to notice, or if they did thought nothing of it. Strange that.'

'Unless they didn't carry him away.'

'How else would they do it? It's a pedestrian area.'

'And no cameras in the vicinity?'

'They're being checked. I've also asked for those students who might have been for a practice rugby match that day.'

'What makes you think they'd have been playing rugby?'

'They were drunk. When I was a rugby-playing student I used to get drunk after practice too.'

'That's not part of a health and fitness regime, surely?'

'No, but it's part of student life.'

Honey had a sudden eureka moment. 'Wait a moment. I remember where I've seen her. She was in the restaurant the other night with another girl and the four young men Mary Jane brought back with her. They were all drunk.'

Doherty paused before unlocking the car. 'So she could be lying. She does know their second names?'

Honey shook her head. 'They're students. Who cares about second names?'

CHAPTER FOURTEEN

C.A. Wright had a sister. Nobody had been aware of this until he got murdered and the next of kin was traced and informed.

Cynthia Wright had flown over from Paris, stopping off in London to check on her brother's bachelor pad before taking a chauffeur-driven car down to Bath where she'd booked into a room at the Royal Crescent Hotel before contacting the police.

She came bowling into the police station, her cashmere coat flying out behind her and a Pekingese dog tucked under each arm.

Plonking both dogs on the reception desk, she fixed the duty sergeant with a pair of angry eyes.

'I want to see whoever is in charge of the investigation into my brother's murder. Now. Right away.'

The duty sergeant had been preparing to tell her that she would have to wait as the man in charge, Detective Chief Inspector Doherty, had not yet arrived back. Luckily for him Gordon Tomlinson, the landlord of the Saracen's Head, had been out at the cash and carry, though his girlfriend — she must have been half Gordon's age — was there. She said she would ask the bar staff if they recalled the four students. She would also ask Gordon when he got back and get him to ring if he had any information.

Because of this hold-up, Doherty walked back into the station and straight into Cynthia Wright's sights. Doherty felt a sinking sensation in his stomach but tried not to show it. She was wearing a pair of ostentatious clip-on earrings and a matching necklace flaunting a dangling medallion. There was something about women who wore ostentatious jewellery that unnerved him.

'I'm Cynthia Wright. I want to speak to you about my brother's murder and the people you should be arresting,' she snapped imperiously.

Doherty noticed how quiet the dogs were and thinking how strange that was. Small dogs were usually snappy, Pekinese particularly so. He guessed that in her presence they knew when to keep their yaps to a minimum. Miss Cynthia Wright was the one who did all the snapping and the dogs knew this.

He opened the door to the corridor that led to the interview rooms.

'This way, Miss Wright.'

Doherty surmised that the dogs were well house-trained. They weren't wearing Huggies, and he supposed that even if they weren't house-trained it didn't matter that much. The room they entered didn't belong to him. It was his job to ask questions, not to clean up dog mess.

'I'm sorry for what happened to your brother,' he said after pulling a chair out for her then sitting down himself. 'If there's anything at all I can do . . .'

'Yes. There is.' He watched her mouth snap shut. Like a guillotine, he thought, the sort used in an office to chop paper in a straight line. Or the French version used to chop off aristocrats' heads! 'You can question these people. One of them must be responsible.'

He listened because it was his job. He nodded in the right places. Like her brother Miss Wright was not a likeable person, but he would deal with her grievances.

She threw what looked like a collection of letters on to the desk with such force that they slid halfway across towards him.

'Poison pen letters from people who wished ill on my brother.' Her bottom lip curled back as she relayed exactly what she thought of these people. 'Wicked people, all of them. They should be locked up just for what they said in those letters. My brother was a true professional and dedicated to his job. He had awards for his work and he only spoke the truth. Anyone can tell you that.'

Doherty avoided eye contact whilst he fingered the letters, fanning them out like a hand of cards. He guessed that he wouldn't find much difference between the letters: hate letters and, from what he'd gathered from both Honey and Casper St John Gervais, the chairman of Bath Hotels Association, not without good reason. He was doubtful of finding anyone with anything nice to say about the deceased. The man had been far from flavour of the month — or even the chef's special.

From what he'd found out so far, C.A. Wright had been a leech, a lecher, and a libellous bag of unmentionable detritus. Casper's words, not his, though Honey had concurred.

He ground his teeth as he thought about it then tried to stop. His dentist had warned him about doing that. 'You'll ground them down to the stubs,' he'd said in a voice as cool as his hands.

Doherty had never met this C.A. Wright except when laid out on the stainless steel in the mortuary — which was just as well for Wright. He might have had a word with him otherwise— well, not so much a word. More of a warning. A policeman needed to be impartial in his work, but the fact that the deceased had propositioned Honey regarding a sojourn in a bedroom closet rankled. The impartiality went flying out of the window on broomsticks when things got personal. And things had got personal, so it was just as well that Wright was dead.

He picked up one of the letters. Each letter sported a Bath postmark. Each of the letter writers had also inserted their home address — as if they'd really expected Wright to get in touch and apologise or withdraw the wicked words he'd written.

Pushing both her dogs from beneath her arms and on to her lap, jamming them together with her beringed fingers like a pair of bookends, Cynthia Wright pointed out the obvious.

'As you will see, Chief Inspector, they all reside in this city. In Bath. I specifically filtered these out from the rest.'

His ears pricked up. 'The rest? You mean there are more?'

'Quite a few. No reflection at all on my brother and his work, of course. Colin made enemies of people who couldn't take criticism. He was a professional, Chief Inspector. A man of high standards. People peeved with his deliberations on their establishment phoned or wrote in very abusive tones, as you can see,' she said, flicking a beringed hand at the cascade of letters, 'He's had many threats, including murder, that's why the case can so easily be solved and why I am here. One of them murdered him. Mark my words.'

Doherty sifted through the letters, running his eyes down each one in turn. They were certainly abusive and the threat to kill was mentioned in all three.

'And you say there were phone calls . . . ?'

'Yes,' she snapped. 'There were. One in particular.' Snatching the letters out of his hand, she thrust one at him. 'That one there. Read this.'

He did as he was told. Not that he feared this woman. Just taken aback. For now. The threats added a new dimension though overall he wasn't really that surprised. He himself wished the guy was still alive so he could deal with him too. And he wouldn't be gentle. In fact he wouldn't be able to help himself.

The letters were predictable, but feeling Cynthia Wright's beady eyes on him, he made a big show of reading each letter in turn. All three threatened to kill her brother. From what he knew of the man he guessed every other letter he'd had from offended people was in much the same vein. This one he was presently reading, however, held one different line.

'I'll have you the next time you visit Bath. You just see if I don't . . .'

He looked at the signature. It was signed Walter Morden. Next to his signature Walter had drawn a skull and cross-bones with a dagger running through it — similar to the way the skewer had been pushed into the deceased.

'Tell me,' he said, suddenly remembering Agnes Morden and her missing daughter. 'Did you know any of your brother's girlfriends?'

'He didn't have any girlfriends. Not regular girlfriends. He was too busy with his work.'

'Did he ever mention any names? Did you see any girls, especially young girls? Especially one named Cathy Morden?'

He got the photo Mrs Morden had given him out of the drawer. 'This girl?'

Doherty noticed a slight change in expression. The eyes hardened as her expression turned from arrogant to blank.

'I've never seen her before. As I've already told you, Colin was too immersed in his work to bother with girlfriends.'

* * *

In the centre of Bath, Gordon Tomlinson, landlord of the Saracen's Head, leaned down and whispered to his girlfriend, a stunner of a twenty-six-year-old who had replaced his middle-aged wife only two months before. 'I think that's them.'

'The same ones that were here last Wednesday morning. Are you sure?'

She'd spoken to the copper who'd called in because Gordon had been out at the cash and carry. She'd liked the copper, Doherty. She remembered the name because it was also that of her favourite rockstar. She'd also liked his rangy look and the two days' worth of stubble on his face. She liked rugged. She liked rough.

Gordon licked his lips, wishing he didn't have such a grungy taste in his mouth, and wishing Samantha, his live-in lust, wasn't so pushy. He'd taken up with her thinking she'd be less pushy than Clara, his wife. Clara had pushed him hard. He was sure he had indents from her hands in his back the way she kept pushing him.

When she'd announced she was off to Spain to find herself, he'd been stunned. After two months he'd never felt happier. After four months he'd begun feeling lonely. Samantha had come along when he'd been at his lowest ebb. Two months together then Sam had moved in.

He couldn't quite get a handle on why she'd moved in with him. After all, she wasn't a bad looker. But perhaps you're not so bad yerself, he decided. 'I mean, just look at those shoulders,' he'd said to himself as he eyed his reflection in a full-length mirror.

Gordon's eyesight wasn't quite what it had been. Neither was his body. His upper torso was shaped like a wedge of cheese. In his youth he might have had quite a body. Nowadays he looked as though he'd swallowed a barrel of beer — albeit a small one but still enough to disrupt the firmer contours of yesteryear.

Sam was nudging him, pushing him to decide, just as Clara had done.

He'd been taken aback when she'd told him about the visit they'd had from the police.

'Are they the ones?' she asked again. 'Come on. Are they?'

Gordon gulped. He didn't really want anything to do with the police, but the thought of going up to an empty bed was totally unpalatable.

He knew the four lads all right. They were regulars and he'd laughed and joked with them about rugby, about women, about drinking.

Sam had told him about the copper calling and asking if they would give him a call if the students came in. Normally Gordon wouldn't have given the matter the time of day, presuming the crime to be something trivial, but given that this was in connection with the murder of some bloke found out in a grave at Much Maryleigh his sense of duty had been jogged from unploughed depths. He couldn't believe they could have had anything to do with it, but they were a lot more subdued than when he'd last seen them, sipping their bottles of Budweiser slowly. They looked as though they were discussing something worrying. Gone were the loud voices, the confident air of young men on the threshold of life. Something was troubling them and he could guess what it was.

'Well?'

Sam was nudging him again. Thinking of the cold bed he almost shivered.

'It's them,' he whispered back.

Leaving them unaware of his attention, he went into the back room, picked up the phone, and dialled the line that went straight through to Detective Chief Inspector Doherty.

CHAPTER FIFTEEN

Honey was trying to make the best of the situation with the orphaned Bobo while considering the details of the murder of C.A. Wright. It wasn't so easy to be positive about Wright. Like most of the people in the hospitality trade, her opinion was that he'd been a number one stinker. There was no other way to describe him.

Casper phoned her to say that Doherty was making progress. This meant that Casper, in his capacity as chairman of Bath Hotels Association, had been chasing Doherty's ass. He wanted results. He wanted his clean and pleasant city to resume its worldwide respectable image. Poor Doherty.

Casper was filling her in on the details, the basics of which she already knew. These had to be the four students responsible for stuffing Wright into a large teddy bear. She could see the funny side of it. Wright deserved stuffing — though not so gently.

She pretended to be listening intently. 'He's interviewing four students, so he says. Four rugby-playing students.'

'You sound regretful,' she said to Casper.

'Well . . .' he said, sounding quite peeved. 'I do like to watch local rugby. Those boys are so fit — and very nice.'

She reminded him that they may have committed murder.

'I know, my dear . . .' He sounded as though the bottom had fallen out of his world. It was typical. Casper was fine about the out-and-out villains of the world being arrested but he had a soft spot for beautiful people, especially young men who performed on the sports field. He sighed heavily. 'What a shame.'

Guessing that Doherty wouldn't be in touch for some time, she concentrated on Bobo, thinking to herself that the nice thing about having a dog thrust upon her was walking through the park, getting fresh air plus the exercise she'd always promised herself. The negative that she tried not to think about was carrying a pooper scooper and the requisite plastic bag.

The moment she was outside, standing with the dog outside the Green River, woman and dog looked each other in the eyes.

Honey stood with hands on hips. Bobo stood four-square looking up at her and wagging.

'Are you reading my mind?' Honey asked the dog.

Bobo gave one yap.

'Right. Off with your pants.'

Taken unawares, the chin of a passing gentleman wearing a tartan cap and golfing trews dropped like an elevator from the seventeenth floor.

'I beg your pardon?'

'Not you. Sorry,' Honey said hurriedly, popped the nappy behind a plant pot and hurried off.

Bobo trotted along with more of a spring in her step. The disposable Huggies designed for a newborn to three-month-old baby would not be replaced until they got back.

Henrietta Park formed a patch of greenery in the midst of the city, and had big trees, rolling lawns, neat paths, and benches to sit on. A magnet for office workers eating their lunch, it was shady and surprisingly quiet for a park in the middle of a city. Big it was not.

Dogs had to be kept on a lead in city parks under threat of a fine if they were not. Long walks were best taken on the perimeters of the city: fields where the towpath ran beside the river and canal, or footpaths leading off the main road into Bristol. And then there was the required pooper scooper and the plastic bag.

Clean up after your dog.

Quite right, thought Honey. The signs were everywhere. The city was no place for dogs and neither tourists nor locals relished stepping in nasty things. She wondered at the outcome of the will. Bobo deserved a bit of space, she decided. Living with her mother was out of the question and so for that matter was living with her. In fact the dog wouldn't be happy living with anyone who resided within the city. No matter what the terms of Dora Crampton's will, the dog would be better placed in a home in the country. So Honey told herself as she wandered the paths through the park, musing on murder, mutts with incontinence problems, and matters relating to the smooth running of a Bath hotel.

Deep in thought she didn't at first notice she was being summoned.

'Excuse me!' came a shout.

The summons just couldn't get through the whirligig of stuff in her mind, didn't sink in. The shout was for someone else.

'Excuse me.'

Slowing her pace, she looked over her shoulder.

A very tall man sporting ash-blond shoulder-length hair was running up behind her, his gloved fists powering him forward like a steam train, his long thin legs kicking out behind him.

Running entered her own head — away from him with all due speed. He looked weird. He looked strange.

She paused for a second, her head to one side debating whether to flee or face him. Kids were told never to speak to strangers. Perhaps she shouldn't either. Bath attracted some pretty quirky-looking types and this guy certainly had a quirky look about him.

She looked him up and down, rating him on a one to ten for weirdness. He was close to ten and no lower than an eight on the scale.

Apart from the over-long hair, which was of such gossamer fineness it let through the sunlight, he had an all-over tan, skinny arms, and very skinny legs, a definite winner in a knobbly knees' competition.

She blinked when she took in the white shorts he was wearing. 'Skimpy' was the best way to describe them, though 'too tight' and 'too small for decency' were right up there with it. The matching vest was a mere formality. White socks, running shoes, and fingerless gloves plus a sweatband around his forehead finished his far from fetching ensemble. She concluded that the shop must have been out of his size at the time he'd taken up jogging.

Just in case she'd made a mistake and he wasn't really addressing her, she did a swift sweep around. An old lady sitting on a bench out of earshot feeding the pigeons, a woman wearing a tangerine skirt and lots of beads was doing a series of Tai Chi movements under a tree, and two toddlers were running around while their mothers smoked and chatted. Nobody else was close by. What to do? Scream or humour him?

The spidery man with the peroxide hair had come to a halt on the path in front of her blocking her progress and had addressed her. His hands were bunched into fists which he held at his waist. The stance made her think that he might sprint off suddenly; either that or he had it in mind to throw a left hook. She tensed just in case she had to duck. On second thoughts she decided he was around sixty years of age and she should be able to handle things — even a punch on the jaw.

'Were you speaking to me?' she asked, sounding casual when in fact she was still considering doing a speedy dash in the opposite direction.

'Ye . . . sss,' he said between rushed breathing. 'Are you that bird who does the crime thingy with the hotels thingy?'

His narrow chest heaved from concave to convex like a pair of punctured bellows.

She thought she knew the thingy he was referring to. 'If you mean the Hotels Association thingy, then I am. Crime Liaison Officer last time I looked.'

'I want to speak to you.'

'You already are speaking to me.' Honey met his look with firm resolve though inside she was about as firm as a warm jelly.

'I wanted to tell you that I wrote that letter on a whim.'

A letter? What letter? Perhaps he was speaking to the wrong person. She hoped he was.

She shook her head. 'I'm sorry. I don't know what letter you mean.'

'I want it back,' he blurted. It sounded as though he'd been psyching himself up for this.

The pale cheeks either side of his overlong nose were laced with fine veins that were getting redder by the second.

Honey took a step back and eyed him. The self-awareness, self-defence, and desperate scenario course she'd attended had advised keeping things light. At the time she hadn't been able to envisage when exactly she would ever use what she was taught. There was only a very outside chance that she would find herself in a hostage situation. This was very likely the closest she was likely to get so she shrugged and did a little laugh. It wouldn't hurt to put a little practice in. 'I know nothing about any letter.'

'Yes, you do,' he snapped. 'I want it back!'

This was crazy. He was crazy.

Shaking her head, she laughed even more — not a manic laugh, just a gentle "hey, let's be friendly and funny" kind of laugh. My, that course she'd gone on was coming in handy. Unfortunately, things didn't come out quite as she'd planned.

'You're crazy! I haven't a clue what you're talking about . . .'

He had staring eyes, pale and limpid. The pink veins in his face took on a rosier glow, almost as though they were being fed by sub-dermal heat ducts. 'If you won't give it to me . . .'

'I cannot give you what I do not have,' she said, shaking her head and wondering what opportunities there were for people skilful at negotiating techniques.

The blond jogger burst her bubble. In one swift move he'd snatched Bobo's pink leather leash.

Taken totally by surprise, Honey yelped as it blistered through her palm.

'You can't do this,' she yelled, desperately trying not to envisage a carefree lifestyle without Bobo.

'Yes, I can!'

She couldn't believe what he did next. Jerking the leash as though it were a yo-yo, Bobo was propelled upwards landing in the crook of his arm.

'You can't do that,' she shouted as she ran after him, not sure whether she was referring to him taking the dog or using the helpless mutt like that.

Leaping into his stride, he shouted at her over his shoulder. 'You're not getting your dog back until I get the letter.'

'Hey! It's not my dog. Bring her back this minute!'

'Ha!' she heard him shout.

The jogging outfit was a blur of white as he sped off with Bobo beneath his arm.

'Bobo! You traitor!'

The women chatting and smoking glanced over, paused then went back to what they were doing.

She took a few tentative steps, but stopped as a very important thought came to her. His stride was greater than hers, plus she had the pooper scooper.

'Hey!' she shouted again. 'You'll get fined if you don't have one of these.' She waved the red plastic scoop and the plastic bag in the air. He took no notice of course.

'You'll get fined if she does a poo-poo on the grass,' she yelled somewhat lamely.

He didn't stop, of course, and disappeared out of sight.

'And you haven't got any Huggies,' she added with a smile. 'Pity your laminate floors or your woollen rug.'

Her smile turned to a grin. Bobo's kidnapper was totally unaware of what he'd got himself into. He'd left her holding the poop-scoop and the plastic bag, and the baby's disposable pee pad was stuffed behind a flowerpot outside the hotel.

With raised spirits, she shoved the lot into the nearest bin, smacked her hands together, and made for home.

There could be repercussions, of course, but she'd cross that bridge when she came to them. First things first, there was no need to tell her mother what had happened. Since lumbering her daughter with the dog, Gloria Cross had absented herself from the Green River Hotel and from the end of the telephone. She'd gone undercover and would not emerge until the will was read and the dog's future cast in stone.

And there was no chance of paying a ransom. None of the deceased's old friends were keen on giving Bobo a home anyway, so for now it seemed best to let sleeping dogs lie.

Best of all, she was shot of the dog. Her smile was as broad as the sunshine and the avenue of blue sky all the way down Pulteney Street. She smiled broadly to passers-by and tipped a wink at elderly foreign gentlemen whose legs were kaput but whose fantasies were still active judging by some of the winks she received back.

See? If you're happy you make other people happy. Just see what positive thinking does for you, she told herself, unable to stop her silly grin from spreading.

'Poor mutt,' she muttered to herself, and she didn't mean the dog. She hoped the guy who'd taken Bobo owned a very expensive antique Persian rug — or fitted carpet newly laid. Either way, it wasn't going to stay pristine for long. Bobo was moving in!

As for the letter? What letter? Was it something to do with C.A. Wright?

CHAPTER SIXTEEN

'Something about a letter.'

Honey was mumbling her thanks to Bobo. She'd heard it said that looking after a dog was a big responsibility. It tied you down. You couldn't go anywhere or do anything with a dog in tow. And once it was gone? Whoopee!

She was on her fourth vodka and tonic — hence the mumbling and the pleasant fuzziness invading her head.

'So, he kidnapped your dog in exchange for this letter? And now you're celebrating.'

She looked at him with a silly grin on her face, the same one she'd been wearing since Bobo's kidnapping. If she'd been more sober, she might have wondered why Steve Doherty was eyeing her so thoughtfully. Normally she cottoned on to when his mind was ticking at time bomb speed. Usually all this talk of a daft dog being kidnapped would have been greeted with a raw mix of disbelief and humour. But he wasn't doing that, he was being very serious.

Honey, on the other hand, was finding it very difficult to be serious. She was on a high, blasé and celebratory — hence the drinking. Her vision wobbled a little when she nodded.

'That's what he said. A letter. A letter I told him I know nothing about. I think it was something to do with C A Wright.'

She giggled, shook her head too vehemently, and nearly fell off the stool.

Doherty set her back on it again.

'Now listen to me,' he said firmly. 'I need to locate this blond jogger you're on about. He may know something. Think carefully about what he said to you.'

'I thought you'd traced the students. I thought you suspected they did it but wouldn't own up?'

'You thought wrong. The four students have an alibi. They were in the Saracen's Head until three. The girl left them there at two. The post-mortem states death occurred no later than three. It couldn't have been them, plus the deceased had one hell of a lump on the back of his head. I'm presuming that he might have been sobering up and the murderer wanted him comatose.' He paused and slid a fresh drink across the bar. 'Drink this.'

She drank without being asked twice then screwed her nose up. 'There's not much vodka in this.'

'There's no vodka in it. OK, the dog's gone, you're very happy about it and want to celebrate, but I need you to listen to what I'm saying and I also need to know about this runner.'

'Jogger.'

'Runner, jogger, whatever. Did you hear what I said about Wright?'

She nodded. 'Lump on the back of the head.'

'Someone had hit him before he was killed, possibly while he was doing the sightseeing thing in the Roman Baths. Deke Hattersley, one of the students, went back in following an argument with Wright. He could have hit him. We can only charge him with grievous bodily harm — though he denies doing anything, just finding him there.'

Honey swigged back the straight tonic feeling saintly that she hadn't insisted on having a shot of vodka added. 'So you're hinging your suspicions on the writers of the letters that Wright's sister brought in?'

'Correct.'

'Is she pretty?'

Doherty's eyes tightened when he looked at her and small wrinkles — hinting at both pleasure and amusement — radiated from the corners.

'You jealous?'

There hadn't really been much time or room for jealousy in their relationship thus far. OK, Doherty worked with female police officers, but she'd never let the fact fudge her feelings.

'Of course not.'

'You'd love her. All fluffed-up hair and a pair of matching . . .'

He moved his arms and hands like men do when they're about to describe a favourite part of a woman's anatomy.

The look on her face must have said it all. Throwing back his head he burst out laughing.

'A pair of Pekingese!' he said, revelling in his school boyish humour.

'Dogs?'

He nodded. 'Dogs.'

Feigning contempt, she pretended that there were better things to see in the club and took a gander around — not that you could see much.

The air in the Zodiac Club whirled in its blue and smoky way, heavy with the smell of grilled steak, onions, and garlic prawns. Around one or two in the morning she'd leave this place smelling of it all.

Judging by Doherty's demeanour, Cynthia Wright was made of the same mould as her brother. Better than that, Doherty had not found her attractive. He would never have described her as he had if she was. Neither would he have used the over-flamboyant description for what turned out to be a pair of Pekingese dogs.

Dogs brought Bobo to mind. Somewhere in the city Bobo would be tiddling on someone else's floors. OK, she'd get round to finding the little mutt, but in the meantime her Turkish rugs and flagstone floors would be safe from Bobo's excitable nature.

'You're not mad with me?' Doherty didn't like silences. He didn't like long silences and he didn't like short ones either. She'd learned fast that Doherty didn't like confrontation in his relationships. He liked everything to mosey along, but it didn't hurt to throw a little gripe now and again.

'I might be.'

Suddenly he took her chin between forefinger and thumb and looked deeply into her eyes. She managed to focus but felt as though she were swimming.

'You've got come-to-bed eyes.'

'Beats having to say anything.'

She held her breath as she awaited the question she thought he would ask her which was, '*I've got half a bed to spare. Are you in it or what?*'

But he didn't ask that.

'Now, Honey. I want you to think very carefully. Did this mad jogger mention a name when he asked you about these letters?'

OK, she was disappointed. Cuddling up to Doherty would round the evening off nicely. She pulled her thoughts together, or as together as she could.

'I don't recall him mentioning any name, his own or anyone else's. He reckoned I could get hold of this letter. He kept pressing me, I kept denying, and eventually he nicked Bobo.'

'I see.'

Letting go of her chin Doherty frowned and looked away. She couldn't see the expression in his eyes, partly because he wasn't looking in her direction, and partly because he was going all blurry around the edges.

Taking a deep sigh, she mused on the imagined scenario at the place the kidnapper called home.

'Oh, boy! Is he going to regret that! Did I tell you that Anna left behind a pack of babies' disposables and that Lindsey fitted one on to that dog? Bet you that guy doesn't have a pack of them in his place. Bet you he'll be out buying some pretty damned sharp!'

She laughed but stopped abruptly when she saw the way Doherty was plucking at his bottom lip, his eyelids half covering those delicious dark blue eyes of his.

She kept looking at him whilst juggling her thoughts into cohesive order. Something was going down here. Doherty hadn't laughed and didn't look amused. In fact he looked dubiously thoughtful — which was very worrying. It meant that the doggy kidnapper had hit on a sore spot.

'There is a letter? Is that what you want to tell me? There is a letter?'

He gave her that melting look, the one that superseded the serious detective bit and made her go weak at the knees.

He took a deep breath. 'There are three letters, all signed and all from people in receipt of one of his reviews. Cynthia Wright has letters from all over. It is possible that this guy you met might have been from out of town when he wrote his letter. Perhaps he had a hotel elsewhere but moved here, saw Wright, and took his revenge.'

Honey's humour died an instant death. She'd taken another look at the letters, viewing their provenance in a more positive light. Three letters, three identities, and three addresses; they couldn't help but find the yellow-haired man who was holding Bobo to ransom and now a lot more. They would take some going through, checking on the whereabouts of the letter writers, but eventually the people Doherty had at his disposal might very well hit the right one. The upside was that she might be instrumental in solving the murder. The downside was that the dog would be back in the fold in double-quick time.

'Has he contacted you at all since?' Doherty asked.

Honey shook her head. The fuzzy head brought about by the drink she'd consumed wasn't feeling so good now. 'Well . . . he's been ringing the Green River. I told him again that I knew nothing. I mean, anyone can ring there and he knows that I'm Crime Liaison Officer for the Hotels Association. He insisted that if I didn't get hold of his letter and hand it over I would never see Bobo again.'

'You shouldn't look so pleased about it. Your mother won't be happy.'

'That's a point.'

'So how come he didn't give you his name? If he wanted the letter back that badly, surely he would have given you that?'

She shrugged. 'Beats me. It's almost as though he expected me to know who he was.'

'Your description is pretty imaginative: a tall, skinny blond bloke wearing diminutive clothing and sporting a fake orange tan.'

'Did I say it was a *fake* orange tan?'

'It sounded as though you didn't quite believe it was real.'

'I didn't think he was quite real. He was odd. Really odd.'

Doherty ordered himself another drink, jerked his chin at her by way of offering her another. 'Tonic water only.'

Her brain wasn't quite in tune with her mouth so she didn't argue about the drink he was ordering for her.

He passed her the glass. 'Here. I'm going to be generous. You can have a double tonic water.'

'You're so kind.' She knew it made sense. Her lips were like rubber and moving without direction.

He gave her that knowing look that seemed to say, '*I like a woman who knows her limits*.'

Honey swiped her forehead with the back of her hand. Her head was hot, the back of her hand cool. Normally she was fully aware of her limits. If only she'd instigated the ruling a lot earlier in the evening. Drinking too much in her profession could mean entering a downward spiral that was nigh impossible to escape. She'd seen plenty of others take to the bottle though usually because of personal problems. Infidelity and marriage breakdown came top of that list as a reason for hoteliers overindulging in the stuff they were supposed to sell. Another reason was lack of business. She'd known one guy who couldn't work out where his wines and spirits were going — until he realised that his bar was empty of customers and he'd been standing there, bored beyond belief, helping himself.

Honey screwed up her eyes. 'I wonder what turned Wright to drink?'

Doherty shrugged. 'Could be anything. Divorce, bereavement, unfulfilled expectations . . . or even something happening that left him feeling guilty. Perhaps all these people he upset.'

Honey frowned at him. 'Nah! Not him. Wright didn't have a conscience. He had a lot of other things, but not a conscience. Not him.'

'One last drink?'

She nodded. While Doherty went out to the men's room, she got the barman to make hers a double vodka, reasoning that the two straight tonics had sobered her up no end. So why are you drinking, she asked herself? She provided an instant answer: 'To forget.'

'What was that?' Doherty had come back.

'I was just thinking out loud. Wright might have drunk to forget.'

It was an outright lie. She was thinking of the kidnapped dog. The question of Bobo was suddenly a lot more worrying. There was something about Dora's will . . . and the dog. Adding both items together it was safe to say that her mother would not be pleased. Now what could she say to explain why Bobo wasn't around? Not a lot.

She slurped back the drink. Down in one.

Doherty was saying something but she struggled to understand.

'The thing is, I've already . . .'

She pretended that she knew where this was going.

'Wright?' she murmured blearily. Her head fell against his shoulder.

Doherty rested his chin against her soft, dark hair, drinking in the scent of apple blossom shampoo mixed with garlic prawns and chargrilled steak.

'I'll take you home.'

He managed to get her on to her feet, her cheek resting on his shoulder. She let him think she was far worse for drink than she actually was. It was nice to have a strong man to lean on, though her legs did feel . . .

'Did I ever tell you about the dog I had when I was a kid? His fur was the same colour as your hair. Did you know that?'

She didn't know and she didn't hear. Doherty smiled to himself. 'Let's get you to bed.'

Placing her arm up around his neck he passed his across her back.

'I want to go to bed,' she said mournfully.

'That's exactly where I'm taking you.'

A few people heard and smiled knowingly.

He didn't bother to say that he was taking her home to her own bed and that they shouldn't have such filthy, and inappropriate, minds. He didn't really care what they were thinking, and besides he might *not* take her home to her own bed. Whatever bed she ended up in it was certain that all she'd do was sleep.

Clint, Honey's oft-time washer-up, wasn't on the door tonight. Doherty was grateful for that. He could do without a snide comment or smirk and Honey could do without the gossip it could cause amongst her employees.

Fitting Honey into the front seat of his Toyota MR2 wasn't the easiest job in the world.

Muttering under his breath he made another attempt to put her right. 'Other people just pass out and go floppy like a rag doll. Do you have to be so bloody awkward? Even when you're drunk?'

'Is it midnight yet?'

'Not quite.'

'Do I smell of garlic?'

He sniffed. 'No. Not yet.' Doherty smiled down at her. 'Your place or mine?' He flipped a coin. 'OK. Mine.'

The action was flippant. He didn't know whether she was needed to cook breakfast in the morning. He knew there was a duty roster at the Green River but didn't know who was doing what or how many guests were currently in residence. After thinking it over, he decided it made sense to phone the Green River Hotel and enquire who was 'it' in the morning. Hopefully one of the employees would answer. He hoped it wouldn't be Lindsey. He and Honey had been an item for a while and so far Lindsey had seemed unfazed by their relationship, which had mostly been kept at a distance from her though she was far from being that green. However, he was about to say that he was taking Honey back to his bed . . .

It was a very nice bed — a French sleigh-type bed, six feet wide and made of solid walnut. He'd bought it on a weekend trip to the September street market in Lisle, courtesy of the Channel Tunnel rail link. Because of its bulk it hadn't been possible to bring it back on the train so he'd paid to have it transported from there, but the bed's size and ambience had been worth it. You could fit six in that bed and it still wouldn't be crowded; not that he'd ever had six in that bed, and not that he ever planned to do so. There was a thick line between fact and fantasy. Anyway, Honey looked pretty good in it all by herself, her hair splayed out all over the pillow like the rays of the sun — though dark of course, but still, nice.

When he pulled a sheet over her, she made a noise closely resembling the purring of a cat and curled down, making herself comfortable.

Doherty sighed. 'And now. For my next trick . . .'

He looked at the phone long and hard before picking it up. With a bit of luck it wouldn't be Lindsey who answered, but unfortunately for him his luck had gone walkabout. Lindsey answered the phone.

'Shit.' That was to himself. 'Linds!'

The idea was to sound hale and hearty. Instead he sounded nervous.

For Chrissakes, why?

He reminded himself that Lindsey was an adult. These were modern times. OK, he was having a thing with her mother. So what?

'Hi, Steve. I take it my mother is with you?'

His tongue tripped over the words. 'Kind of. She just doesn't know it at this moment in time.' That sounded OK. Cool. In control.

'Is she staying with you tonight?'

Sleeping! She meant sleeping.

He gulped. Come on. Bring on the macho male.

Well, he kind of went halfway to that.

'That depends. Tell me, is she scheduled to cook breakfast in the morning? If she is, I'll get her back to you. If she isn't I think it's best she stays in bed.'

'No. Let her sleep it off. Doris is in and Smudger has also promised to be in early. He has to prep for the Agatha Christie lot.'

'That's great. I do think she needs to sleep it off.'

'I take it she told you that she lost that dog?'

'Yeah. I think she's been celebrating the fact, which is why I thought it best that she sl—stays with me.'

He threw back his head, exasperated that he'd tripped over the obvious word, the one he should have seen coming.

It's OK, he told himself. It's OK. You weren't lying. He'd tripped over the word sleeping, but he was just being considerate. That was the picture he was trying to paint and Honey had been drinking swifter than usual, so everything was cool, everything was OK, and . . . shit . . . Lindsey was saying something.

'That's terrible. That poor dog. Honestly, my mother can be so selfish at times.'

Lindsey's criticism of her mother surprised him. She'd always seemed so good-natured, so in tune with whatever her mother was doing.

'You sound sympathetic to the missing Bobo,' he replied. 'I thought it had problems, not trained properly from what I understand? Not like police dogs. They're very well trained. Best trained in the world.'

The truth was that he knew nothing about dogs, but at least talking about dogs took them away from the subject of him and Lindsey's mother.

'Well, Bobo wasn't trained. She just didn't get brought up properly at all. Her mistress didn't get round to exercising and training her right.'

'You can't know that for sure.'

'Are you kidding? Did you ever meet Dora in the flesh? Exercise was never on her agenda.'

Doherty replied that he had never met the woman so couldn't really say. He wanted to end this call. He wanted to snuggle up beside Honey even though she was out of it. Lindsey made him feel guilty.

However, Lindsey had opinions about everything, knew a lot and sounded very knowledgeable about dogs. Come to think of it, Lindsey was knowledgeable on a lot of subjects.

'So you're OK about your mother staying over here?'

'Sounds as though you've got no choice, and Steve . . .'

'Yeah?'

'I *am* over eighteen. And so's my mother.'

'I know that. What I meant was . . .'

He didn't know what the hell he meant. Honey had once said that her daughter sometimes made her feel as though she were the one who was eighteen and Lindsey was the mother. He now knew just what she meant.

Lindsey was still giving good advice. 'Give her a hot glass of milk, a couple of aspirin, and tuck her in. Then run for cover in the morning.'

'You're telling me she's going to be grouchy.'

'Well you know that film where the cute creatures turn into ratty little critters when they're put in touch with water? That's what my mother's like after taking too much booze on board.'

He pulled a 'so what' face because what she said was no great surprise; everybody was grouchy if they woke up in the morning with a hangover. But he was actually feeling more at ease with his girlfriend's daughter until . . .

'Undress her first,' Lindsey added.

Doherty blanched. Lindsey was actually telling him to take her mother's clothes off! Feeling the heat rush to his face, he rallied his nerves and decided where this should go. Firstly, he needed to divert the conversation, to lay on the excuses as to why this was happening thick and fast.

'I'll do whatever you say.' He bit his lip. 'I mean,' he said, frantically searching for a plausible get-out clause, 'carrying her across Reception in a less-than-sober state doesn't show a good example to the staff or the guests.'

'That's not what I was getting at. My grandmother's still here. If she doesn't leave soon I swear she'll turn into a pumpkin — or I will.'

Doherty paused. 'I'll rephrase. I don't want to bring your mother's reputation into disrepute with your grandmother. So what's she doing there?'

'She's holding a séance with Mary Jane and a few of her friends. They're trying to get in touch with Dora.'

'Did she leave much money?' Doherty asked, presuming that her friends were going to ask the dead Dora about her will.

'That's not the problem. They're worried about who gets to inherit Bobo. My grandmother promised she'd look after the dog. She didn't mean it could move in with her. And before you ask, no, she doesn't know that the dog's been kidnapped. She thinks my mother's out for a late-night walk with her at this very minute.'

'Did your mother say anything about this blond jogger wearing the small shorts and vest?'

'She did. Pity she didn't get his name.'

'Never mind. He's got to show up on one of the letters Wright received. We're looking into it.'

'Really? I thought you'd be sticking to the letters from ex-businesspeople in Bath.'

'We've already interviewed them. They don't match the description of the dognapper.'

'No blond joggers?'

'Only one man and he's dead.'

CHAPTER SEVENTEEN

Rolling over in the bed, Honey's blurred vision cleared and the tom-toms in her head stopped beating long enough to notice the note Doherty had left her.

The scrap of paper seemed to have been torn from the bottom half of a pizza delivery note.

'Had to go. Sleep it off. See you later. How about we have lunch at the Poacher?'

She sighed, stretched out her arm, and felt the spot where he'd lain. The cotton sheets were already cold.

Oh well, the drums in her skull were still throbbing to a dull beat. She wouldn't have been the best of company anyway.

Wincing, her eyes met the chink of bright light showing where the curtains didn't quite meet. Turning away she closed her eyes again. Guessing it was mid-morning a few more minutes in bed wouldn't hurt. Bliss! A huge bed all to herself.

She should have known better. Every time she wanted some down time: a soak in a bath, or doze in front of a made-for-idiots TV programme, the phone was bound to ring.

Doherty's only homage to antique anything was an ivory-coloured phone from way back in the fifties. Mary Jane had told her that if you concentrated on who you wanted to be in touch, ninety-to-one your wishes would come true.

She wished for Doherty.

Doherty it was. How great was that?

'How's the sleeping beauty?'

'Is that what I am?'

'The sleeping or the beauty?'

She grinned into the phone. Doherty wasn't the greatest at giving compliments but the message was in the way he said it.

'It's the thought that counts,' she said to him. 'You were thinking about me so you called.'

'I was also going to tell you that I was calling on the three phantom letter writers. Are you interested in coming with me?'

'Give me half an hour. By the time you get here my eyes should be back in their sockets.'

'I'm on my way.'

* * *

This morning she was in heaven, heaven being naked in Doherty's shower and thoroughly enjoying the warm water cascading over her. Warm edging towards cool was the temperature of choice when your head was playing host to a group of bongo drummers.

The shower was spacious; a wet room tiled in black marble and smelling of spicy gels and shampoos.

Although firmly installed in the Alpha Male category, Steve Doherty was a man who had a penchant for the finer things of life. Despite his sometimes-dishevelled appearance, he was never grubby. Rugged was the best description for him.

The big comfort in his bathroom was provided by a pair of fluffy towels, big enough to make a quilt out of. She could easily have wrapped herself up in one of them and lain down on the other. She'd slept but not that well. However, she had made him a promise to accompany him to interview these three letter writers.

Fishing for her clothes was no big deal. She found them neatly folded on a chair, which in Doherty's estimation was superior to a hanger and a clothes rail in that it was closer to hand.

Doherty tended to put things down rather than put them away. On reflection he seemed to have an aversion to hanging things up. Come to think of it a lot of men were pretty much the same way.

She had no make-up with her and anyway Doherty wasn't that type of guy. Rooting through the bathroom cabinet she did find a cream of some description, the label long rubbed away. It smelled OK and had the consistency of moisturiser. A little seemed to go a long way. Her face felt soft. Screwing the lid back on the pot she put it away.

By the time Doherty arrived she was dressed and ready to go.

He pulled into the kerb outside his place in Camden Crescent in the low-slung Toyota Sport he loved so well. The sun was out so the top was down. Wisps of hair were blowing across his face, though only gently, she was pleased to see. Nothing gale-force.

Doherty wrinkled his nose. 'That smell's familiar. Is everything all right?'

'Smell?'

At first she wasn't sure what he meant, then she twigged it.

'Oh! You mean my face cream.'

'Is that what I can smell?'

'I expect so. I didn't have anything with me so I borrowed some from that pot with the blue lid.'

'Oh!'

The way he said 'Oh!' should have alerted her that something was wrong. But she let it go. Anyway, he'd already swung out into the traffic — more swiftly than usual it had to be said. A cyclist swerved. A car honked its horn.

Whatever smell she might have been harbouring was blown away.

'So where are we going?'

'Widcombe. Trudy Wendover lives in one of the static mobile homes up there. She couldn't say much to enlighten me about our friend Mr Wright except to say that she hated him, wished he was dead, and could we pin a medal on the person who did it. Besides that, she had an alibi; in fact all the letter writers had a plausible alibi. It's a long shot, but perhaps she or one of the others might know who our blond jogger is.'

Mrs Wendover's home site was confined to the over fifty-fives. Net curtains hung at the bay window of her mobile home. They twitched as they drew up. On seeing who it was, the curtain was dropped and the door opened.

Mrs Wendover had a shapeless figure and mousy hair, and although her bone structure was excellent, she had the pale, unmade-up face of someone who was beyond caring.

'Detective Chief Inspector. How delightful to see you.'

She held out her hand. Doherty shook it.

'This is my associate, Mrs Driver.'

Mrs Wendover looked her up and down with hooded eyes, her chin held at an imperious angle. Honey decided that when it came to looking down her nose, Mrs Wendover was top of the tree.

'Delighted to meet you. Would you care to take tea?'

Anyone else might have asked if she wanted a cuppa, but Trudy Wendover was apparently top-drawer material. At one time she must have been quite a Chelsea-type girl, well brought up and privately educated. Despite living in a static mobile, she had not let the side down.

'Stiff upper lip and tight corsets,' Honey murmured to Doherty.

'We wouldn't want to put you to any trouble,' Doherty said as they were shown into Mrs Wendover's living room.

Everything in it was white: white carpet, white furniture and white walls. Overall it looked quite smart though Honey wondered how the devil she managed to keep it clean. It wouldn't suit her at all. Wouldn't suit her guests either.

Mrs Wendover settled herself into a comfortable armchair. Close to her feet a Persian cat slept in a basket lined with pink satin quilting. Sensing there were visitors, it stretched one smoky grey leg and opened one yellow eye. Deciding that they were of no particular interest or immediate threat, it went back to sleep.

'That's Sylvia,' said Mrs Wendover.

Doherty sneezed. 'Sorry,' he said, wiping his nose. 'I'm allergic to cats. I think I'd better take a rain check on the tea.' He dabbed at his nose with a man-size tissue.

Honey was about to say that she'd never known he had a problem with animals. That was before she realised that he was using an excuse not to take tea. They had two more people to see.

The cat decided the time was ripe to exit its basket. After stretching languorously, it furled its tail around Honey's ankles while Doherty asked Mrs Wendover about the blond jogger.

'No,' she said, shaking her head emphatically. 'I can't say I have.'

Honey looked down at the cat. 'Has anyone ever threatened to kidnap your cat?'

'No!' cried Mrs Wendover, sucking in her breath as she bent to scoop her beloved and expensive-looking cat up from the floor. Eyeing Honey with outright suspicion, she stood there wide-eyed, the cat hugged tightly against her face.

Honey regretted frightening the woman like that and tried to explain. 'The blond jogger we're seeking kidnapped my dog.'

'And we think he too may have written a threatening letter to Colin Wright,' added Doherty.

Mrs Wendover stiffened. 'My letter was not threatening! It was the truth. Wright ruined my life. It broke my husband's heart when he read that awful review. Not everyone sets great store by reviews or depends on them for their business. But we did. I don't regret writing that letter and I am certainly not sorry that Wright is dead!'

'Can we speak to your husband?' asked Doherty.

Mrs Wendover's lips curled into a defensive snarl. 'You can if you wish, though you won't get anywhere. My husband has dementia. He can't even remember who he is, let alone the likes of that scoundrel Wright and what he did to us.'

Doherty made his apologies for troubling her. They left.

'Well, that's telling us,' quipped Honey laughing as they headed back to the car and off towards Salisbury Plain. 'C.A. certainly didn't get an A plus for good will to all men — or women.'

The weather was getting warmer. Just for once she didn't mind travelling with the hood down. Doherty's little Toyota made short shrift of the miles, the fields were green, and the sun was causing a white mist to rise from the damp grass.

They stopped at a café on their way along the A36 before heading off across the long green curves of Salisbury Plain and the monolithic structure of Stonehenge.

The second letter writer lived in a pretty cottage that might once have had a thatched roof. The roof was now of dark red "Rosemary" tiles, small but pretty and made prettier by scalloped tiles of the same sort along its lower edges. Tiles had replaced thatch on a lot of cottages: understandable really seeing as they were pricey to replace every twenty years and pushed up the cost of home insurance due to the risk of fire.

The moment she opened the door there was something just too familiar about Adelaide Cox. Not a day under sixty, she was well turned out, though in a blousy way. Her hair was big, blonde, and in a seventies style; her skirt was too tight, and her sweater too low-cut. A pink chiffon scarf was tied around her throat, its ends fashioned into a bow on the right-hand side beneath her jaw.

She beamed on recognising Doherty from his last visit. 'Oh, it's the nice policeman.'

She didn't acknowledge Honey at all.

'This is . . .' Doherty began.

'How lovely to see you again,' she gushed, cutting him off. 'Now do come in and tell me how I can help you further.'

Adelaide Cox exerted a firm grip on his arm as she propelled him into her home. Honey squeezed through the gap she left. The woman showed no sign of regret when she almost closed the door on her.

They were shown into a chintzy parlour where china birds of various colours, shapes, and sizes perched on every available surface. A real live bird — a budgerigar — twittered from a cage on a stand.

When Mrs Cox smiled her botoxed lips dominated her face. Honey felt her stomach tighten. The woman was a younger version of her own mother.

A charm bracelet rattled on her wrist when she waved her hand in the direction of a fat, chintz-covered sofa.

'Do sit down, Detective Chief Inspector. Doherty, wasn't it? I don't think you gave me your Christian name when we first met. You know mine of course,' she simpered, her eyes twinkling as she propelled him to where she wanted him to sit, pressing him on to one half of the sofa. Adelaide took the other half. Feeling as useful as a chocolate fireguard, Honey was left standing by a table. There was no way Adelaide Cox was going to include her in the conversation, she obviously wanted Doherty to herself.

Listening to Doherty getting similar answers as they had had from Mrs Wendover without being asked to comment was irritating. Her concentration began to wander around the room finally settling on the newspaper sitting on the table. It was turned to the personal page, the one where men and women advertised for company.

Honey ran her eyes over the long list of "*gay divorcee*", "*trim, slim woman in her fifties seeks fun companion,*" and "*merry widow. Likes dining out, foreign holidays, and cosy nights in for two.*"

There were men of course. There'd be no point in the pages if they weren't included, but they were fewer in number. Most were women who wanted male company, romance, and intimate twosomes. One glance at Adelaide Cox was enough. She definitely fitted into the seeker of romance category.

The evidence of that was also on the table: two pens; one green, one red. Some of the advertisements from men looking for company were circled green, others crossed through with the red pen. Green was obviously for 'go'. There weren't many. Red predominated.

Bending her head slightly so she could see better, she also took in what looked to be the beginnings of an advert Adelaide herself was writing.

Curious to see how Mrs Cox described herself, Honey bent her head some more.

"Attractive lady, 45 years old . . ."

Forty-five was stretching it. Sixty more like.

Adelaide Cox was totally absorbed in what Doherty was asking her so didn't notice Honey's incredulous look. She was too busy offering Doherty tea and cake which he was firmly resisting. One of her knees was pressed against his.

Doherty was handling it well. 'Sorry. I have to think of my waistline. I wonder if you can help me, Mrs Cox . . . ?'

'Call me Adelaide.'

'Adelaide. I'm looking for a man . . .'

'So am I . . .'

'. . . Who may also have sent a derogatory letter to Wright,' Doherty went on, shifting in an effort to put at least an inch or two between them. 'It's very possible you may have known him in the days when you and your husband still had your business. He's tall, blond, and quite athletic I think.'

'Well,' said Adelaide, finger on chin as she thought it through. 'I don't recall such a gentleman — though it does sound as though I should. He's around my age.'

'A neighbour? A boyfriend perhaps? With all due respect to your deceased other half, I'm sure you're not wanting for male company.'

She simpered as girlishly as she could get away with. 'You naughty man.'

'Anyone at all?'

She shook her head. 'No. I'm sorry. I don't recall anyone like that.'

Honey harboured wicked thoughts in her mind about Adelaide Cox. She wanted her to know that a woman could live an interesting life without a man in it. And, secondly, that it was she who occupied the other half of Doherty's bed and there was no room for three.

However, she was here for a purpose and that purpose was paramount. She herself had already racked her brain, trying to recall if she'd ever seen the blond jogger working in or owning a hotel or some other catering outlet. Casper had also racked his brain and came up with a big fat zero, and if Casper couldn't recall such a dramatic-looking man in the hospitality trade, then he didn't exist. The chairman of the Hotels Association prided himself on recalling every member past and present. The only conclusion Honey came to was that the jogger had to be something to do with the individuals who had been upset by Wright, especially those who had lost their business or partner because of the effect of his scathing reviews.

Doherty nodded thoughtfully as he reached for his teacup.

'He sounds like a fit man,' said Adelaide Cox. 'Do you think he's single?'

'I wish I knew,' said Doherty, setting his teacup down on the table with obvious finality. He got to his feet. 'We were hoping he might be related to somebody. Is there anyone else connected with you or your husband that looks remotely like that?'

'No. And such a shame,' she said, shaking her head and pursing her bright pink lips. 'I would remember somebody who looked like that, but there's nobody, nobody at all that I can recall. I only wish I could help you further.'

'Never mind,' said Doherty. 'Let me know if you do recall anyone who matches that description.'

Adelaide caught his arm as she also rose to her feet. She smiled up at him.

'Do drop in again if you're passing. There's always a cup of tea and a piece of cake waiting for you, and who knows, I may recall something that might help you with your enquiries.'

Saying goodbye and thank you took Doherty a while, so Honey was outside the front gate before he was. Seeing as she was having a fit of the giggles and only just managing to keep it under control, this was just as well.

Doherty opened the driver's side door and saw her expression.

'Wipe that grin off your face.'

Honey spluttered. 'There's more than a slice of Victoria sponge on offer if you ask me.'

Doherty looked at her reprovingly. 'I'm not keen on Victoria sponge. Too light and fluffy. A piece of rich fruit cake turns me on every time.'

'She wanted you to herself and you loved it.'

Doherty started the car and glanced behind him before setting off down the road.

'You could have stepped in and warned her off.'

She smiled. 'And split up a blossoming friendship?'

They took the road back to Bath that wound around the town of Warminster, just a few miles from Longleat where lions and all the creatures of the wild strolled through the magnificent park behind high wire fences.

Beatrice Dixon lived on the outskirts of the town in a modern semi-detached house built when the Bay City Rollers were still topping the charts, just a few years before Margaret Thatcher had become Prime Minister.

The house had big windows designed to let in the light, but for some reason the occupant had blotted it out. Vertical blinds afforded total privacy in the case of 36 Marlborough Row. The garden was simply planted, the borders straight and emblazoned with marigolds of uniform height.

'Doesn't this house strike you as a little . . . regimented?' Honey asked Doherty.

Doherty gave it the once-over. 'You mean straight up and down?'

'Stiff and unbending. Not a curve in sight.'

'Yes, there is.'

Honey looked at him. 'Where? I don't see any.'

He grinned at her. 'I see you.'

'Cheeky!'

Beatrice Dixon was as straight and unbending as her house. She was dressed plainly, without the addition of a brooch or necklace. Her sweater and matching cardigan were grey and her skirt was of grey wool criss-crossed with thin brown checks.

Her face was plain and bare of make-up, though her skin looked peachy soft and she had natural pink spots on her cheekbones. Short hair clipped close to the scalp clung to her head like a tight-fitting swimming cap. Her nose was long, her mouth was wide, and her eyes were too close together.

It was a silly thought and probably an old wives' tale, but Honey recalled that you could never fully trust a person whose eyes were too close together.

Miss Dixon looked straight at them, saying only an abrupt 'Yes?' Then she stood there, waiting for them to speak, to make the first move.

Doherty explained why they were there and asked if they could come in.

'You may recall I came here before,' Doherty reminded her.

Beatrice Dixon took a few seconds to think about it while regarding them with undisguised hostility, her piercing eyes looking them up and down as though searching for hidden weapons.

'I told you all I know,' she snapped, and for a moment it didn't seem as though she was likely to allow them over the threshold.

Doherty did conciliatory rather well.

'There's just something else you may be able to help us with. There's another person we want to ask you about.' Doherty looked over his shoulder as though nervous that other eyes were watching from behind any number of curtains. 'It's a bit public out here. Are there many neighbours home at present?'

A pair of deep-set iron-grey eyes scoured the street at his back, immediately alert to the slightest movement, immediately hostile. Honey construed that neighbourliness did not come high on Mrs Dixon's agenda.

Opening the door a little wider, she stepped back into the dark confines of a narrow hallway.

'You'd better come in.'

The interior was as plain as its owner, the walls of the living room a bland beige, the furniture dated but serviceable. A flower-patterned rug lay before a copper-hooded gas fire. The curtains were only a shade darker than the walls and family photographs lined the mantelpiece. A painting of a young girl hung on the fireplace wall. It looked as though it were a copy of a photograph in a frame just beneath it. The girl was pretty, smiling from both the painting and the photograph.

They were not offered a seat.

Standing in the middle of the room Beatrice Dixon folded her skinny arms across her less-than-expansive chest. When it came to talking about figures, Beatrice Dixon had the unmistakable shape of the number one; straight down. No curves and a fried-egg bosom.

Doherty questioned her about the blond-haired runner.

Her response was terse. 'I don't know him.' She began to make towards the door. Their welcome hadn't been good and their stay was destined to be short.

'You don't recall any hotelier who looked like him? No family member? Your husband's family perhaps . . . ?' Doherty offered.

'I'm not married.' The response was as terse as before.

'My apologies. I didn't know that for sure.'

'Why should you?'

Doherty changed direction. 'You hated C.A. Wright?'

'Yes. Me and a hundred others.'

Doherty played the conciliatory card again. 'His reviews and his manner were pretty nasty, so I hear.'

'Very.'

Honey was hearing all this at the same time as studying the painting. It sometimes helped to bring a personal thread into an investigation. Being a woman, she might get further with this than Doherty. She jerked her chin at the painting. 'She's very pretty. Is she a relative of yours?'

The full force of Ms Dixon's chill grey eyes was brought to bear.

'That's none of your business. It's just someone I know. Now. If there is nothing else?'

They were sitting in the car when Honey stated the obvious. 'You won't be getting any Victoria sponge from her!'

Doherty grinned. 'Win some, lose some.'

Honey sat back, her brows knitted. Something about the painting niggled her. Why have a photograph made into a painting of "just someone you know". Mothers had photos of their babies turned into paintings. She repeated her thoughts to Doherty.

'So what are you saying here?'

Honey chewed it over before spitting it out. 'Their bone structure was the same. I bet you Ms Dixon was a looker when she was younger. I bet she looked a lot like that girl in the painting.'

'You're saying they're related?'

'Maybe they're mother and daughter.' She paused. 'By the way, what was in that jar in your bathroom?'

'Haemorrhoid cream.'

CHAPTER EIGHTEEN

It was bin day. The local council were collecting household waste which the good citizens of Bath had divided into plastics, glass, textiles, and ordinary stuff for the landfill site.

The gulls that usually roosted close to the river or floated on it were sweeping low and screaming for lunch. The air was a mix of the stench of rotten vegetables and pizza toppings.

One or two gulls were too brave for their own good, swooping down on the men collecting the garbage. The men shouted and waved their arms to beat them off.

Honey and Doherty stood watching. Doherty was watching the gulls. Honey was endeavouring to gulp as much fresh air as she could muster.

She took a deep breath. The beat of the tom-toms was gradually fading away.

'So. What next?'

Doherty pursed his lips. His eyes were narrowed and fixed on the screaming gulls — almost as though he had it in mind to shoot them down with a crossbow. Well, they did make a lot of noise. And they were a menace.

But that wasn't why his eyes were narrowed. 'I'm thinking. First, does your jogging friend have anything to do with this murder? It could be that he's nothing to do with it. It could be that we made a wrong assumption. Second, and where is Colin Wright's overnight bag. Third . . .' He paused. His stomach rumbled. 'Where shall we go for lunch?'

'Well . . .'

Before she had time to put forward her suggestion, Doherty's phone sang a snatch of the 'The Dawn Patrol' from *The Jungle Book*. He'd taken to downloading various ring-tones of late.

'Variety is the spice of life,' he'd said to her when she'd questioned his motive. 'It gets me through the day.'

She listened to what he was saying. 'You've found it?' Basing her judgement on the way he was looking at her, she guessed that Wright's overnight bag had been located. He turned to her. 'Follow me.'

'Where are we going?'

'We're retracing old ground. Wright's bag has been found in a slurry pit.'

'Yuk.'

'The farmer was clearing it out. Normally he wouldn't do it for years, but he's sold his cattle and is going in for organic planting. Luckily for us he's already swilled it off. He's also opened and handled it. Normally that would be a big no-no, but any forensic evidence is likely to have been obliterated by the slurry anyway.'

On the way there they chewed over the details. Whoever had killed Colin Wright needed to hide the bag. From what Doherty had been told the slurry pit was a mile or so away from where the body was found. The perpetrator, not privy to the farmer's plans to go organic, wasn't to know that the slurry was about to be sucked out and thrown around the field prior to ploughing and planting. Throwing it in would have worked if the farmer hadn't implemented his plans so soon after the bag was thrown in. It hadn't had time to sink to the bottom but was sucked out and in the process blocked the intake.

'Going through his bag may not tell us much. I think we need to take a close look through Wright's things. I think I would also like to take a look around his pad in London.

His sister Cynthia has the key. I'll contact her and see what I can find. She's also the one who brought my attention to the letters. She only brought in three, but she specifically told me there were more. So why only three? Why didn't she bring in the whole lot?'

'Because she was protecting one of the others?'

Doherty made a humphing sound. It made sense in an odd kind of way. 'If I'm correct I have to ask who was she protecting and why?'

'Perhaps my blond man?'

He shrugged and pulled a so-so face. 'Who knows? Have you remembered anything else about him?'

'The short shorts predominate.'

'OK, I know you're kind of stuck on that, but did he look as though he were hiding something?'

Honey made a guffawing sound. 'Are you kidding? Look, that outfit he was wearing didn't hide anything — and I mean *anything*. It was skimpy and made me blush.'

Doherty raised an eyebrow in surprise. 'Now that must have been skimpy!'

Honey was dismissive. The blond man had been most insistent about a letter, but what letter?

'I could be barking up the wrong tree.'

Doherty shook his head. 'No. Only dogs do that and yours is gone.'

She smiled wryly. 'Precisely. Perhaps he was talking about a different letter? Something to do with dogs perhaps.'

'So you were walking in the park when the pooch got pinched. I take it you were unarmed.'

'Except for my pooper-scooper and doggy doo-doo bag.'

'He obviously thought the dog was yours.'

'I would think so. I keep wondering about that. We certainly could be barking up the wrong tree.'

'Or he could have been barking mad.'

'Was he talking about something else, could be leading us down the wrong path? The tail could be wagging the dog instead of the other way round.'

He looked blank. 'You've lost me.'

'It's easily done as you get older.' She grinned as she said it. Doherty tossed his head.

'Anyway,' she went on, 'as he didn't mention the contents of the letter, we must assume that it had something to do with C.A. Wright. Right?'

'Superfluous thought patterns and dialogue.'

'The thing is, he didn't say it was anything about Wright. Even if it was, perhaps it was one that didn't get delivered. Things get lost in the mail every day.'

'That's true and you're getting me as confused as you sound.'

'And even if it was one sent to your lot, the police, being an earnest bunch, read their mail every day and take notice of everything that comes in.'

Her last remark was greeted with silence.

'I take it that's a no,' she said.

'Not quite. It might be a case of keeping it on file in case something turns up.'

'But there's no guarantee.'

'No comment.'

'I could suggest that it had been delivered only recently.'

Doherty sighed and did a brow-swatting action with one hand whilst the other stayed on the steering wheel. 'You wouldn't believe how many letters we've had from well-meaning members of the public recently.'

She made a hissing sound, as though it hurt. 'You learn something new every day.'

'This jogger has to be well known, especially if he looks as lurid as you describe him.'

'Tight pants. Slim frame. He's noticeable.'

'The uniformed boys must know him. I'll ask about. I'll drop you home.'

* * *

The farm used to raise cattle but, as the farmer Paul Patch explained, his wife had turned vegetarian and was finding the raising of brown-eyed bovines a little distasteful. Bottle-feeding some of the calves hadn't helped. 'She gave them names,' Paul Patch explained. 'That's the worst thing you can do. Even tagging their ears with numbers and referring to number two-four-two as being a pretty little calf is fatal. Giving them names like Poppy, Gavin, and Sookie is even worse,' he explained. 'One step on and you're giving them human characteristics.' He shook his head. 'Not good. So that's it. We're going green, growing things only. I've also gone vegetarian. The wife's idea,' he added with a grimace.

He told them what time he'd found the bag and that he hadn't seen anyone around.

Doherty thanked him for his help. Honey came away with three dozen free-range eggs.

'It won't last,' said Honey once the eggs were stowed away in the small luggage space behind the passenger seats of Doherty's car. 'That man has all the marks of a secret meat-eater. He'll pretend he's off to walk the dog or something and he'll head for McDonald's.'

A call came through telling them that the holdall which had been picked up by the uniformed division didn't contain anything of great interest beyond a leather thong that with adaptation could be used as a slingshot. At present nobody could regard it as anything except what it was: definitely not an offensive weapon.

Doherty's stomach rumbled. 'I didn't have any breakfast.'

'Not a good way to start the day.' Honey had served breakfast as well as eaten some. There was always the odd piece of bacon left over plus a slice or two of toast.

'Fancy a bacon baguette?'

'Hmm. Sounds good to me.'

They stopped at the Poacher for lunch. Honey admitted to liking the place.

Doherty dawdled at the glass-cased noticeboard within which were menu and room details.

'They've got a four-poster room.'

'So does the Green River.'

Doherty's eyes sparkled as he reminded her of the raffle he'd won: a night of luxury at St Margaret's Court Hotel.

'I get it,' she said nodding as she eyed the lunchtime crowd. 'It's better playing away than on home ground.'

They had a simple lunch of thickly sliced ham with salad on a warm baguette. As they ate, Honey's mind went back to their luxury night away. The thought of it was so powerful that she didn't hear everything he was saying, not until he got to his feet and stated that he needed to use the bathroom.

'Yeah. Sure. See you soon.'

He looked amused. 'I should hope so.'

She watched him make his way across the pub, noting that she wasn't the only one. Women were drawn to Doherty. For some reason she didn't mind that and anyway she had a plan to put into action.

The waitress came to collect plates.

'I'd like to book the four-poster room,' said Honey. 'Three days' time. Thursday night. Can you check availability and book it if it's free? Here's my card.'

The waitress said she would do that and came back at exactly the same time as Doherty did.

'Here you are, Mrs Driver. Special occasion, is it?'

Doherty looked at her, smiled, and took a leaflet detailing room rates from his pocket, placing it in front of Honey. It was opened at the page showing the four-poster bed.

'Great minds think alike.'

'Thursday night,' said Honey.

'If I can make it.'

Honey threw him a threatening look. 'You will make it.'

He grinned. 'I will make it.'

He went quiet on the drive back. He'd been doing this a lot of late. He'd also got into the habit of joking around in front of Lindsey, as though nothing in the world was really that serious, including his association with her mother.

His sentences got shorter the closer they got to the Green River Hotel. She was guessing this was a mother and child thing: Doherty was taking Lindsey's mum to bed.

Honey had an urge to remind him that Lindsey was way beyond being a child. She had boyfriends. On reflection she decided it wasn't a bad idea to cut him some slack.

'You don't have to drop me off outside the door,' she said. 'I do have a few errands to run.'

He hunched his shoulders, bracing his arms as he pressed his hands against the steering wheel. 'It's no problem. But I won't come in. I've got a lot to do. Paperwork. You know how it is.'

'Of course I do. I've got plenty enough to do myself. Luckily I've got a daughter who's better at it than I am.'

'So I noticed. Your family has many talents. I even heard that your mother takes part in some of Mary Jane's séances.'

'No jokes about the three witches from *Macbeth*,' Honey said pointedly. 'My mother has a lot of dead friends. I presume the latest one was to do with Dora, the recently deceased?'

'If not her friend and yours, Sean O'Brian,' he said. His amusement at her discomfort was obvious.

'My mother reckons funerals have replaced christenings, weddings, and even divorces in her social life.'

'You can't knock them, funerals, that is; they can be really fun events. I mean, that coffin was something else though, don't you think?'

'My mother and her friends did not approve. What's a few more rainforests between the over-seventies?'

'You would have thought they would have made the boxes — sorry, coffins — stronger.'

Honey burst into laughter. 'Did you see what was printed along the side? "Suitable for recycling".'

Judging by the sudden narrowing of his eyes, Doherty's thoughts had darted off in another direction. Cardboard coffins had led to cardboard boxes and ultimately to the one Cynthia Wright had brought in.

'I sent someone from the local police along to check Wright's pad in London. While he was there Cynthia Wright brought in a whole box of nasty letters threatening all manner of things from hoteliers all over the country.'

'Everything from drowning in a deep fat fryer to death by a thousand cuts?'

He eyed her sidelong. 'I thought I recognised the handwriting.'

She was half-inclined to take his comment seriously until he grinned.

'Very funny.'

'He didn't ring the bell for many people.'

'He preferred them to ring his.'

'Which means . . . ?'

'Quid pro quo — as long as you're female.'

'Ah yes. So you said.'

'His sister insisted that I study every review he's ever done. She's bringing in the disc, though where the hell she thinks I've got the time to go through that lot I don't know.'

An instant thought, so obvious, so enterprising, caused Honey to look directly in his eyes whilst sucking in her bottom lip. Doherty knew the look as thoughtful, inventive, and slick with common sense. Interpreting what she was thinking was no big deal. Reading her mind had become something of a habit and speaking what was in it was very close behind. He looked right back and said it out loud.

'Is Lindsey free?'

Honey too thought it the obvious conclusion. 'I'm sure she'd love the diversion. Can she use your computer? She's in need of a day away from it all.'

He looked puzzled. After all, Manvers Street Police Station was hardly a country retreat far away from the maddening crowd.

There was no need to make a big song and dance about him getting to feel more at ease with her daughter and perhaps make the situation worse.

'She's been a little quiet lately.'

'OK.'

'Before Thursday would be good.'

'Hmm. That suits me fine.'

CHAPTER NINETEEN

It was three o'clock in the afternoon and the Green River Hotel was in that deep trough of slack activity between the cleaning down of the kitchen following the lunchtime trade and the prepping up for the evening.

Today was the day Honey took the takings to the bank — in fact she endeavoured to bank some money every day, a reminder to her bank manager that the Green River was still in existence and that the bank was in with a chance of getting its money back.

She informed Lindsey of her intentions. 'Bank first, sausage shop second. Might even make a coffee with Clare Watkins from the Royal Albert.'

The Royal Albert was an ancient steam locomotive and its two carriages which had long left the rails and now served as a restaurant on a railway siding near Frome.

Lindsey carried on reading last month's copy of *Bath Life*, but said she would hold the fort.

Youthful and attractive, it surprised Honey that her daughter appeared content to look after her mother's business rather than get a job with her own peers. But there it was. Lindsey was the most responsible member of the three generations of females who made up the immediate family.

It was on Honey's tongue to plead gratitude, but today there was something else on her mind.

'Do you fancy some time out?'

Lindsey looked up. Her eyes were velvet brown, deep pools in a creamy-coloured complexion.

'Where are we going?'

'You. Not me. Dawn said she's willing to take over.'

'That's fine,' said Lindsey, setting her magazine to one side. 'She's working out pretty well.'

Dawn had come to them from a holiday complex in Antigua. Lindsey was right about her having worked out well. Dawn bubbled with enthusiasm. Honey was of the opinion it had something to do with being born and raised in a land of endless sunshine. She was like a battery and still running on years of sunshine permeating her skin.

'What it is,' said Honey, feeling oddly nervous under her daughter's searching look, 'is that Doherty is in need of a favour.'

'Whatever. What time does he want me round there?'

This was not a normal Lindsey response. Her daughter was usually a little sassier than that with a longer dialogue.

'Soon as you can?'

'Whatever,' she said again. Having tired of the *Bath Life* magazine, Lindsey reached for a pile of invoices filed in plastic-coated files.

Honey tried again.

'I shouldn't be long. If your grandmother comes in tell her Mary Jane has gone out too. I saw her earlier.'

'Sure,' mumbled Lindsey, slamming one file down on top of another.

'I hear they had a séance.'

'No big surprise,' Lindsey muttered. 'All witches together.'

Well, this was something new; Lindsey was in a mood. Honey frowned. This was decidedly worrying. Lindsey had never been moody. Even as a babe in arms, she'd been a cheery sort who seemed to cope well with the inconsistencies of adult attention. Honey had never considered herself a natural born mother, just a loving one who'd always gone out to earn her own crust of bread under difficult circumstances. She'd been an independent modern woman out of necessity. Carl, Lindsey's father, was absent more than he was present. He had hobbies, he had challenges to face, and he'd had girlfriends. Basically, Carl had never grown up. His intention had been to stay blond and beautiful forever, the Peter Pan of the over-forties. Unfortunately, after he'd drowned, Lindsey had been left with just her doting mother and dotty grandmother.

Seemingly having got bored with the files, Lindsey resettled herself, running her fingers through her hair, thus fiddling it into instant disarray. Usually she was staring at the computer screen. Today she was staring into space, seemingly devoid of concentration. She wasn't usually like that. She was good at concentrating. It was second nature.

Honey knew when something was wrong.

'What gives?' she asked.

'Nothing.'

Honey knew all the signs. The word 'nothing' in teenage speak meant something very irritating indeed. She was right there.

'I don't believe that.'

'I'm under considerable pressure.'

Honey placed the canvas bag containing the takings next to her brown leather shoulder bag on the reception desk. Reaching out she rubbed her daughter's shoulder.

'Boyfriend trouble?'

Lindsey snorted. 'I wish.'

'Things can't be that bad.'

'They are. Think of worst-case scenario.'

Honey shrugged. She'd had too many worst-case scenarios in her life. Lindsey's could be a world away from those and still bad.

Prying her daughter's fingers from mussing up her hair, she took both hands between hers.

'Spill the beans, sweetheart.'

'Gloria's given up on you. She's diverted her attention to me. In short, she's trying to fix me up with a guy who ticks all the right boxes. All *her* right boxes, that is.'

Honey's grip tightened. 'She saw Archie?'

'She *screamed* when she saw Archie.'

Honey sucked in her breath. 'My God. This is serious.'

Darn right it was. Lindsey's terminology was enough to light the touch paper of worrying moments.

Gloria Cross had never really left her thirties behind. At seventy-plus she was still as meticulous with her appearance as when she'd been twenty-five — perhaps more so. The nose piercing she'd recently had done was a case in point. Honey had pretended not to notice but didn't get away with it.

'Do you like it?' her mother had asked.

She'd nodded dumbly, unable to tear her eyes away from the sight of it. Her mother's nostrils were large and brought to mind a goat that an old friend of hers had owned. Her hair was blonde and received the attention of one of Bath's top hairdressers on a weekly basis. The rest of her body received the best of care from her favourite beauty salons and botox treatment centres. Getting old was a challenge to be risen to as far as Gloria Cross was concerned. Everything to do with age was kept at bay and that included being called 'grandmother'.

Gloria Cross kept up a fast-moving social life. She also had a hobby in that she considered she had a penchant for matchmaking. She thought she knew men far better than her daughter — hard to believe she thought that at all seeing as she'd been married four times.

'You need a man,' her mother had proclaimed.

'I've got one,' Honey had retorted.

'He's a mere dalliance. He's not husband material.'

She was, of course, referring to DCI Steve Doherty.

There were times when Honey felt a great need to pinch herself at the same time as ripping up every copy of *Pride and Prejudice* — and everything else in the Jane Austen collection if she had her way — and throwing it all into the river.

Deciding that her daughter wasn't going to give up Doherty, she'd refocused her attention (and presumably skill) on her granddaughter.

Lindsey was far from pleased. '"I've found you a professional man." That's what she said to me.'

'Oh! One of them. Is he that bad?'

Lindsey gave her mother the sort of look old ladies reserve for young men on crowded buses who haven't thought to give up their seat for the elderly.

'He wears glasses and has neat dark hair.'

'Is that so bad? A lot of good-looking men wear glasses and have neat dark hair.'

'He also wears bicycle clips. And flannelette striped pyjamas. I cannot envisage a great love life with a man who wears flannelette striped pyjamas.'

'How do you . . . ?'

Honey's question was cut short.

'Whoa there! Before you ask me how I know, it's not from personal experience. Gran told me his mother buys them for him.'

'Ouch!'

Lindsey sighed. Honey did too until she rediscovered that little chink of light that might raise her daughter's spirits.

'Did I just mention that Doherty had asked a little favour?'

'Uh-huh.' Lindsey nodded.

'He's got access to a load of reviews Wright did on Bath hotels. We're sticking to Bath because it was his favourite hunting ground, if you know what I mean. I think he liked sticking it to the little people.'

'And hotels in Bath are mostly run by little people.'

'Correct. What he wants someone — you — to do, is to go through the reviews and list the bad ones on a separate file. Is that possible?'

The look daughter gave mother could be loosely interpreted as '*Are you kidding? Am I a whizz at this or what?*'

'They're waiting for you and I'm reliably informed that the computer is close to the water fountain. You OK with that?'

'Variety, as they say, is the spice of life.'

Lindsey gathered herself together, smoothing her hair and attacking the computer keyboard with renewed energy in order to finish off what she was doing.

There being nothing else constructive Honey could add to Lindsey's predicament with her mother, and things seemingly improved, Honey made a sharp exit, money in bag and bag over her shoulder.

The city was busy. The weather was fair and it felt good to be out walking the pavements with visitors from all over the world. She felt like smiling at everyone in sight, that was until she spotted a trio of Agatha Christie fans bearing down in her direction.

There was something formidable about a threesome of old ladies, especially these three.

Not wishing to have to field questions on the ongoing enquiries regarding C.A. Wright, she ducked into a shop doorway, opened the door, and went in.

The shop smelled a little musty and there were collecting tins everywhere. Lying next to them were piles of forms and pens. Head bowed she pretended to be filling one in.

'Goat or cow?' somebody asked.

She looked up into a smiling, moon-shaped face.

'Pardon?'

'A goat or a cow? You can sponsor a goat or a cow. Five pounds will secure.'

She was trapped. She chose a goat.

By the time she left the shop the old ladies had gone. Looking back towards Oxfam, the charity shop she'd entered, she saw the assistant who'd taken her money looking out at her. She was smiling, no doubt pleased that she'd sold a goat to someone who had basically been in hiding.

CHAPTER TWENTY

Lindsey's perusal of the CD containing C.A. Wright's reviews drew a big blank.

'I got sick of reading them,' she said. 'The good ones were sickly and the bad ones were vicious.'

'There was no in-between with Colin Wright,' muttered Honey, yet again on her way to the bank though only with half the amount she'd banked yesterday. That was it with the hospitality trade: up one day and down the next.

It was just possible that the blond jogger was another disgruntled member of the catering trade, she thought, though she herself had never seen him before and no one else seemed to remember him. He was, she decided, an enigma.

She was in the process of stepping out of the revolving door, one foot still inside and one out on the pavement — and suddenly there he was! Mr Blond Jogger himself. She couldn't believe it.

'You!'

Mr Blond Jogger looked apologetic.

'I'm sorry,' he said, his right hand gripping the handle of a red tartan leash. 'I brought your dog back. I shouldn't have taken him.' He had a face like a bereaved bloodhound.

'Her,' Honey corrected, feeling smug that Bobo had wreaked revenge on her kidnapper. The feeling didn't last when it hit her that it would be her floor next to receive Bobo's lack of direction — unless Lindsey could find some more nappies.

Although her mother had guardianship of the dog and she herself was basically responsible for it, she couldn't help niggling Mr Blond Jogger by way of revenge.

'And it isn't my dog. I was looking after her for someone. It really doesn't matter who looks after her. You've got her, you keep her. A weekly clean with Domestos should sort you out.'

In a frenzy of denial and seemingly glad to be back, Bobo yapped and jumped up and down, her little paws clawing at Honey's brand-new tights.

Honey growled. The tights would have been good for a few days, if not a few weeks. Now they were only fit for straining sprouts.

The blond jogger was looking nervous. A trio of crescent-shaped lines beneath his eyes jerked nervously.

'Perhaps I could come in and we could discuss the matter further,' the blond jogger said hopefully, his jowls following his eyebrows in a swift upward sweep.

The sight of him in his running gear was enough to make anyone nervous, so Honey held back. What was he capable of? How threatening was today's outfit and was he respectable enough to be seen in her hotel? It seemed that he was. He was not exactly smart but perfectly respectable dressed in faded jeans, a green sweater, and a khaki-coloured waistcoat plus a red bandana worn as a headband with the ends trailing down the back. Overall, he didn't look bad — quite normal in fact if you could accept the straggly hair feathering on to his shoulders.

An old saying came to mind: less is more. In this man's case it was spot on; the less he showed the better he looked.

'I'm sorry about what I did,' he said and sounded apologetic if a little weary. Cleaning up after Bobo had to be the cause of that.

Honey folded her arms, forced her mouth into a straight line, and fixed him with an accusing glare. 'It wasn't very nice.'

Beneath the surface she was bubbling with laughter. She had wanted to say, 'I much appreciated you doing it, better your carpets get ruined than mine'. Besides, her mother hadn't noticed the dog was missing. She wouldn't have been pleased if she had.

'My name's Ken Pollock,' he said and offered his hand.

Honey was careful to note that he wasn't holding the leash in that hand where he could easily slide it across on to her wrist. She reminded herself that it had to happen; the dog was her responsibility.

She was about to take it, then reconsidered.

'Why should I shake your hand? You stole my dog.'

He looked at her askance. 'But you just said she wasn't your dog and you didn't sound as though you cared much.'

His accusation made her a little indignant.

'That's not the point. You kept on about a bloody letter that I knew nothing about. You're at fault. Now you come by here expecting everything to be hunky-dory as though nothing really happened. Have you any idea of the anguish you've caused? This poor little dog was owned by my mother's best friend who died recently. It was a terrible, terrible thing to do and you should feel ashamed of yourself.'

She considered her outburst good enough to win her an Oscar. Acting was an important aspect of running a hotel. Many a guest had received her sugary sweet smile when she'd been steaming inside. It made a big change to do things the other way round, vehement on the outside whilst inside she simmered with amusement. She hadn't felt any great anguish at all. But still, you must play the part, she reminded herself, and you played it bloody well.

The gaping mouth and round-eyed staring shock on his face confirmed she must have hit the right button. Ken Pollock blanched, his pale face turning paler than his hair. The poor man's sharp intake of breath and shocked expression said it all. He looked as though she'd jumped up and down on his body. He was on the ropes, as they said in boxing. If she boxed clever, she might get something out of this: the amateur sleuth's interpretation of a knockout — or at least an admittance of defeat.

Standing with hands on hips, chin held high and punching straight, she gave him it full blast, raising her voice.

'So, Ken Pollock. What the hell was this all about?'

At her shout, passers-by jumped from the pavement, their cameras leaping out of their hands. Tourists in a horse-drawn carriage turned to face her. The horse shied. The driver threw her an angry glare.

Pollock knew exactly what he'd done wrong. All she needed now were his reasons.

All the same she wanted to laugh, ripples of it barely held at the back of her throat.

His gaunt face, pale at the edges and pink in the middle, turned sheepish. He suddenly seemed smaller.

'I knew you had friends in the police force.'

Honey frowned. 'I'm not terribly sure what you're talking about.'

'The con. The money. Everything!'

He hadn't mentioned murder. She decided it must be an oversight.

Slinging her shoulder bag over her shoulder, she took hold of his arm. The bank and her uptight bank manager would have to wait. 'How about we discuss this further over a cup of tea?'

He looked instantly relieved and nodded vigorously. 'I would absolutely love that, if it's not too much trouble.'

She didn't know how he did it, but somehow on their passing through the revolving doors, she found herself in reception with Bobo's tartan leash around her wrist. Bobo was stuck in the revolving door.

She called for Lindsey.

'Bobo's back. But stuck.'

'Leave it with me.'

Smoothly, she took the leash from her mother, let it go, and waited for the door to revolve again.

'The leash is jammed between one section and another. She can't run away.'

'I'm not sure she'll want to. She's wagging from head to toe,' said Honey, feeling a mixture of both relief and annoyance. The dog went straight for Lindsey, adoration shining brightly in its eyes.

Lindsey seemed as glad to see the little dog as Bobo was to see her. 'Great. I'll break out the Huggies.'

'Now,' said Honey, cupping Ken's elbow while guiding him behind the reception desk and into her office. 'Let me and you have a little chat.'

Bobo also attempted to follow. Honey stuck her foot out.

'Not you, doggie. You go with Auntie Lindz while me and this man take a cup of tea.'

Bobo went willingly with Lindsey. Honey knew it was only a temporary solution. Lindsey was on reception duty and a yapping dog with incontinence problems wasn't good for the image.

A few minutes later, barely giving them time to exchange names let alone notes, Lindsey brought Bobo back, a baby's disposable nappy fixed firmly around her nether regions.

'Aha!' said Ken, eyeing the disposable underwear with a look of pure revelation. 'I didn't think of that.'

'Bobo has a problem but at least we know how to deal with it. Now what's yours? I warn you right now that it had better be good. You need to give me a good reason for stealing this dog.'

Ken Pollock made himself comfortable and drank the first cup of tea down in one. 'That's better. Now let me see.'

She was finding it hard not to stare at his chest which was even more concave than she'd first thought. He rasped with each upward heave of his bony ribcage. The dog curled itself over his foot.

'She's very affectionate,' he said and smiled before continuing with his wheezing and the act of collecting his various thoughts.

'I think she likes you. Perhaps you're her ideal owner.'

He winced. 'Oh, I don't think so,' he said, shaking his head.

CHAPTER TWENTY-ONE

Honey was on the phone to Doherty the minute Ken Pollock had left the premises, explaining that Bobo was back and that the blond jogger had nothing to do with sending threatening letters to C.A. Wright.

'He wanted to draw your attention to the Cardboard Coffin Company. He's accusing them of using substandard material that rots away pronto once it comes into contact with water.'

She imagined Doherty's puzzled frown.

'I thought that was the whole point,' he came back with. 'The coffin is supposed to rot and then the body. Isn't that what this natural, eco claptrap is all about?'

'That, and saving the rainforests. Ken says they're overcharging. He also reckons there's some kind of cartel going on. It sounds preposterous I know, but stranger things and all that . . .'

'Have happened at sea — or something.'

'Right.'

'What's he basing this on?'

'Something about the caskets being used twice. He reckons they're reusing the coffins.'

'Aren't they marked recyclable?'

'Well, yes. But I don't think . . .'

'He's a crank. He has to be. Besides, I've got more important things to do than ask questions about cardboard coffins.

'You do sound like you're in something of a hurry.'

'There's been developments. Deke, the guy who went back into the Roman Baths and was found standing over Wright, is related to one of the complainants.'

'Which one?'

'Adelaide Cox. She's his aunt.'

* * *

Thursday night came and the deal was on: they were staying at the Poacher. First they dined on guinea fowl followed by rum truffles with Cornish cream. The food was good. So was the wine.

'An old friend came in today. She's been having family problems. Her daughter's a little wayward.' It wasn't really relevant to the case, but Honey felt a need to lighten up, to be close to normal in fact.

It must have been her tone that made Doherty looked at her expectantly.

'Daughters are problems?'

Honey sighed. 'It seems I've been lucky having Lindsey.'

Doherty said nothing. He was looking down at his unfinished wine with a slight pout on his very appealing lips.

'Is there something you want to say to me?'

He looked up. 'A confession. I have a confession to make.'

She tilted her head to one side and eyed him inquisitively. At the same time she held her breath. Confession was said to be good for the soul, but that depended on the depth of sinning they contained.

'When we were here the other day, I didn't just pick up a brochure — well I did, but only as an afterthought. I was asking the manager whether he knew C.A. Wright. I showed him a photo. I also showed him one of Cathy Morden. He said he was new here but that he'd show them to the rest of the staff. Nobody knew Colin Wright, but they did know Cathy Morden. She used to work here. Lived in.'

Honey was astounded. 'She was working here, just a few miles from her mother, and she never let her know?' She shook her head. Teenagers were not easily understood. Their inexperience of life was no excuse for hurting those that loved them.

Doherty shrugged. 'That's the way it seems.'

Pushing back the dirty plates, he made space for the two photos on the table in front of him. Cathy Morden's looked as though it had been taken on the day she'd left school: fresh-faced and smiling towards the future. C.A. Wright was unsmiling, his chin up and staring directly at the camera; his version of a professional portrait for heading his column or on the dust jacket of a book.

The waitress arrived to take their plates. At first, she did it swiftly. On seeing the two photos she slowed down.

'That's Cathy.'

Doherty looked up. 'You knew her?'

The waitress nodded. She was dark-haired and not much older than Cathy if she was at all.

'She didn't stay long, just long enough to scrape together enough tips to go away and make a life for herself.'

'Do you know where she went?' asked Honey.

Inside she felt total empathy with Agnes Morden. She'd feel just as sad, just as helpless should Lindsey ever go off without a word. Devastated was the only word to describe what her mother must be feeling.

The waitress shook her head. 'No. It was a bit sudden. I think she suddenly came into a bit of money so she left quicker than she thought she would. Gone off with one of her sugar daddies, I expect.'

Mention of sugar daddies sent a chill coursing down Honey's spine. 'You're saying her boyfriends were a lot older than her?'

The girl, kiss curls of black hair sticking like limpets to her cheeks, placed one set of red-varnished nails on her trim hip and nodded. 'I should say so. She was always with an older bloke. Used to meet them in that old tomb in the churchyard. She reckoned it added a bit of "frisson", whatever that is when it's at home.'

'Do you know any of the boyfriends' names?' Honey asked.

The waitress winked. 'One or two. Him for a start.' She nodded down at the photo of C.A. Wright.

'Him?' Honey stabbed her finger at Wright's photo. 'You saw her with him?'

'Yes. Among others. I think he gave her money. Was she underage?'

Honey shook her head. 'No. Do you think you can . . . ?'

'Hold on.'

Doherty's hand landed on hers, cutting her short.

'Can we speak to you in the morning about this?'

The waitress nodded, smiling as she glanced from one to the other. 'Staying the night, are you?'

'Yes.'

Her eyes twinkled. 'See you in the morning.'

'Steve! How could you?'

Doherty hunched his shoulders. 'What?'

'You heard what she said. Wright was having some kind of ongoing liaison with Cathy Morden, exactly as her mother feared.'

'For Chrissakes, Honey, this is not a missing person's case, and even if it was, it's not my department. We're looking for the murderer of C.A. Wright.'

'I feel sorry for her mother.'

'But we're not here to . . .'

'There's no need to remind me. I know what we're here for,' she snapped.

It came out sounding worse than she intended. Normally she might have apologised, but under the circumstances she did not. A missing daughter touched a raw nerve. She'd sympathised with Agnes Morden.

'You don't understand. You've never been a . . .'

'Parent?'

She had been going to say that he had never been a mother — which was true. But he was a father.

His face softened. 'I'm sorry. It's my fault for leaving the photos here the other day.'

She forgave him easily. He was giving off vibes — very warm vibes, although all they were doing was having a night away in a country pub. A very nice country pub, but a pub all the same. And yet he seemed to be setting great store by it. OK, he did have a thing about four-poster beds, but even so . . .

'The girl will turn up,' he said with some finality. 'Teenage girls like to worry their parents. It's par for the course.'

In a bid to ease the sudden tension between them, Honey cast her eyes around the restaurant. There were oak beams in abundance and antiques/junk shop finds dotted around as decoration. The tablecloths were white, the lighting low, and the ambience was first class. For a pub restaurant it seemed to have everything going for it, and yet there was something about the atmosphere . . .

'A penny for them?'

'Sorry. Did I drift that far away?'

'You did. What were you thinking?'

'I was thinking about C.A. Wright, that master of the poison pen. He was into everything: blackmail, seduction . . . how about murder? I wonder if he was into that too.'

* * *

'I can barely get up these stairs,' Honey stated as they made their way to their room.

'Lie down on the bed a while. Take deep breaths. You'll be OK. It's a four-poster.'

'I know. It was me told you that.'

The room was pretty much as depicted on the brochure. The bed was of dark mahogany, the coverlet burgundy and gold, and the open window looked out on to the field that had become Memory Meadow.

Replete with food, there was nothing left to do for a while but talk. The conversation centred around the case, batting the particulars backwards and forwards until a detail that had appeared as a tennis ball was transformed into a shuttlecock. That was the way it was.

Honey had bagged the bed. She lay down full stretch, arms folded behind her head. 'Perplexing,' she said, puffing out her cheeks then exhaling on a long zephyr-like breath.

Doherty sat on the bedroom chair in front of the window, his eyes boring into the night beyond the window. He sat there as though as wooden as the chair itself, just staring thoughtfully.

She guessed he was thinking about what she'd said, mulling it over, that and the fact that the waitress had recognised the photo of C.A. Wright. What deduction could be drawn from that?

Honey waved her fingers at him in a bid to break his concentration. 'So. Cathy was here and Wright was here. Where does that leave us?'

'Nowhere really.'

She rolled on to her side and looked at him.

Doherty stretched his arms above his head and yawned. His body went limp as he slid down into the bedroom chair, putting him in danger of sliding off completely.

'Hey,' she said, watching him. 'Do you have something to say?'

He took in a deep breath before he responded. 'OK. Yes. I know you want to hear it so here it is. I felt sorry for Agnes Morden. I didn't doubt she was right about Wright making a pass at her daughter, but there was no evidence to suggest she went off with him, with anyone in fact. Now it seems that it was kind of half-true. They weren't living together. By the sound of what the waitress said, he called by, spoke to Cathy, and they met up. Still, what was her reason for not returning home?'

'Mother and daughter had an argument?'

Doherty pulled a disapproving face. 'Is that any reason for her to shove off and not get in contact?'

Fingers linked on top of her head, Honey shrugged nonchalantly. 'Happens all the time. It's a mother-daughter phenomenon. Daughter wants to do something, mother objects, daughter wants to do it all the more. They argue, mother puts her foot down, daughter goes off in a huff.'

Doherty jerked his chin in understanding. 'I bow to your superior knowledge. But did Lindsey ever go off in a huff and not come back? Even for a short while?'

'No.' She paused as an old memory came bounding back. 'That's a lie. She did leave home for a whole day and vowed never to come back.'

'So how long was she away?'

'Less than a day. She came back PDQ because she was hungry and her grandmother was threatening to take her to a shop selling tartan kilts. My mother thought they looked fetching. My seven-year-old daughter had set fashion views, even back then.'

'She wasn't a teenager.'

'No. But I was.'

She caught Doherty's questioning look and felt obliged to enlighten him.

'I left home once or twice myself when I was a teenager. My mother was getting on my nerves, interfering in my life, wanting to choose my clothes for me. Can you blame me for taking off?'

He shook his head. 'No.'

Honey smiled. Doherty knew her mother almost as well as she did. Gloria Cross was not the easiest person in the world to live with; her four husbands had found that out and moved on — or died.

Honey frowned. 'I would hate it if Agnes never got to see her daughter again.'

'I can understand that.'

'C.A. Wright has a lot to answer for.'

'If I'd met him, I would probably have killed him myself.'

'You would have done. Still, he has been murdered. I can't help being reluctant to find his killer. Mr Wright was not a likeable man.'

'I'm hearing you.'

She could count on Doherty to understand where she was coming from, and she certainly didn't wish to appear unconcerned about C.A. Wright's death. The case had to be solved even though she hadn't liked the man, but the fact was they'd come so far and no further in this case. Fingers clenched above her head, she eyed a spider weaving a web in the corner of the room. On closer inspection she could see he wasn't weaving at all but interring a fat fly in a mesh of silk. The fly was embalmed and totally immobile — fresh meat in the larder for a future feast. A bit like the bodies buried in Memory Meadow, except that in their case they would be devoured from within as well as without.

Honey shuddered at the thought of it.

Doherty noticed. 'What's up?'

'I was thinking about the cardboard coffins and Ken Pollock saying that they were substandard.'

'I can't think that it matters seeing as it all ends up as mush.'

'Yuck!' Honey shuddered again. 'I don't mind worms. It's maggots I can't stand.'

Doherty sat bolt upright, hands resting on his thighs and looking at nothing in particular. Or at least, that was the way it seemed. Like a cat spotting a bird, he was very still and very alert, leaning forward at a forty-degree angle with the chair back. His hands were clasped together in front of him. His jaw was rigid.

'Turn off the light,' he ordered.

'Wow,' she said. 'I'm your girl.'

The room was plunged into almost total darkness. There were few lights at this end of the village. Squares of light fell from the bedroom windows at the Poacher and on to the road. Beyond that was the churchyard and the new kid on the block next door to it, Memory Meadow.

Raising her hands, ready for action, she approached him on bare feet, aiming for his back, that broad muscular back that felt hard beneath her fingers.

Sighing she laid her hands on him. 'Your shoulders feel as hard as iron. How would you like me to . . . ?'

'Shhh,' he whispered. 'Take a look over the road there. Can you see a light?'

His muscles tensed beneath her fingers.

Cursing whatever was happening over the road, she looked anyway, her fingers inching stealthily from neck to collarbone. Normally there would be nothing but darkness beyond the lights of the hotel falling on the road. Black outlines of trees blended like spilt ink into the sky.

She was ready to go to bed and do more interesting things but Doherty's tension could not be ignored.

Her fingers faltered just at the exact moment when her eyes narrowed. Something was flickering at the far end of Memory Meadow, at what seemed to be the opposite end of the field to that part where Sean O'Brian had been buried.

'Now who might you be?' murmured Doherty, not to her but to himself.

Honey was good at reading minds. Doherty's was sometimes an open book, like now. His curiosity was aroused. All other kinds of arousal were put on the back burner until later.

She got up from the bed. 'I'll get our coats.'

'They should have a torch in Reception,' said Doherty as she handed him his coat. He pushed his arms into his sleeves as she held his coat for him. His eyes were still fixed on the flickering light in Memory Meadow.

'No need. I've got one.' A quick search in her coat pocket and her fingers touched what she was looking for. The bright blue of a clutch of LED bulbs burst into life. 'Lindsey thought it might be useful for when I can't find my car keys in the dark.'

'Neat. Come on.'

'Hey,' she said, suddenly grabbing his arm. 'You don't think they're grave robbers, do you?'

'Like Burke and Hare?'

The Edinburgh grave robbers were the last thing on her mind. 'Don't be stupid. I was thinking of what Ken Pollock said about bodies being dug up and the coffins being recycled.'

Doherty rolled his eyes. 'Give me strength.'

'You don't think so.'

'He may have thought he saw bodies being dug up, but he was referring to the time before the field was turned into a cemetery. There were no bodies here then. He's confused.'

Honey decided he was probably right. Ken Pollock was a bit of a nut. He'd rambled on about people digging the place up, but his recollections had been confused and in no chronological order, or at least, none that were instantly recognisable.

He'd espoused the fact that people were wandering around the field and digging things up in the middle of the night.

'They had lamps,' he'd said. 'And electrical things to lift bodies from the ground. They'd hummed and sometimes made bleeping noises.'

They hadn't had a clue what he was talking about, and an in-depth discussion hadn't taken them anywhere except Memory Meadow, where cardboard coffins were being reused. It hadn't occurred to him that people keen on recycling wouldn't worry too much about that. The coffins were supplied as a matter of form. People were used to bodies being boxed up, not just wrapped in a shroud or bundled off in their best suit on the pallbearers' shoulders.

Suitably attired and armed with nothing more offensive than a torch, they left their room and bolted down the stairs.

It was late and the tables in the restaurant had been set for breakfast. The night porter nodded at them as they headed for the door. 'Midnight walk?'

Honey threw him a winning smile. 'We've got our key. OK?'

He nodded, smiled and threw her a wicked wink. Only two types of people went walking in the dark together. Passionate couples and murderous ones. He obviously thinks we're the former, thought Honey. And he could just be right!

No main road ran through the centre of Much Maryleigh. There was no village green where winsome lassies and ladies lingered. The road was a loop that started at the main A46 two miles away, passing through the village and looping back out again on the other side.

The night was just cold enough to turn their breath to steam. The lights of the Poacher had been turned off, leaving just a glow from the reception area falling out on to the road. Once they were on the other side by the grassy verge, their footsteps fell into darkness; not a shred of moonlight to see by.

'Keep to the wall and keep down,' whispered Doherty.

Honey did as he said. Feeling the rough edge of the wall she followed him, stopping where he did without them colliding.

Except for what must have been the light they had seen, currently at ground level, the darkness was unremitting. The only time they could see clearly was when a pair of headlights from the far-off road pierced between the towering leylandii that someone had planted when they were only eighteen inches high. They were now around eighteen feet and threw dark, dense shadows.

The sound of digging and falling earth came from the direction of the light and whoever was digging there.

Another flash of far-off headlights picked up the outline of the disused mausoleum on the churchyard side of the wall, the old tomb, as the waitress had told them. Honey had wandered into the churchyard on their last visit whilst Doherty had visited the pub's washroom. She recalled a busted padlock, the heavy oak door, and the strange calmness inside. That was all there was inside, just calmness, no body or foul deed, though the place cried out for a dark and dirty deed to be done there.

She was about to poke Doherty in the back and mutter, 'Hey. There's that pretty tomb, the one Cathy used to meet her boyfriends in,' but she didn't get the chance. The sound of shovel digging into soil stopped abruptly. The night air was heavy with silence. She sensed someone was holding their breath; she certainly was.

'Hey. Is somebody there?'

Whoever was there had sensed their presence. She didn't recognise the voice. Unknown male, breathing heavily whilst involved in physical exertion; it could apply to anybody.

Doherty was part of the darkness and yet she knew he had tensed. Like her he was holding his breath.

She remained still, taking comfort that she was behind him — the very best place to be in case the somebody who spoke had a gun or leapt forward with fists flying. Just because they couldn't see him didn't mean he couldn't see them. It depended on the light.

She made herself small, curling into not much more than a foetal ball. She reckoned Doherty was doing the selfsame thing. It was like having a solid wall in front of her and deeply comforting. Cowering down behind him she pressed snugly against his bum.

Whoever it was must have satisfied themselves that they were all alone. The sound of digging and falling earth recommenced.

She lifted her head and tried to peer through the darkness over Doherty's shoulder. She had the sense that there were different shades of darkness as in one shade of darkness for solid, immovable things, and another kind of darkness for things that moved.

Curiosity made her less cautious. Balancing on bent knees, she eased forward, eyes narrowed, trying to see the impossible. In doing so she overbalanced. Her right hand landed in the dirt that was piled up against the wall. One hand wasn't enough to support her. She landed on Doherty's back, pressing down, knocking the breath out of him.

The digging stopped abruptly this time. There was the sound of something landing in the earth followed by the rustling of bushes. Then there was stillness.

Doherty got to his feet and moved forward. Honey followed.

'Turn on your torch,' he barked.

Honey obeyed. The stark light from the LED bulbs picked out a pile of earth and broken concrete. She flashed the light over the bushes. Beyond the bushes in the distance, she could see lit windows of the luxury houses on the new estate. There was no moon but for one instant she thought she saw movement against the backdrop of lit-up new homes.

'Can you see anyone?' asked Doherty.

'I'm not sure. It could have been just a shadow.'

'Give me that.'

He took the torch from her, shining it down into the hole, picking out the dried-out brickwork of what had once been a cesspit.

Honey pointed out that there'd been a digger working here when they'd last visited.

'Huh.'

The word were meaningless, but the way Doherty said them she knew he was thinking on his feet. Something had struck him.

A chill wind was blowing through the laurel hedge. A warm bed and a hot man beckoned, though from the looks of it Doherty had forgotten about the four-poster bed.

It seemed appropriate for her to do some thinking too. Wrapping her coat more closely around herself, she thought things through. Nothing momentous seemed to come into sight so she voiced the only thing she could think of.

'So why use a shovel now after using a digger?'

'This looks like a disused cesspit. Bypassed once everything round here got connected to the main drains. It's a dead cert that happened when the houses were built. We had reports of the digger being vandalised. You may also recall that it was fitted with a bucket with teeth on and for a very good reason. They were demolishing this. It probably fills up with water during rain. Somebody, possibly a child, could fall in and drown.'

Honey peered over Doherty's shoulder. LED lights were bright but the torch only had a narrow beam. The beam skittered over dark mounds of earth, broken concrete, and debris like some digitalised Tinkerbell.

'There's still a lot of stuff down there,' Honey remarked, her eyes following the dancing beam to wherever Doherty directed it.

'That's because somebody has been filling it in.' His tone of voice echoed around the cesspit walls.

She reminded herself that this wasn't a grave. There could have been any number of reasons why someone wanted to scupper the efforts of the men ripping the pit apart.

'Perhaps somebody thinks they're not shifting themselves fast enough. Perhaps somebody has an almighty health and safety issue here.'

Or burying something. Burying a body. Burying loot. Burying . . .

No matter which way she looked at it the word burying was involved.

Doherty suddenly thrust the torch at her. 'Hold this. I'm going in.'

Loose earth and more rubble tumbled into the square of blackness with Doherty's legs and then his whole body.

She attempted to pass him the torch.

'No. You hold that. Pass me the shovel then hold the torch steady on where I start digging.'

He focused on the narrow beam of blue light. Muck and rubble sucked at his ankles.

She sensed his excitement. His need to know was infectious. Eyes wide and unblinking, she got on to her knees, rested one hand on the edge of the pit, the other holding the torch.

The shovel made a tearing sound as he dug into the mix of rubble, muck, and effluent.

Honey wrinkled her nose. 'It doesn't smell too sweet.'

Totally absorbed in what he was doing, he didn't answer, which wasn't entirely unexpected. That was how he was once he was on the scent of something interesting, even when it didn't smell good.

A few shovelfuls of earth were thrown on to the opposite side to where Honey was kneeling. A few shovelfuls more . . .

Suddenly he stopped and reached for the torch, bending over with his back towards her, the light between his body and the ground.

Honey was immediately plunged into darkness.

The wind was turning colder and it was beginning to rain.

'What is it? What have you found?'

Doherty turned round, flung the shovel out of the pit, and reached for her hand.

'Give me a tug.'

With a bit of effort from him bracing one leg against the wall, she did manage to pull him out.

He was brushing something off in his hand and had given her the torch. Even before she saw it clearly, she knew what he was holding was his phone; knew he was reporting a serious incident.

'Is there someone down there?'

His face was in semi-darkness, his features bluish and demonic by the stark light of the torch and the phone.

'Wait and see.'

CHAPTER TWENTY-TWO

Ned Shaw was sitting with his shoulders hunched and his hands clenched. His head was bowed and he wasn't saying anything except that he wanted his lawyer.

Resting his clasped hands on the desktop in front of him, Doherty leaned forward. The preliminaries had already been gone through. Now they were down to the nitty-gritty.

'Cathy Morden was employed as a waitress at the Poacher. You must have seen her there.'

Ned stayed stock-still and said nothing.

Doherty focused on the thinning sandy coloured hair of Ned's bowed head. Ned was wearing a dark green T-shirt. His arms were brown from working outdoors and covered with a fine layer of corn-coloured hair.

'How often did you drink at the Poacher?'

Again, no response.

'Twice a week? Three times?'

A nerve flickered close to Ned Shaw's hairline. His whole body tensed. Doherty interpreted the warning signs, the muscles hardening like springs, the fists clenching more forcibly.

Doherty prepared himself in much the same manner, half expecting Shaw to throw a punch or even pick up the chair he was sitting on and throw that. He knew the man had a violent history. He'd lash out at anyone and with anything.

Doherty could almost taste the atmosphere in the interview room. It was like cordite or gunpowder: one spark and everything would explode. He didn't want things to go there. He wanted co-operation. He wanted closure on this and he wanted a calm road to the ultimate goal.

There were two things he could do: keep Shaw in a cell overnight and try again tomorrow — in effect try to wear him down until he said something, preferably confess to the murder. Or he could go with the softly-softly approach, man-to-man and gently does it.

Deciding he didn't have the time to pussyfoot about, he decided to plump for the second option. There was a chance he could get duffed up in the process, but he had a panic button. He decided to go with it.

He nodded at the uniformed constable. 'Get us two cups of coffee, will you? No sugar for me. Sugar for you, Ned?'

Ned raised his eyes but didn't say anything.

Doherty leaned back in his chair. 'I think Mr Shaw would like sugar.'

Realising what Doherty was asking him to do, the constable stalled, the young face a little stiff. Doherty was doing the unconventional.

'Well, go on.' Doherty nodded. 'Don't keep us waiting.'

A frown appeared on the fresh and slightly pink young face, but he didn't linger. He'd received an order from a superior officer; he had to obey.

Doherty flicked the switch on the recorder. It was an old model in that it still used tapes. An order had been put in for a new one but due to an overstretched budget, the purchase had been put on hold.

'Damned thing,' Doherty muttered, all the while aware that Ned was watching him do it through slitted eyes. Ned was trying to get the measure of him, wondering what he was going to ask now they were off the record.

'Tell me the truth, Ned,' he said. 'Off the record.'

Ned grinned knowingly. He'd had a few brushes with the law before the rape charge: petty crimes mostly, enough to make him familiar with the process of police interrogation.

'I s'pose you're gonna offer me a ciggie next,' he said.

'The rules on no smoking are strict. Sorry I can't offer you one.'

Inside Doherty was almost whooping with joy. The man was speaking. Nothing serious, but it was a step in the right direction.

Body language was everything. He kept his cool, hands no longer clasped tightly together but resting palms down on the desk. His expression was neutral.

'Look, Ned. I'm asking you whether you'd seen the girl, who she might have been friendly with, who she argued with. All that kind of stuff.'

What Doherty had interpreted as a nervous tic stiffened into a sneer.

'She was a cock teaser!'

The terminology wasn't exactly unexpected. Ned Shaw had maintained that his rape victim was just that. The jury had found him guilty, and Ned had done five years with good behaviour.

Doherty polished the edge of the desk with his finger, watching it leave smudges along an area of about twelve inches. A little movement helped ease the atmosphere before he made the number one statement.

'So she led you on, things got out of hand, and you killed her. Dropped her into that cesspit and attempted to fill it in to hide her body.'

'Like hell I did!'

'You were there the other night. I saw you running away.'

'Not me, you didn't.'

Ned's face was turning redder and his eyes, which had been slits, were bulging.

'She led you on. You just said so. Things went wrong . . .' Doherty continued.

'Not me. It wasn't me she was leading on. It was him, that bastard Pierce,' Ned shouted suddenly.

Doherty could smell the other man's sweat. Ned wasn't just angry, he was scared.

'I did my time, Mr Doherty. My family went through enough. I wouldn't go there again. I didn't touch Cathy Morden. I swear it.'

There were times when just the tone of a man's voice was enough to make Doherty assume innocence rather than guilt. Vice versa too.

'OK. OK,' he said slowly. 'So you reckon it was Pierce.'

Ned nodded. 'He boasted about how young girls fancied him. Silly sod. She was just a kid away from home for the first time and out to enjoy herself. Feeling the power of freedom. That's all. I reckon she laughed at him behind his back . . .'

'But you're the one with the track record, Ned,' Doherty pointed out.

Ned stared at him like he had before, everything about him tensing.

The constable edged his way back in with the coffee.

'Sorry, guv, I think I put sugar in both,' he said as he put the coffee down on the table.

Ned didn't seem to notice that anyone had entered. He was frowning and shaking his head, leaning forward suddenly as though he couldn't quite believe what he was thinking. 'Christ. That was why he didn't want us to rip it out.'

Without Ned noticing, Doherty switched the recording machine back on and nodded to the constable to stand by the door. Ned Shaw wasn't out of the woods yet and anything could happen if the decision was made to keep him in all night.

'You knew Cathy Morden. Do you know where she is?'

Ned blinked. Doherty had surprised him.

'I thought she was in . . .'

'No,' Doherty snapped as he shook his head. 'She is not.'

Ned Shaw stared at him. He was sweating, his tongue flicking over the moisture hanging on his top lip.

'So who was it?'

CHAPTER TWENTY-THREE

The Poacher was busy during a lunchtime, filled mostly with locals, mainly the retired plus a few that were merely passing through.

Honey made herself comfortable in the window seat, a good spot from where she could watch happenings within the bar plus the comings and goings outside.

There was only space for two people or one person and a very large handbag, and seeing as she didn't want anyone joining her, she spread herself out a bit.

'All right there, me dear. Ain't I seen you 'ere before?' The speaker was tall with rounded shoulders. He was wearing a green padded waistcoat and matching wellies. He swept a corded green cap off his head in gentlemanly fashion.

She hadn't wanted to be recognised as having visited before, but he was old and probably only vaguely recalled seeing her before. Anyway, she looked up and smiled. 'You could have done.'

'Can I buy you a drink?'

She didn't usually accept drinks from strangers, but in his case she did. Besides, he was white-haired and around her mother's age, so no threat whatsoever.

'So,' she said after sipping her orange juice. 'I take it you've lived here a long time.'

He chugged back a mouthful of strong cider, his flaccid lips almost covering one side of the glass.

'Seventy-five years man and boy. I was born 'ere.'

'I suppose you've seen a lot of changes over that time.'

He grimaced his disapproval. 'You bet I have. Suburbans. That's what we've got 'ere now.'

His tone was enough to tell her that he didn't approve of smart new houses and smart Alec people from the towns.

After some rummaging in his inside coat pocket, he brought out a pipe — one of the old briar types that used to make men look brainy but now made them look like dinosaurs.

'I don't think you should be . . .'

Honey was just about to point out that smoking was no longer allowed in bars when he tipped the pipe so she could see inside the bowl. There was nothing in there.

'I just like to feel the stem between me teeth,' he explained.

Village pubs were hotbeds of village gossip, which was why Honey had come here today all by herself. She figured Doherty had already got himself known with the locals and although she'd stayed here overnight with Doherty, she hoped she wasn't so clearly remembered.

Sam Trout, as the old gentleman was called, went on to tell her about how he'd protested when the posh houses for 'pen-pushing toffs', as he'd put it, were built.

'Used to be the village green. Kicked footballs about on it when we were boys. Went courting there too,' he added with a twinkle in his eyes. 'Got my first kiss there. Much more besides.'

The twinkle was building to starbursts of fondly remembered lusts. Honey cleared her throat and prepared to get him back on the right track.

'What about the people who live in the new houses; do you know any of them very well?'

'Of course I do.' His expression changed, his bushy grey eyebrows lowering over bloodshot eyes. 'I lives in one of them with me daughter and her husband. That's what you have to do when you're older — live with yer family; once the wife was gone it was all I bloody well could do. Had to live somewhere. Couldn't do all that housework by meself. I'm not that sort of bloke.'

Honey nodded in understanding. Not only did blokes of Sam's generation consider themselves above doing domestic work, but they also lacked the skills. Brought up to be head of the household and to go out and earn the daily bread while the wife stayed at home. Spoilt by doting mothers, they'd expected their wives to do the same. Tradition. That's what it was.

Listening to old Sam brought a terrifying thought to mind: how long until her mother got to the stage when she could no longer live alone, in other words, how long before she moved in with her? She shuddered at the thought of it. Hopefully the dreaded day would never come. Who knows, Gloria Cross, the glamour puss of the Darby and Joan Club, might be swept off her feet by some millionaire octogenarian and flown off to somewhere like Tampa or Orlando — a place of sunshine where all the snowbirds go for the winter.

Sam got another round of drinks. She thanked him before taking a sip of orange juice.

'Well not all your neighbours can be that bad,' she remarked.

He shrugged. 'Just some.'

Sam Trout's red-rimmed eyes homed in on a guy at the bar who had knocked back one pint after another. Such heavy drinking seemed inappropriate seeing as it was only lunchtime. The man was middle-aged and dressed in a pale green polo shirt with almost-matching trousers and two-tone loafers. His shoulders were hunched and his folded fore-arms were resting on the bar. He was staring into his drink desperately, as though hoping it would give him answers for questions only he knew.

'He's certainly knocking them back,' Honey remarked.

'Stupid sod,' Sam spat. 'He thinks he's a bit of a Jack the Lad, a dead cert with the women. He wants to take a look at 'imself in the mirror. Look at that gut he's got already — and it'll be getting bigger the way he's knocking back the booze. Don't know where he gets all his money from. Not legally, I should think. He's got the look of a villain, that one.'

Sam wasn't that quiet a talker. The bloke at the bar heard some if not all of his comment and turned his head. Strands of dark blond hair straggled over a pinkish forehead. Bright dots of colour sprouted on each cheek and seemed to be spreading.

His bleary eyes fixed on Sam.

'There's an old saying about not bringing your own idiots to a country village. The village have got plenty of their own. Isn't that right, Sam?'

Eyes blazing with indignation, Sam Trout half rose to his feet and pointed a bony finger.

'Well, you're something worse than a village idiot, Peter Pierce,' he shouted. 'Peter the Pervert. That's what they call you.'

The knives and forks of lunchtime diners paused midway to open mouths. All eyes turned in the direction of Sam Trout and the man at the bar.

Honey was fascinated. Amazing what lurked between the quiet façade of a country village, she thought.

The man at the bar turned red with rage, specks of saliva foaming at the corners of his mouth.

'If you were a few years younger, Sam, I'd take you outside and punch your bloody lights out!' he shouted.

'Well come on then. You wouldn't hold back from beating an old bloke anyway — not from what I 'eard,' Sam bellowed.

The man at the bar began to lumber forward, his face red and his fists clenched and tight to his chest — like a boxer about to land a killer blow.

The barman, who had seen and heard everything, moved with purposeful intent. Raising the flap at the end of the bar, he rushed through, his strong hand outstretched to cup the elbow of the man at the bar. 'No more drinks for you, Peter. Time you were going home. Go quietly or you'll not find a welcome in here again.'

'I can find my own way,' snapped the man addressed as Peter, shaking the barman's hand from his elbow. He made as though for the door, but did a sudden sidestep, lashed out and crashed against the table Honey and Sam were sitting at, sending their drinks tumbling to the floor.

'I'll have you, Sam Trout,' he said, thrusting a finger just an inch or so away from a spot between the old man's eyes.

Sam's old face set into a fierce glower. 'You better be careful what you're saying, Peter Pierce. This here's the girlfriend of that copper that was here before. I've told her about you. Told her about the way you chase young women half yer age. Disgusting it is. Plain disgusting. And I told her about you protesting about that cesspit. There was no need of it. Church funds would have benefited from the sale of that, but you weren't having it, were you? That's the bloody trouble. You newcomers thinks you rule the bloody place. Well piss off, Peter. Piss bloody off!'

Honey made the brave move of standing between the two warring men. 'Sam. Calm down. There's no point in getting flustered about this.'

Absorbed in calming the old chap down in case he gave himself a heart attack, she didn't at first notice the look of alarm on Peter Pierce's face. If she had she would have realised that referring to her policeman boyfriend hadn't gone down too well.

'You'd better go,' she said turning to Pierce.

The look he gave her was unexpected. He looked terrified, his eyes glassy and his pink cheeks steadily paling.

Without another word he slunk swiftly away, the door hushing closed behind him.

Eating, drinking, and talking steadily resumed while Honey sat collecting her thoughts, one finger tapping thoughtfully on her knee. Why the worried look? It had to be

Sam mentioning that the last time she'd been here Doherty had been with her.

'Fancy a chew?' It was Sam.

'What?'

'Of my pipe. A pipe does wonders for the mind. Helps sort yer thoughts, it does.'

Honey barely glanced at the chewed end of the pipe as she shook her head. 'I don't think so. Thanks all the same.'

'Suit yerself.'

'I was wondering. You said something about that man protesting about the cesspit being filled in.'

'That's right. Said it was his. Said something about it being on his deeds, though that's a load of old cobblers.'

'Why do you say that?'

'When they were first going to build the houses, they would have started them next to the church right where that cesspit is. His house — the one he was going to buy — would have had that in his back garden. But the protests kept going and we got the builders to build the houses where they are now. He didn't argue about it then so why the bloody hell — begging yer pardon — he started moaning about it now, I don't know. But he's got a thing about that cesspit. Got a thing about that field if you ask me. He were always in it, wandering around with that damned metal contraption of his.'

'Contraption? What metal contraption was that, Sam?' she asked.

'One of them things for finding old coins with.'

'A metal detector. Is that what you mean?'

'Aye,' he said, with a jiggle of his pipe. 'That would be what it were called.'

'You do know that the police have found a body in the cesspit?'

The pipe jiggled in Sam's mouth before he replied. 'No wonder he didn't want them to demolish that pit. That's where he must have put her, young Cathy. Killed her and buried her there after she'd resisted his advances.'

It wasn't beyond belief that what he said could be right, on the other hand rumours fly like sparrows around a village. If the man Doherty was interviewing, Ned Shaw, hadn't done the job, then Peter Pierce might well be a possible contender for prime suspect.

'Does Mr Pierce have any family?'

Sam took the stem of the pipe from between his teeth. 'His wife Carol, though of course she ain't his first wife. And two boys. Just like 'im they are. Big 'eaded. Not like village lads at all. Think they never got over their mother leaving 'ome, though you couldn't blame 'er you know, being married to 'im. Peter Pierce. Peter the Pervert.'

Honey cleared her throat and reminded herself that there wasn't always truth in village gossip. However, giving someone a nickname like that you had to wonder, didn't you?

'Liked the young girls,' Sam repeated, clamping his teeth down tightly on his pipe.

'Did he like Cathy Morden?'

Sam eyed her wickedly and chuckled. 'She was a right little charmer. Could wind him round her little finger, she could. And he fell for it. Silly bugger. As if she'd be interested in the likes of him.'

Honey thought of Cathy's mother. Agnes was beside herself, waiting for confirmation that the body in the cesspit was her daughter, praying it wasn't but doing what she could to prepare herself for the worst.

'Was she seeing any of the village boys?'

He looked at her with a lopsided smile, the pipe fixed at a jaunty angle; a bit like Popeye the Sailor.

He shook his head. 'Not that one. I used to meet them in that old tomb . . .'

'The mausoleum?'

'That's the one. It's a grand place for meeting a lass; used to do the same meself in days gone by. That old door never did shut right, but it was warm if you jammed it in the 'ole.'

He tipped her the wink. What he said contradicted what the waitress had told her, but villages are ripe with gossip. Cathy Morden could have been nobody, anybody, or everybody.

She looked at her watch. Old Sam would tell her some juicy tales of his youth. It might be fun to hear them, but not now. Not when she was getting some insight into village life.

She checked her phone, half expecting to see a message from Doherty, but there was none. She took another sip of her drink.

'Was the present Mrs Pierce a village girl?'

'Not bloody likely.' Old Sam looked repugnant at the very thought of a village girl marrying the likes of Peter Pierce. 'He got her the same way he got his first wife: went to one of them dating agencies. Not natural as far as I'm concerned. I mean, you might look at a catalogue to choose a new washing machine, but not a woman. That ain't right.'

Honey understood where he was coming from. She'd tried that approach to meeting a man herself once. Three men had been referred to her. One had described himself as a 'dapper businessman'. Turned out he was five-foot-two and sold brushes from door to door. The second had described himself as an adventurous and fun-loving outdoor type. The caravan he was living in occupied the corner of a field halfway up a mountain in Wales where the nearest neighbour was a farmhouse two miles away. Candidate number three had seemed OK at first until one of his kids had phoned him saying that their mum wanted to know when he was coming home.

Setting her own experiences to one side, she focused on the job in hand.

'So he divorced one then married another.'

Sam looked thoughtful. 'I suppose so. Mind you there didn't seem much of a gap between the two. Gettin' divorced don't 'appen overnight, do it?'

She agreed that it didn't.

'So what happened to his first wife?'

Gripping the pipe between his teeth, Sam managed to sup at his drink without letting the pipe go. It was quite a feat in Honey's book. Quite funny to watch him doing it too.

'Patricia,' he said once he'd wiped his mouth on the back of his hand. 'Ran away with a bloke that taught her golfing. Never even knew she was interested. Funny thing is though that the boys never hear from her. As I told you, Peter got two boys. He tells everyone who enquires that him and his wife thought it best that she made herself a new life and didn't interfere with him and bringing up the boys. Best to make a clean break, he told everybody. Seems strange to me.'

It seemed strange to Honey too. It appeared that Peter Pierce was not a nice man and the more she found out about him, the more she suspected him of having done some pretty bad things. There was Cathy, there might even be a wife. What if she hadn't gone to Australia? What if, as Sam suspected, she'd never played golf? Nobody keeps their hobbies a secret — not unless it's something best kept between the pages of *Penthouse* magazine.

Outside the sun had deigned to appear and the clouds looked to be falling from the sky and into the horizon.

Retrieving keys from her shoulder bag was always something of an adventure, there being so many bits and piece to forage through before finding them.

Lunchtime being three-quarters of the way through, the car park was emptying of customers. Whilst cars were coming and going it made sense to keep a lookout and stay close to the perimeter. Now less busy, it was possible to traverse on the diagonal without being mown down.

Head bowed, hand still groping in her bag, she did exactly that. At the same time as searching for her car keys she took on the secondary task of locating her phone. Doherty was bound to call shortly confirming the identity of the corpse found in the cesspit. She guessed that it was Cathy Morden, though for the sake of the girl's mother she hoped it wasn't. After her brush with Peter Pierce and Sam's comments, she was beginning to suspect otherwise.

'Damn! Where the devil . . .'

She found the keys. She found the phone. Clasping the keys in one hand she slung her bag over her shoulder. The phone glowed blue the moment it was switched on at the same time as it belted out 'Bohemian Rhapsody'.

'Hello.'

It was all she had time to say. Suddenly she heard a screech of car tyres. Momentarily blinded by sunlight bouncing off a profusion of chrome radiator and fender, she backed into a parked car and staggered. Her shoulder bag swung as she overbalanced. It landed with a thwack on the ground, spilling contents all around and she went down with it.

Knees grazed, bruised from contact with the car she'd bumped against, she could have lain there dazed, waiting until she'd sorted herself.

But the idiot driving the speeding car had angered her.

'You bloody idiot,' she shouted, raising herself on one knee and waving her fist.

Blood trickled from one nostril and into her mouth. She barely noticed. A blue Range Rover over-endowed with chrome swerved out from the car park and onto the road, a road that wasn't usually that busy. The Range Rover had chanced his luck. On this occasion his luck had run out. There was a loud bang as a large horsebox, the dead smart sort big enough to house a family of Romany gypsies, had ploughed straight into the front of the Range Rover. Steam was gushing out from beneath the bonnet. Whoever was in it wasn't getting out — at least not until the fire brigade was called and he was cut out.

A whole flurry of lunchtime diners and drinkers flowed out of the Poacher. At least one of them had some medical knowledge judging by the way he seemed to take charge, hovering around the smashed-up door of the dark blue Range Rover.

Honey got to her feet.

'You all right, love?' someone asked her.

She nodded, her eyes still on what had happened. More to the point, she wanted to know who would want to run her down.

'Who is it? In the car?'

The woman helped her retrieve her bag and the items that had fallen out of it. On top of that she pointed at the receding Range Rover.

'That's Peter Pierce's car, though he shouldn't have been driving. I saw him at the bar knocking them back. He's had a skinful. Still, bad luck to bad rubbish.'

The woman handed Honey her very battered phone, which was now no longer a unit but split into two pieces. The sliding lid had parted company with the rest of it. The blue light no longer sparked into life when she pressed the 'on' button.

She frowned. 'Damn. I liked that light.'

'Never mind. You can always get another,' the woman said helpfully. 'Do you need to phone someone? You can use my phone if you like.'

Honey nodded. 'Two people. If you don't mind.'

She phoned Lindsey first, explained about the accident and then asked her to research local businessman Peter Pierce, resident of Much Maryleigh.

'Will do. How far do you want me to go back?'

'As far as you can.'

'OK. Anything else?'

'Yes. Check whether he's listed with any dating agencies.'

There was a sudden pause as though Lindsey was holding her breath as she considered the implications of this.

'They'll want me to go on their register if I'm to find that out. He'll be put forward as a possible match. Every man on their books is put forward even if he might have two heads and a sting in his tail.'

'Do whatever you have to do. Pierce met his second wife through a dating agency and there are rumours he still resorts to meeting women that way. He married wife number two soon after his divorce came through.'

'OK, but I'll use your name.'

'Do that. And check up on the whereabouts of his first wife, Patricia Pierce. It's rumoured she ran away to Australia with a golf pro, but nobody knows for sure. Check the membership lists of the local golf clubs from about ten years back — if that's possible. If she was learning how to play golf her name should be there.'

'Not necessarily from ten years ago. Club memberships aren't obliged to keep lists from that far back, in fact the Data Protection Act wouldn't allow them to.'

'OK. Do what you can.' She sighed. 'I've got a funny feeling about this. The boys are still with their father but never receive word from her. That's odd in my books. Blood's thicker than water and all that. First things first though, check on the dating agency.'

'That's fine. I'll do all you ask of me, but I must warn you, there could be implications.'

'What kind of implications?'

'You could end up wearing a carnation and carrying a copy of the *Bath Chronicle* under your arm. That's what people do if they've been introduced by a dating agency, the old-fashioned type at least.'

'I'll have to chance it. I'm determined to nail his ass!'

'Whoa!' yelped Lindsey. 'So what's he done to turn my mother into the harpy from hell?'

'No. But he did just try to kill me while under the influence of alcohol.'

CHAPTER TWENTY-FOUR

The national news had headlined the body found in the cess-pit. Just like in a relay race, the local television station had picked up the baton and was running with it, though on a more personal note.

Agnes Morden was being interviewed on the local television news about the body recovered from the cesspit next to St Luke's Church.

'How do you feel about the news that the body is not that of your daughter?'

Honey watched with increasing pity for the poor little woman who had lost so much since she and her husband had moved to Bath. She herself was still coming to terms with the fact that it wasn't Cathy Morden in that cesspit. On the other hand, the identity of the woman was not yet known.

Honey tuned into Cathy's mother.

Agnes sighed heavily. 'In one way I'm relieved, but obviously, I'm desperate to know where my daughter is. She's all I've got now since her dad died.'

'Poor woman,' said Lindsey, expressing her mother's thoughts and wearing the same concerned look.

Honey reached for the remote control and turned it off. Like Agnes Morden, she was feeling a little let down, but for an entirely different reason. She'd been so sure that the body would been that of Cathy Morden or even Patricia Pierce. To hear that it was not had certainly taken the wind out of her sails.

'A homeless woman,' Doherty said to her. 'She fell in. Shame she wasn't conscious and saw what else was down there. She would have been a rich woman. A Celtic torque — whatever that is — a cloak clasp, cups, even a sword. I understand from an expert that it's worth a small fortune. Somebody buried it fifteen hundred years ago. She said it was probably being hidden away from the Saxon hordes who were invading following the withdrawal of the Roman army.'

'Sam Trout!'

Her exclamation made him jump. She explained what Sam had told her, describing the metal detector as something that hummed most of the time but beeped on others.

'He wanted to keep it for himself. As for the homeless woman . . .' Doherty spread his open palms. 'It appears she fell in by mistake. She was *not* murdered. I'll confirm later.'

He had breezed into the Green River Hotel just long enough to fill her in on the details and chug back a cup of coffee. His priority had been to ask her if she was OK following her brush with Peter Pierce.

'Stop looking me over as though you can see through to the bruises,' she said in answer to the all-encompassing look he gave her.

'But I like doing that.'

'Back to business. Where does that leave us with the murder of C.A. Wright?'

Doherty shrugged. 'Lost in the desert, though I do have one glimmer of hope; I think that our friend Deke did give Wright a bashing in whilst he was out cold. However, I don't think he killed him. Wright was transported out of the city without anyone really giving the giant teddy bear much attention.' He shook his head. 'I'm not happy about this, but I have to accept it. I'm going to ask all four students more questions. I might get somewhere, there again I might not. I'll just play it by ear.'

Honey poured more coffee for herself. 'That's my theories and my womanly intuition out of the window. My money was on it being Cathy Morden. Failing that, Patricia Pierce.'

'Sorry, doll. You were wrong on all counts.'

'So what next?'

'We're waiting to ask Peter Pierce that question. It's too much of a coincidence that he was protesting about the cess-pit being demolished.'

'Pretty telling that he tried to run me over when he found out that I was with you — thanks to Sam Trout.'

Frowning, she stroked a hair on her chin as she considered all the bits and pieces that made up the whole of this. 'I would have thought he would have wanted it demolished. Don't they fill those places in?'

'Yes, the deceased would have been buried, but not quickly enough. Apparently, the bricks were scheduled for a reclamation yard. Old bricks are sought after for building and repairing listed buildings. Pierce was panicking. The body would be discovered. The treasure trove was buried beneath him. We're looking for Pierce but so far no joy. Somebody's hiding the bastard. I just know it.'

'What does Pierce actually do for a living?'

'Maintenance. Apparently he's got a full crew working for him maintaining buildings like flats and things. The main thrust of his business seems to be in the heart of the city. He does a lot for the local council. Good rates and workmanship as far as I can make out.'

Honey was thoughtful. 'I was wondering if Wright could have been killed by a woman.'

'I take it you mean Cathy's mother. You're letting your imagination run away with you. How would she get him out here? She couldn't have carried him to her parked car, not unless she had a disabled badge.'

Doherty shook his head. 'None of our suspects are incapacitated to that extent.'

Pulling a frustrated face she shook her head. 'OK. I'm talking rubbish.'

'You just want this finished,' he replied. 'So does Casper, by the way. I didn't know he was sunning himself in Majorca.'

The thought of Casper St John Gervais wearing shorts and sunglasses in sunny climes brought a smile to Honey's face. 'Casper doesn't do sunbathing. He does pale and interesting whilst looking elegantly superior.'

Doherty nodded. 'True. Anyway,' he said, tipping the last of the coffee into his mouth. 'I've got to go.'

He said he would swing by later if he had anything to report. 'But between now and then you can come into the station if you're out and about. I've got a surprise for you.'

She raised both eyebrows. 'That sounds interesting.'

He grinned. 'We need to communicate more.'

Doherty swung out through the swing doors in one direction at the same time as her head chef, Smudger Smith, came swinging in the other, heavily burdened with a three-foot long salamander. The way he was carrying it, with both arms and resting on one shoulder, reminded her of the pall-bearers at Sean O'Brian's funeral.

'You could have used the tradesman's entrance,' she said to him.

'It's locked. Isn't it great though?' he chortled, face pink with effort and grin almost splitting his face in half.

Honey smiled. Only a chef could be so pleased about a gas grill.

He disappeared into the kitchen. Regardless of regulations about having a gas fitter sort out the connections, Honey was in no doubt that the grill would be up and running by six this evening; Smudger kept a supply of tools for such eventualities. He was self-sufficient and totally sure of his own expertise.

Lindsey was scouring the net; so far, she'd entered her mother's particulars on every local dating site she could find.

'They're a bit slow to respond. I expect they're checking you out,' Lindsey informed her mother. 'No luck on the golfing angle for the wife. Unless she had friends who went golfing with her, the actual clubs don't keep their records that long.

'Hmmm.'

'However, I do have some info on our friend's business dealings. Wrightway Holdings. They appear to own commercial properties, i.e. shops, cafés, and units on trading estates as well as running a maintenance service.

'Back to the drawing board.'

'It would seem that way.'

* * *

Peter Pierce looked as though he'd gone ten rounds being punched by a heavyweight boxer. His face had obviously taken most of the impact.

Doherty was surprised to see him on his feet and said so.

'I thought you'd be in here longer.' He was referring to the hospital ward, but the hospital needed the beds and Peter Pierce was out on his ear.

'Sorry I can't hang around here talking to you, Chief Inspector,' Pierce replied, not meeting his eye, 'but I do have children and a home to go to.'

'Not driving, I hope?' Doherty kept the tone light, not that it cut much ice with the man presently buttoning up his shirt.

Pierce had the look of a man with a hangover, bloodshot eyes, dark circles, heavy bags, and a waxy complexion. His eyes narrowed.

'You bloody coppers. Never miss the opportunity to arrest people, do you?'

'Only guilty people.'

Pierce wouldn't know it, but Doherty was having trouble keeping his temper. Honey hadn't known how he'd reacted when he'd heard the news. In his early career he'd been the 'Angel of Death', the bearer of bad news to the relative of the victim of a road traffic accident. It was a nasty job, but nothing compared to how it felt to the relative of the dead person or even an injured person. It made him angry; it made him want to lash out.

Pierce's prim lips curled into a girlish smile.

'Well, I know I'll be found guilty seeing as she's your girlfriend. She keeps bad company, she does. Old Sam Trout is best avoided. So out of my way, Chief Inspector. I've got work to do . . .'

Doherty grabbed him.

'I'm going to do you for dangerous driving,' Doherty snarled. 'At least. And then it's a summons regarding the treasure trove you found.'

Pierce adopted a pained expression as though he had no wish to deal with the likes of him.

'I could sue you, Doherty, for police brutality,' he snarled. 'Is that what you want?'

Doherty could smell the man's sweat, but more so than that he could smell his arrogance. 'You don't know what the word means.'

'OK, I got drunk. We all do now and again.'

'I think you've done more than that, Pierce, such as not declaring treasure trove.'

Pierce laughed in his face. Doherty pushed him away.

'Get out of here.'

Pierce smirked as he threw his jacket over his shoulder.

'You've got nothing serious on me, copper. Nothing serious at all.'

Honey's comment about Pierce looking fearful before he'd driven into her only came back to Doherty later. Wouldn't it be great, he thought to himself, if I could link Pierce to Wright's murder?

But he couldn't. As far as he knew their paths had never crossed.

At least, that was before Lindsey reported back.

* * *

'That's it!'

Lindsey had found the link at precisely the same time as another body had been found beneath the homeless woman and the treasure trove.

Doherty phoned to tell her. 'It's Patricia Pierce. No doubt about it.'

'I've got something to tell you,' said a breathless Honey, excited by what she was reading on the computer screen. 'Patricia Pierce enrolled with a dating agency. One of the men she met was Colin Wright.'

'But she was married.'

'So? If you were married to Peter Pierce, a guy with a penchant for young ladies, wouldn't you seek pastures new?'

Doherty didn't argue. He was aching to get Pierce back into custody and any excuse would do if it held up, gave him enough time to look into things.

'I'll see you later.'

The call was disconnected.

'Is he pleased?' asked Lindsey who looked as though she'd expected some praise for her efforts.

'Ecstatic,' returned Honey, though she still wasn't quite sure about all this. 'So Pierce might have murdered his wife, but did he murder Colin Wright, and if he did, how did he get him out of a crowded city without being noticed?'

The revolving doors suddenly spun round like a carousel and like a prancing horse — or at least a strutting one — her mother made an entrance.

'It's settled,' she said. 'Dora left instructions that whoever offered to give Bobo a good home was the best home. I've found her a new home.'

Honey immediately recognised Tracey Maplin who gave a little wave.

The terrier, which had been snoozing on a pile of clean laundry beneath the reception desk, leapt out from hiding, throwing herself into the welcoming arms of her new owner.

Honey held up a pile of disposable baby nappies. 'Do you want these?'

Tracey Maplin shook her head. 'No, we're seeking the great outdoors. I've bought a Volkswagen Camper, one of those old sixties-style ones with a split screen and multi-coloured bodywork. Bobo and I are off on the road. First stop, Glastonbury Festival.'

Honey and Lindsey said, 'How nice.' Gloria Cross was showing her teeth in a rictus smile.

'That's good.'

Honey had to agree that it was.

* * *

'So how did he do it?'

Peter Pierce was in custody. His story was that he'd found out about his wife's affair. She'd been telling him she was having golfing lessons when in fact she'd been meeting C.A. Wright. They'd had a row. She'd run off to the field that was now Memory Meadow. Her husband had run after her.

'It was an accident. She slipped, fell in, and hit her head.'

So far Doherty could say nothing to contradict what Pierce was saying. It was difficult to tell for sure that it had been nothing but an accident. At the very worst Pierce would get off with manslaughter.

Doherty kept at it. 'And you buried her. I take it Colin Wright found out.'

'I don't know what you mean.'

Pierce was confident. His voice didn't falter and he wasn't sweating. Even his brief seemed surprised at how calm he was, slipping him little looks now and again as though checking that he was still needed.

'Your wife met Wright through a dating agency some five years ago. I would suggest that they'd planned to run away together. When she didn't turn up, he came looking for her. Wright was the suspicious type. He knew how to needle people. He needled you. He put on the pressure and he began to blackmail you. You paid. He went away, but then he came back. He wanted more.'

Through all this Pierce said not a word. Now he smiled.

'I've only two words to say to you, Mr Doherty. Prove it.'

* * *

Doherty had related all this over tea and scones while sitting at a table in Abbey Churchyard.

He folded his arms, sending the sleeves of his leather jacket into a mass of wrinkles, and narrowed his eyes, principally watching the people wandering around Abbey Churchyard, in and out of the Pump Rooms and the Abbey, or sitting at one of the many cafés drinking coffee and eating hamburgers.

'Nobody seemed to notice anyone carrying a large bear. How ridiculous is that? He had to carry it out of here or have a vehicle near at hand. Our best bet is that he was some kind of contractor and had a van parked here. If there was breakdown of one of the appliances in one of these cafés or over in the Pump Rooms . . . Pierce had a maintenance company after all.'

His voice trailed off. They'd checked as far as they could. Abbey Churchyard was not a high security risk. There were no security cameras because the city was touchy about infringing people's civil liberties in places where there was no need. Nobody recalled seeing a tradesman's van in an area that was predominantly pedestrianised.

'There has to be some other way . . .' Doherty said wistfully.

Honey swallowed and licked away the jam and cream on her lower lip.

'He also owned some catering outlets. Did you know that?'

He looked surprised. 'No. I didn't.'

'My feeling is that if there was no tradesman's van to lump Teddy Devlin into, and nobody saw him carrying the bear, then he couldn't have carried it very far.'

She'd been just about to take another bite of the second half of the scone, when the significance of what she'd said suddenly hit her.

'That's it.'

Doherty had also grasped its significance.

'Somewhere around here,' he said gravely, his head turning this way and that, searching for the right place at the right distance.

Honey twisted right round, looking behind her at the small café at the foot of the narrow building set in the shady corner behind them. The property was owned by the city. On reaching the end of his lease, the last owner had been given notice to quit even though he was willing to renew and had never missed a rent payment. Someone in the city council had thought it a good idea to let it to a more upmarket concern. The hoardings advertising its availability were still *in situ.* The address was familiar. The previous owner had been selling everything off.

She related all this to Doherty.

'So who was the previous owner?'

Doherty didn't waste any time. He got someone to check. 'A property company in London. Absent landlords. Pierce oversaw everything.'

'That's why Smudger couldn't get the salamander,' she blurted. 'That's why it got delivered later.'

Doherty had never been involved in the hospitality trade, but he was becoming a little more au fait with the terminology. He recalled Honey saying something about a salamander and him thinking that her chef had become interested in reptiles.

'This was where he was coming?'

She nodded. Their eyes met in mutual understanding.

'Let's go in.'

* * *

There was blood on the floor, of course. It turned out to be Colin Wright's blood. Pierce hadn't managed to get back there to clean it up. He confessed that he had thought about leaving the country, but he had his two boys to consider.

'I meant to bury him in the cesspit along with everything else, but first I needed to get the loot out. Unfortunately, I got drunk and chucked it in the wrong hole. By the time I discovered what I'd done . . .'

'Poor old Sean O'Brian was being buried.'

''Fraid so.'

* * *

Honey and Doherty agreed that he was not a nice man.

'But I am,' said Doherty.

Honey raised her eyebrows, an amused look on her face.

'Is that so?'

'Very.'

After dipping into his pocket, he slid a small velvet box across the bar. They were sitting at the bar of the Zodiac. The air was smoky and the hour was late, but it felt warm, it felt good, and the ambience was as juicy as smoked salmon and rare rib of beef.

She had a hollow feeling in her stomach as she opened it. The sapphire was big enough and surrounded with diamonds.

'So! What do you think?'

'Blue's my favourite colour.'

'Great. So that's all right then.'

Honey nodded. 'Does this make it official?'

'Depends what you mean by official.'

'Who do we tell?'

'Who do you want to tell?'

Honey grinned. 'Can we keep it between us — until the time is right.'

His eyes twinkled. 'It's our engagement. We've got all the time in the world and anyway, it's our business. Nobody else's.'

THE END

ALSO BY JEAN G. GOODHIND

HONEY DRIVER MYSTERY SERIES

Book 1: MURDER, BED & BREAKFAST
Book 2: MENU FOR MURDER
Book 3: WALKING WITH MURDER
Book 4: THE JANE AUSTEN MURDERS
Book 5: MURDER BY LAMPSHADE
Book 6: MURDER BY MUDPACK
Book 7: MURDER AT THE ROMAN BATHS

Thank you for reading this book.

If you enjoyed it please leave feedback on Amazon or Goodreads, and if there is anything we missed or you have a question about, then please get in touch. We appreciate you choosing our book.

Founded in 2014 in Shoreditch, London, we at Joffe Books pride ourselves on our history of innovative publishing. We were thrilled to be shortlisted for Independent Publisher of the Year at the British Book Awards.

www.joffebooks.com

We're very grateful to eagle-eyed readers who take the time to contact us. Please send any errors you find to corrections@joffebooks.com. We'll get them fixed ASAP.

Printed in Dunstable, United Kingdom

71681295R00143